MAFIO$O
PART THREE

Melodrama Publishing
www.MelodramaPubishing.com

FOLLOW
NISA SANTIAGO

FACEBOOK.COM/NISASANTIAGO

INSTAGRAM.COM/NISA_SANTIAGO

TWITTER.COM/NISA_SANTIAGO

Order online at
bn.com, amazon.com, and
MelodramaPublishing.com

www.melodramapublishing.com

Library of Congress Control Number: 2017909508
ISBN-13: 978-1620780824

First Edition: April 2018

Printed in Canada

MAFIO$O

PART THREE

NISA SANTIAGO

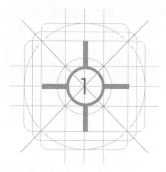

January 2015

The pearl white Benz S63 AMG was the perfect gift from Scottie, and Maxine flaunted the car through the streets of Brooklyn with a broad smile. Her Benz was a start to a new life and a new beginning. After all the years she'd spent in prison, it felt good—damn good—to be on the winning team again. The look on Layla's face when Scott curbed her ass was priceless to Maxine. Layla had been outsmarted and replaced. That bitch was canceled. Maxine wished she had it all recorded.

Maxine felt her revenge had just begun. It takes time to kill a person and keep them alive. Maxine wanted Layla's days to be filled with misery and angst. She wanted Layla to mourn her murdered children and long for the strong embrace from a husband who would never again be hers. Maxine wanted Layla to kill herself because the pain was too great.

Maxine knew that kind of suffering. When she was found guilty and sentenced to prison for a murder she didn't commit, she remembered going numb and then her body began to shake uncontrollably from fear. Her heart felt as though it would implode. Although Maxine made it through those dark days, she still couldn't find it in her heart to forgive Layla.

No, Maxine wanted Layla to continue to suffer and to lose her remaining kids, financial support, and her sanity. Layla was the type of heartless bitch who deserved to live in public housing and drink forties for breakfast. Maxine was the type of bitch to make that happen.

Though it was a cold, windy day in Brooklyn, the sun was rising in clear skies. It was a new year, and that meant new things. A fresh start. And things couldn't get any more new and fresh than the Benz Scott had bought her. It felt like old times again—like when she was nineteen years old, living her life and doing big things as a hustler's wifey.

With Mary J. Blige blaring inside the car, Maxine sang the lyrics to "Be Without You." She navigated the Benz onto her mother's silent and still block with the sun still rising. Most of the neighborhood was still asleep on the cold Sunday morning. When the Mary track ended, the only sound Maxine could hear was the January wind tapping at her window.

Maxine took a deep breath. Reluctantly, she had put her mother on the backburner since she had returned from the cruise. She knew she should have come to see her sooner, but her new lifestyle had her caught up. She had been gone for several weeks running around with Scott, celebrating Christmas together and then the New Year. Maxine was there to help him deal with his business and family issues. There was no way she could leave his side and allow Layla or any other bitch to weasel in. Too much was at stake, and no matter how good it felt to snatch Scott back from Layla's conniving fingers, her work was far from done.

Maxine had something important to discuss with her mother. The woman was getting older and more fragile, and Maxine was worried about her. She felt she couldn't live on her own for too much longer. During telephone conversations Maxine noticed that her mother was increasingly confused about how to complete simple tasks. She was showing signs of memory loss and found it hard to concentrate. Mrs. Shirley had noticed the behavior changes first while they were on the cruise, and as soon as they got back she called Maxine and voiced her opinion. At first, Maxine was in denial because her mother would have a lot of good days. But now, Maxine could no longer deny that her mother's mental health was declining.

She wanted to convince her mother to put her house on the market and tell her about the excellent assisted living home on Long Island she and Scott found for her. Lots of wealthy widows and notable retirees lived at the high-end facility. It was expensive, but Scott could afford it. The grounds were lush, and it boasted five-star amenities in their lavish rooms, great food, regular entertainment, and social events and trips for the senior residents. Everything was set. The only thing her mother was to do was move in.

Maxine climbed out of the car looking flawless. Her SJP over-the-knee boots hit the pavement as she approached the home dressed in slimming jeggings and a mink coat over her sweater. Her clothing was ridiculously priced from head to toe—a far cry from the prison garb she'd once sported.

Maxine used her key to enter and put on coffee. Everything was quiet and neat downstairs, but the place still smelled like mothballs. She had gotten used to it. It was home, and it would always be home until she put the place on the market. With the coffee brewing in the kitchen, Maxine made her way upstairs and walked toward her mother's bedroom. The door was ajar, and the hallway was silent. She didn't even hear the TV on. Maxine assumed her mother was sleeping.

When she walked into the bedroom, she received the shock of her life. Maxine immediately stood frozen with terror when she saw a man standing over her sleeping mother's bed with a .50 Cal in his left hand. He was wearing black latex gloves, a disturbing sign of bad things to come. He scowled at her, and she returned his scowl with a hard glare. Her eyes shot down at her mother lying underneath the blanket; she was still—was she dead? Thankfully Maxine noticed her mother's chest rise and fall. She was still alive—for now.

"What do you want?" Maxine asked the stranger quietly.

The man put his index finger to his lips, signaling he wanted her to be silent. He was now in control. Maxine was terrified. That was a big gun near her mother's head, and he was an intimidating looking figure—black and scary with cold, dark eyes, looking like he'd been through some insane things. He was dressed in all black, wearing a hoodie over his head, black jeans, and combat boots. His eyes were burning a hole into Maxine.

He pointed toward the hallway, directing her to exit the room. She hesitated for a moment. There was no way she would leave her mother in the bedroom with this crazed looking stranger. He didn't like it. He put the gun to her mother's head and scowled heavier. Everything about him said that he wasn't bluffing.

Maxine backpedaled toward the bedroom door, her eyes shifting back and forth from him to her sleeping mother. She was begging with her eyes for this stranger not to do anything stupid. He removed his gun from the old woman's head and followed Maxine out the bedroom door. Now his gun was trained on her. Quietly, he followed her downstairs and into the living room. Maxine felt powerless. What did he want? And who was he?

With it now just the two of them downstairs, the man tucked his gun into his waistband and lunged at Maxine, striking her with a staggering blow to her face. The hard bash sent Maxine flying into the wall. However, she didn't scream. Her face tightened with anger, and she wanted to react, but she was at a disadvantage.

A million things went through her mind. Was this an assassination? Was it set up by Layla? It was possible. Layla had become enemy number-one, and she had her resources. Maxine was suddenly filled with regret. Scott had warned her to always travel with his security detail and not take any chances, but she hadn't listened. Sneaking away from his bedside to visit her mother alone might have been a fatal mistake.

Maxine looked at him defiantly and said, "Tell Layla that Scott will kill everything she loves for this. She knows how he feels about me."

He looked puzzled by her statement. "What the fuck you talkin' 'bout, bitch? Who the fuck is Layla?" He had heard the name before, but he couldn't place it. A lot of time had passed.

Now she looked puzzled. "Who sent you?" she asked him.

He smirked and growled, "You did . . . you sent me."

Fed up, she shouted, "Who are you?!"

"Wacka, bitch!"

Suddenly, it felt like the blood had drained from her body and her heart had stopped. The name sent chills down her spine. He was her hired gun. She had only heard about him through Shiniquia. They had never met. She had never seen his face. Wacka was so elusive that he didn't want his mother sending any pictures of him to Shiniquia while she was locked up. He didn't want his image circulating through the correctional facilities. He wanted no one to know his face.

How he was still alive and how he'd found her was a mystery to Maxine. But the biggest mystery was why he was suddenly mad at her. What did she do to him? He had been paid in cash for each hit he had carried out, and if he or his family got caught slipping, then their deaths were due to his murderous occupation. He took the money and provided his service, and whatever madness and darkness followed was on him. She was innocent of any wrongdoing toward him and his family. She didn't ask Layla to kill his whole family. Layla had sanctioned the hit on her own.

"I'm sorry for what happened to Shiniquia and your family . . . your sister was cool, and I liked her," she said.

He frowned. Fuck her apologies. He wanted her to suffer and feel the same pain he had felt, but before the blood-spattered get-together was to begin, it was interrupted. Scott and his goons arrived onto the block in two black SUVs, thick with manpower.

Wacka wasn't expecting this, but he wasn't going out like a bitch. He was a killer who refused to be the one in front of the gun.

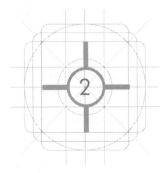

2

Scott woke to find Maxine gone. He got out of bed naked and donned a long black robe and lit a cigar. Not seeing Maxine in the room worried him. He called her cell phone a few times, but it went straight to voicemail. Scott figured she must have forgotten to turn it on. It irked him how unattached she was to her phone, even after he'd continually explained how valuable a cell phone is in case of an emergency. The pit of his stomach felt queasy; something was off. He knew she was stubborn and had gone off to visit her mother while they were in New York. She didn't leave with her security detail, and that upset him. She was in Brooklyn alone while he was in a Manhattan penthouse suite.

No matter how many times he warned her about Layla's thirst for vengeance, Maxine would just shrug it off. What would it take for Maxine to see just how cunning Layla was? Layla always got her revenge; she just couldn't rest without it. If twenty-plus years in prison didn't make that crystal clear to Maxine, then Scott wasn't sure what it would take.

Scott didn't want to lose Maxine a second time, so he called down to his goons and told them to ready themselves and bring the vehicles around. He would meet them downstairs in ten minutes.

He opened the closet door and got dressed. He had so much to worry about—but last night with Maxine—that was incredible. The sex seemed to get better every week. The way she made him come was mind-blowing. The intimacy with Maxine was taking him places he had long forgotten.

Their chemistry was off the charts, and they had sex almost every night. Once again, Maxine had captured his heart.

This morning, he had something special planned for Maxine—another reason he was upset about her leaving. Maxine had her ways, but how had she slipped by his men without them knowing? Were his men that incompetent? If so, then they all would be dealt with.

Scott hurried to get dressed and put his Glock 19 in his shoulder holster. Before he exited the room, he reached into the drawer and removed a small item. He held the black velvet box in the palm of his hand and opened it. Inside was a multi-million-dollar, nine-carat pink diamond solitaire ring. It was exquisite. He was planning to ask Maxine to marry him. He didn't care he was married already. Layla had become irrelevant in his life, and he would soon divorce her. He felt that Maxine was always the one he should have been with.

The plan was to have breakfast and champagne, and he would subtly place the diamond ring into the champagne glass and surprise her. It was a corny move, but then again, Maxine liked corny things. The ring in the champagne glass was once implemented long ago by him when he'd proposed to Layla. But this time it would be done during breakfast instead of dinner. Unfortunately, his romantic surprise was put on hold. He had to find Maxine first.

He climbed into the backseat of the black Escalade, and the two-vehicle caravan headed toward the Brooklyn Bridge to Brooklyn. His security detail was heavily armed and alert, and every move they made was cautious. The man in the front seat carried a Heckler & Koch G36C. His goons traveling in the other truck were each armed with 9mms and .45s. Scott wanted no more risks with his life. Deuce had gotten close to him twice, and he would not allow a third time.

With Whistler and Deuce still alive, Scott had changed all his residences, stash houses, and routines. What was night, he turned into day—what was left became right. He switched it all up to protect the organization and his family.

The drive to Brooklyn was an easy one on an early Sunday morning. During the ride, Scott felt the engagement ring in his pocket and thought about his future with Maxine. He was making the right choice with her, right? He loved her. He always had. So why did he allow her to take the fall for Layla twenty something years ago? He was young back then; foolish and unwise.

There were things about Maxine that had changed, and he admired that. Her newfound temperament was a turn on, but it also was becoming a pain in the ass for him. Once he found her, he would drill into her head that what he says goes! There would be no more traveling without her security detail. He was at war, and she could become a casualty, just like his three children had.

Scott and his security team arrived at Maxine's mother's place, and he saw her pearl white Benz parked out front. Quietness engulfed the narrow street, and Sunday morning brought out the church folks and weekend employees. Everyone else was into their third dream or hung over from last night.

Scott and his men exited the vehicles, and he approached the front door flanked by a few goons.

"Fuck. We got company, I see," Wacka growled as he glanced out the front window and saw the barrage of goons walking toward the house. He kept his cool and removed the pistol from his waistband. If he had to die today, then he wasn't going out without a fight.

Quickly, he grabbed Maxine and placed her into a chokehold and put the gun to her head. He was outnumbered, and he needed another way out of the house. He dragged Maxine to the back door to see if there was another exit. She struggled slightly, and his chokehold tightened around her, causing her to gasp somewhat. He was strong—stronger than the average man—and he was ready to blow her brains out and make his getaway if necessary.

Unfortunately for Wacka, the fenced-in yard had only one way out, and it was through the front. On the other side of the fence was a brick tenement building. Fuck, he wasn't able to climb walls! He had only one option—one way out, but he had leverage. He had Maxine as a hostage.

Fuck it!

Just as Scott was approaching the door, it swung open, and he and his men caught the shock of their lives. Wacka glared their way, holding Maxine in a tight chokehold with his gun pressed against her temple. Immediately, everyone's weapons lifted in his direction, but Scott stood in the middle of the standoff, looking at Maxine caught up in a murderer's grip. The two locked eyes and she was trying to keep her cool, but she was in a perilous predicament.

"Just do what he says," Maxine pleaded in a feeble voice.

Scott wanted to reach for his gun, but Wacka quickly threw out demands. "Y'all niggas back da fuck up!"

"Chill, playboy. We can talk like men here," Scott replied calmly, taking a few steps back from them. He wanted to rip the man's throat out, but he had to keep his cool. The man had the upper hand.

"We ain't got shit to talk about!" Wacka shouted. "I'm walkin' out the front door wit' this bitch in my arms."

All eyes were on Wacka, and things were heating up. He gripped Maxine tightly, his finger was on the trigger, and the barrel of the .50 Cal was a dulling pain against her temple. She knew it all could go wrong in so many ways. Her primary concern was her mother and her safety. The last thing she wanted was bullet holes riddling her mother's front door and turning the home she grew up in into a war zone.

"Let her go, and there's some hope for you," Scott said.

Wacka chuckled at the order. "You a funny nigga, but I ain't fuckin' laughing or playin' wit' y'all niggas. One of y'all niggas flinch wrong, and I'm blowin' her fuckin' brains out!"

Wacka stepped farther out the door, still in complete control over Maxine. Scott and his goons could only glare with their weapons on standby and wait for an opportunity to strike. Wacka wasn't leaving them much of an open window.

"Nigga, I'm ready to die today and go out for mine," said Wacka. "Y'all niggas feel the same way?"

If he had to, he'd join his family and go out in a blaze of glory. How could he survive this? Could he kill Maxine and still get off a shot at Scott and make his escape? The odds weren't in his favor. Wacka knew he would be riddled with bullets after the first shot. He didn't want to die with unfinished business. He wanted to slaughter the entire West family, including Maxine.

"I want y'all muthafuckas to put y'all guns on the ground and step back," he ordered them.

They hesitated. It wasn't happening unless Scott told them to. They were taking too long, so Wacka started counting, "Three, two . . ."

"Put them down," Scott told the men.

Reluctantly, the men placed their weapons onto the ground and took a few steps back.

With Maxine in his hold, Wacka slowly made his way toward his car, with Scott and his men standing down. As Wacka moved to his vehicle, another unexpected thing happened, and it brought tears to Maxine's eyes. Her mother loomed in the doorway. She had finally awakened from her sleep, and there she was, standing near the chaos in a floral nightgown looking confused. She saw the men and then Scott, and stared at her daughter being held in some man's arms.

"Maxine, get your narrow tail back in this house, chile. You got school tomorrow," she said. It was the early stages of dementia.

"Mama, go back inside please . . . it's cold out here," Maxine replied.

Her mother refused to listen. She was nosey, seeing the men in her front yard was odd, and then there was Scottie, the same young gangster she didn't want her daughter hanging around. She was troubled by his presence. She was gradually losing her memories, but she could never forget that face—the face of the man who charmed her daughter and turned her good girl bad. He had been the distraction in Maxine's life that caused her to go astray.

"You need to leave," she said to Scott, oblivious to the horror unfolding around her.

Wacka continued to hold Maxine hostage at gunpoint and forced her to his car. Maxine could only look on worriedly, knowing she was most likely going to die. Wacka shoved her into the car and shouted out his warning to Scott and his men. "If y'all muthafuckas try to follow us, this bitch is a dead bitch."

"You're gonna kill her anyway," Scott growled at Wacka. "Let her go!"

Wacka smirked. "Today, I'm God, nigga . . . maybe I will; maybe I won't."

"I'll find you, nigga. I got peoples and resources all over this fuckin' planet. You won't be able to hide."

Wacka stood undaunted by the threat. Scott was no one to him. He had seen hell personally, and he felt that even the devil himself couldn't take him down. The look he shot back at the man making the threats was deeply disturbing.

Scott recognized the look. The crazy bastard was suicidal, and Maxine's chances of survival were very slim. So he pleaded, "Take me instead. I'll be a better hostage to you than her."

Wacka wasn't taking the bait. "No deal, nigga."

He continued to hold Maxine tight and forced her into the driver's seat. His gun went off, and he quickly flattened the tires to each SUV, ensuring that Scott and his goons wouldn't follow them. Wacka was thinking of everything. He had to, or else he was a dead man. In the passenger seat, he shouted, "Drive, bitch!"

Maxine had no choice. She sped off with Scott looking on in rage and regret. He didn't know if he would ever see Maxine alive again.

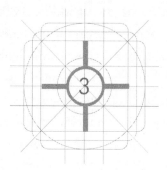

Bugsy and Meyer stood shirtless in the center ring of the gym. Both twins had their hands wrapped, and the boxing gloves were on. Bugsy had on blue boxing shorts, and Meyer was wearing black. Both their bodies were conditioned and lean. Meyer had the large tattoos, though. They draped over 70% of his upper body.

Bugsy glared at his brother, ready to throw some punches and maybe knock some sense into him. Bugsy was upset with Meyer for taking sides with their mother. He wanted to get the family back together, and if he had to fight his brother in the ring to get a word with him, then so be it. They would spar in the ring with their entourage of goons looking on. Meyer was ready to go head-to-head with his brother, but Bugsy had dreams of being a young Sugar Ray Leonard when he was a kid. But that dream was never a factor in his life. He took up the family business.

The bell sounded, and each brother threw up their boxing gloves defensively. Meyer threw the first punch, but it missed. He then threw a second and third while Bugsy bobbed and weaved in the ring. Bugsy quickly bent his knees and moved his head in a V-shaped motion to the outside of the punch and kept his weight centered. Meyer didn't even see the counterpunch coming. He was hit with a left and then a right. He stumbled, but he didn't fall. He got upset. They threw more jabs at each other, and in doing so, Bugsy quickly said, "You're being foolish, Meyer. What the fuck are you thinking?"

"I'm thinkin' business, nigga . . . building my shit," he replied.

"With our mother? You think that's a smart idea?"

"I'm tired of Pop. He's always clownin' me, and he don't respect me," Meyer griped.

They danced around the ring for a moment, eyeing each other. Bugsy heard him speak but felt everything Meyer was saying was asinine. He threw a few more jabs, they connected, and then Meyer caught him with a few body shots and pushed him against the ropes. Bugsy pushed him off.

"I still need you in Delaware," he said to Meyer.

"Fuck Delaware," Meyer cursed.

"Deuce is still out there, and he's still a threat to us—our family," Bugsy said, followed by an intense swing. Meyer blocked it and backpedaled.

"Deuce ain't my problem anymore," Meyer said.

The statement frustrated Bugsy. "He's everyone's problem. You think this war with him will stop because you and Lucky sided with our mother?"

"We gonna do things differently," said Meyer.

"You're not thinking straight."

"I'm building my own fuckin' empire wit' Ma," he said. "I'm tired of being our father's lackey—his fuckin' doormat. He respects you more than he do me."

"Pop's just got a lot on his mind."

"Well, he ain't gotta worry about me anymore, unless he comes at me the wrong way."

The brothers were doing more talking than sparring at the moment, moving around the ring with their attention fixed on each other. People watched on as each twin showed off his technique, not afraid to get hit and not afraid to go on the offensive. A few more punches were thrown; some connected and some didn't.

"If you gonna be ignorant, then tell our mother to give the money back. She stole fifty million from Pop."

Meyer chuckled. "It ain't happening. That's her money too."

"Scott ain't happy. He's gonna come for it."

"And you think I care?"

He didn't. Meyer saw an opportunity with his mother and sister. In his eyes, that fifty million was his to indulge in too. He thought about the power the money brought them and the things he could buy with it. He wanted to have some fun for once—without Scott looking over his shoulder. Meyer wanted to have a good time. He wanted to go to the strip clubs and make it rain with hundred-dollar bills. He wanted to continue what he'd been doing, which was balling out of control. Deuce, he would be dealt with. But for now, it was his time to shine. Meyer wanted to wear the crown. He wanted to be the boss for once. He wanted his father's respect. And if he couldn't earn it, then he would take it.

Their new organization had a lot of seed money, and they had hired a gaggle of new goons—killers who were loyal to them and not Scott. He felt untouchable.

"You never could see the big picture," said Bugsy with aggravation.

The comment angered Meyer. "You calling me stupid?"

"I'm calling you ignorant!"

The sparring match ended for Meyer. Like a child, he removed his gloves and threw them down to the floor and went on a childish rant about his father, Penelope, and how he hated Maxine.

"I don't trust that bitch! And our father is a fuckin' fool for allowing her into his life," he shouted. "He chooses her over our mother? You're on the losing team, Bugsy, because Pop ain't thinkin' clearly. I can't promise you there won't be collateral damage in a turf war, and the first to go will be that bitch Maxine."

Bugsy immediately threw two quick punches Meyer's way, which landed against his chin and put him on his ass. He stood over Meyer wrathfully. Meyer didn't see it coming. It was a sucker punch, and it created disarray inside the gym. Both sides came charging into the ring, guns were pulled out, and a pushing match ensued between several men. Bugsy's people had known Meyer for years, so they weren't as quick to put a bullet in the boss's son. However, Meyer's goons didn't know Bugsy, nor did they give a fuck about him or Scott. Meyer was the boss, and if he gave the word, Bugsy and his peoples were dead men.

But things went no further than some pushing and heated words between both camps. Meyer picked himself up from the floor and told his men to stand down. They did.

He glared at Bugsy and said, "So that's how we gonna play the game now? Hit someone when they're caught off guard? I thought you were better than that, brother."

Bugsy pivoted and walked away, leaving Meyer grimacing.

Meyer collected himself and exited the ring, his armed goons following behind him. Before he left the gym, he heard Bugsy saying to someone on the phone, "I'll be there soon as possible!"

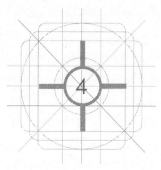

S cott stood there and could only watch Wacka take off with Maxine behind the wheel. He felt helpless at the moment, but he would not stay that way for long. He was pissed that a two-bit thug had gotten the best of him and his men and escaped with the love of his life.

What made things worse was seeing Maxine's mother sprawled out under the doorframe. She had suddenly collapsed. Was it from a stray bullet? He ran over to her to provide aid, but there was no blood, no bullet holes. Inexplicably, she was unconscious.

"Call 911 and clean up the situation," he told Mason.

They quickly went into action. Their guns were placed into the SUV and hidden in a secret stash compartment. The ambulance was on the way.

Scott immediately called Bugsy; he would need his son's assistance too. He held the senior woman in his arms and couldn't stop worrying about Maxine. This madman had taken her hostage, and there wasn't anything he could do about it. He was enraged by the strong possibility he wouldn't see her alive again. It was a hard thing for him to swallow. He wanted to put his fist through a wall and flip over cars.

It didn't take long for the cops to swarm onto the scene. They came from both directions with their lights blaring, and several cops hurried out of their marked cars like it was a movie scene. They were expecting trouble. Neighbors had called in the disturbance and the quiet Sunday morning was looking like chaos in Baghdad.

"Hands up, motherfuckers! Everybody freeze! No sudden moves," an officer shouted at the men.

Scott kept his cool and stayed near the old woman, remaining crouched with her in his arms. He shot an intense look at the approaching cops and shouted, "She needs help!"

In a loud, commanding voice, another officer shouted, "Get your fucking hands up, now!" His gun was trained on Scott's head.

Scott growled under his breath and stood up. He didn't want to become another nameless face on a t-shirt while people marched for justice. Too many black men were dying at the hands of trigger-happy police officers.

Officers went to assist Maxine's mother while Scott was roughed up. A sergeant approached him, and the man wanted to be an asshole today. He cursed at Scott and called him a thug. Scott knew his rights. Neither he nor his men had committed a crime. The only crime committed was Maxine being kidnapped. But he didn't need the NYPD's help for that. He would handle it on his own. And he had lawyers that would chew these officers up and spit 'em out like used gum.

"Is there a problem here, sergeant?" Scott asked him gruffly. "Why are we being harassed?"

"There's been a report of disturbance and gunfire being heard in the area," the sergeant said.

"No guns here. I was here to see a friend, and, unfortunately, she fell ill during our visit," said Scott calmly, adjusting his suit.

The sergeant looked doubtful. Scott was well dressed, and his men didn't fit the profile of typical churchgoers up early Sunday morning. His officers searched the SUVs but came up empty. The guns were well hidden and secured in false bottoms of the vehicles. The sergeant wanted to hold Scott and his goons on suspicion, but they had nothing on them.

"Unfortunately, when we left the house, we came out to find our tires shot out, and we don't know by whom," Scott said.

The sergeant frowned. Something wasn't adding up, but he wasn't a detective. Neighbors emerged from their homes and gawked at the scene. The cold weather wasn't welcoming, and their Sunday morning had started off with a bang. The only thing the cops could do was take down their statements and make sure everything was okay, including the old woman. The ambulance arrived, and EMS workers rushed to her aid.

Scott looked composed in front of the cops, but he was bubbling with rage, vengeance, and concern for Maxine. Each moment he spent on the block detained with the NYPD was a moment too long for him. He wanted to jump into action and make phone calls. He knew the car, and he remembered the license plate number. He wanted his men on it ASAP.

It looked like the president's motorcade had arrived on the Brooklyn block, as the three black Chevrolet Suburban trucks parked across the street. The sergeant and the cops were in awe and watchful. The doors to the vehicles opened, and several black men climbed out. Each one of them looked too dangerous for the cops' taste.

Now who are they? the sergeant asked himself.

Bugsy and his men approached the scene. They moved with authority, not caring for the sea of blue surrounding the area. The only thing Bugsy was concerned with his father's well-being. Seeing Scott in the front yard, he walked that way flanked by his new right-hand men, Choppa and AJ. Two cops tried to interrupt his gathering with his father, but Bugsy looked at them intently and said, "That's my dad, and I need to talk to him."

The rookie cops were inundated with intense stares from dangerous looking men. They reminded them of the Nation of Islam, and the cops didn't want trouble that could give them those five minutes of fame on the Internet. Several neighbors had their phones out recording the commotion. They stepped aside reluctantly and minded their business.

Bugsy approached his father with some unease. "What's going on, Pop? What happened?"

"Take a walk with me," Scott said.

Bugsy and Scott trekked away from the front yard alone. Bugsy was itching to hear what Scott had to say.

"Maxine's been kidnapped."

"What? By who?" he asked.

"I don't know, but I need to find her."

"We'll find her, Pop. I'll get my people on it right away," Bugsy said with urgency in his voice.

Whatever his father needed, Bugsy was ready to provide tenfold. He would not leave his father's side until everything was okay. The two attempts on Scott's life and now Maxine's kidnapping made Bugsy feel edgy. He thought about his woman, Alicia, and to alleviate his worries, he called her to make sure that she was okay.

"I'm fine, baby," she said to him.

"Okay, just be careful and call me if there's something wrong," he said.

"I will. Love you."

"I love you too." He hung up and exhaled. The last thing he ever wanted was to lose her, so he knew how his father was feeling about Maxine's abduction.

Maxine's mother was wheeled to the ambulance on a gurney and placed inside, where they were still working on her condition. She wasn't looking too good. Scott sent one of his soldiers to the hospital with her to make sure she would be okay. Then Scott and Bugsy got into the back seat of the Chevrolet SUV, and they were driven away with their motorcade following.

During the ride to their location, they continued to talk and speculate. Scott was frantic. He did not understand the kidnapper, or why he wanted Maxine. But a wolf recognized another wolf, and Scott knew the man had murdered before. The man's sketchy eyes and bold actions were evidence. Scott and Bugsy concluded that the man had come from Deuce. He had to be one of Deuce's violent thugs. But why take Maxine? The man had Scott dead in his sights. He could have killed him right there, but he didn't. What kind of game was he playing? The troublesome theory they came up with was that the man would torture and kill Maxine to get to Scott. Deuce wanted to see Scott suffer. Somehow, his rival had quickly acquired accurate information on him and Maxine.

"We'll find her," Bugsy said.

Scott didn't reply. He lit a cigar to ease his mind. They had to find her. They had no choice.

Bugsy swiveled his head left and gazed out the back window. He had a chilling thought—a passing notion that it was Layla behind the kidnapping. It made perfect sense to him. His mother had motive to do it, and she knew Maxine's address. They used to be friends, so Layla would know to track Maxine where she would be most vulnerable. He wondered why his father didn't point fingers at her. Maybe he was too upset to think clearly.

Bugsy kept the assumption to himself. If Scott suspected it was Layla, he might kill her. Though Bugsy opposed his mother, the last thing he wanted for her was death. Bugsy knew how far Layla would go to win—and to hurt Maxine was winning. His mother could be a coldhearted bitch. Bugsy suspected she killed Penelope, and now it was Maxine's turn to die. Layla wasn't going down without a fight. She loved a good brawl.

O h shit . . . oh, eat that pussy . . . oh god! Do you, nigga! Do you!"
Layla hollered.

Her manicured hands dug into his bald head, as she arched her back and spread her legs on the comfortable king-size bed. Her muscular and chocolate knight had a tight grip around her lower half, and he was eating her pussy out like a champ. He tasted her sweet and earthly juices. Her pink center was glistening with moisture. Layla felt she *so* needed this. She needed to get her mind off things, especially the separation from her husband.

Her raw sensuality drove him over the edge. The man licked, sucked, tongued, and licked more below. She grabbed his head and held it to her pussy, feeling the warmth of his tongue working her clit and everything else. She was having mini orgasms in his mouth. Her muscles tensed up, causing her to arch her back. He encircled his arms around her thighs tighter so she couldn't get away from him.

"Oh shit, I'm gonna come again! Damn, nigga! Do that shit, nigga!" She panted and huffed.

Layla felt the need to have control over him, and their sexual position shortly transitioned to her on top. Her thighs and pussy straddled his mouth as she gripped her headboard and ground against his face with her pussy quivering. His hands reached up to cup her tits as he took her clit into his mouth and sucked.

When it was all said and done, the chocolate stranger was well worth her time, and her body felt spent from the multiple orgasms. Layla removed herself from the bed, allowing the man to remain comfortable in her presence. His naked frame was barely covered, and his huge endowment showed from under the sheets. It was eye candy for her—maybe something she could deep-throat. But at the moment, she didn't desire that part of him. It was his mouth she fancied.

Layla put their sexual evening on hold to handle some business. She donned a long white robe, lit a cigarette, and poured herself a drink from the makeshift bar. Her chocolate lover gazed at her with admiration from across the room. He wanted more. He wanted to feel her tight and wet cave, her legs wrapped around him.

"Are you coming back to bed?" he asked.

She shot a stern look his way. "Who told you to speak?"

She cut down the hulking ebony hunk with her dominating attitude. If he kept annoying her, then she would tell him to leave. She'd gotten what she wanted.

She traveled to the floor-to-ceiling windows and looked at the city lights. While the cold was biting outside, Layla was comfortable inside the lavish penthouse with her cigarette, her drink, and her hard, chocolate dick. With civil war within the family, she kept her cool and was pushing forward with building her empire. Now that she had the finances, all she needed was loyalty from her children and her goons.

Two out of three wasn't bad, but she wanted Bugsy on her team. He was smart, and with him by her side, there would be nothing she couldn't do. She could take over the world. But Bugsy was his father's son, and he was adamant to remain with Scott. So she had to make do without him.

Layla finished her cigarette and continued to stand by the window. Her attention was on an illuminated Manhattan horizon on a full moon night while she talked on her cell phone. There was so much to do, and she had to be smart about her business and her network. The first thing she did was meet with a team of lawyers and accountants to launder her money—and one-third of it was wired to an offshore account in the Cayman Islands—over sixteen million dollars was sent. Layla felt she needed to build a wall around her, from the streets with Lucky and Meyer, to her band of trusted lawyers and accountants that would shield her from prosecution or financial downfall. The last thing she needed was the feds and IRS knocking down her door and trying to take away everything she'd worked so hard to build.

She'd spent many weeks with her dream team of lawyers and accountants, separating herself from Scott and anything they'd built together. She had enough cash and collateral to do whatever she wanted.

When Scott threw her out on the street like trash the look on his and Maxine's face said that they had broken her. Well, Layla had been picking up the pieces. While everyone was celebrating the holidays, she was making inroads with heads of prominent cartels to see if she could earn a seat at the table. Her name got her a few meetings. Her street smarts, winner's mind, and business acumen would need to seal the deal.

She had to find a new connect and then strategize on moving kilos on the streets. She trusted Meyer and Lucky for that—street dominance. The two siblings were fierce separately, but together, they were a force to be reckoned with.

Drug manufacturing and distribution was a lucrative, but dangerous, business. If you're fortunate enough to outmaneuver your opposition on your way to the top, then you've only won half the battle. The real test was staying there. This feud had sparked Layla's ambition. She didn't want to stand shoulder-to-shoulder with an exclusive club of cartel heads usually reserved only for men; she wanted to be the boss of bosses.

Yes, Layla was building something powerful for herself, and she was determined not to let anything get in her way. She wanted to destroy Scott and decapitate Maxine and see their bodies rot in the gutter. She was a woman scorned, and her payback would be a muthafucka.

Her chocolate lover was still waiting patiently in bed for her to rejoin him for round two of some hardcore fucking. But he dared not to interrupt her while she was on her phone. She gave him a warning to be quiet, and he took heed. Layla's reputation was brutal, and he knew she was connected to some dangerous people. She was becoming a powerful woman in the underworld, and she could easily have someone killed anywhere in the boroughs with the snap of her fingers. So while he waited, he took it upon himself to jerk off while watching her from the bed.

"Not over the phone," she told someone. "Tomorrow evening . . . I'll call you back with the location."

She ended the call and threw back a shot of vodka. She didn't tie her robe together, leaving it open to expose her perky tits and shaved pussy. It was eye candy for the chocolate man waiting for sexual healing.

She lingered by the window for a moment before pivoting with a stern look. "Time to leave."

Her words baffled him. "Leave? Why? Did I do something wrong?"

She didn't need to explain herself. She'd already gotten what she wanted from him.

He removed himself from the bed and looked reluctant to leave. He wanted her badly, and all nine inches of him hung low and strong. But tonight, she wasn't impressed by it. The shop was closed.

"I thought we were gonna fuck," he said.

"I'm not in the mood for it."

"So you get yours, and I don't get mine?" he said.

"You have a problem with that?"

He did. But he would not gripe about it. It would have been suicidal. If it were anyone else, he would have slapped the shit out of her for playing him. He didn't go around licking pussy as a hobby. What the fuck he look like? But Layla's look was intimidating. She had two armed men nearby in case of an emergency—meaning if she needed someone manhandled or killed. And for her personal protection, she had a Glock 17 and a .380 hidden inside the room.

Crushed by her change of mood, he just answered, "Nah, I don't have a problem. I had fun tonight."

She ignored him. He collected his things and quietly exited without a single argument. Layla had the power, and it felt good controlling him like that. He stood six-two, muscles everywhere, and he had arms and a chest so big that it would have made The Rock look small. When the door closed behind him, Layla smirked. Her pussy had been well taken care of tonight.

Power was a hell of a drug for Layla. It felt good to know that she could do and take whatever she wanted from men like him at her beck and call, submitting to her, knowing if they dared come against her they would be violently dealt with. Layla loved the feeling; the power was fascinating, always had been. And with her power, she wanted to crush her husband and see Maxine's head on a silver platter. She had become independent, and now it was time to be a boss bitch.

Layla felt it wouldn't be long until those who betrayed her, embarrassed her, and went against her would be dealt with. She wanted to see them cowering beneath her designer heels before she squashed them like the bugs they were.

W acka didn't plan on abducting Maxine. His original plan was to torture and kill her in her mother's home. He even thought about opening her mother's neck up from left to right with a sharp knife and making Maxine watch her bleed out. Seeing the old lady in her sleep, though, he thought about sparing her. She had nothing to do with his beef with Maxine. But why show compassion? Wacka wished the triggermen that'd come to his mother's home would have given her the same courtesy, but they didn't. They gunned down his family like they were nothing, and now he wanted retribution.

"You don't have to do this, Wacka. I'm sorry for what happened to your family, but that wasn't on me. It was Layla's doing," Maxine said, driving the car on the highway. She had no clue where they were going.

Wacka didn't care for her pleas or pity, or her explanations. He had one motive on his mind, and that was killing anyone who had a hand in his family's murder. He remained stone cold.

Maxine would not give up on not dying today. She thought she could talk some sense into him. "I know we can work something out. Just talk to me."

He stayed quiet, and the gun still was a deadly threat to her. She could almost see down the barrel. One squeeze of the trigger and a bullet would enter the side of her face and blow her brains out. But not at the moment, because she was the one controlling the car on the highway.

Traffic was sparse on the Sunday morning, and Maxine felt time on her life was winding down—tick-tock, tick-tock, tick-tock.

She glanced at Wacka. The gun was so close to her face she could smell the gunpowder. Then she turned to look through the windshield, the car doing sixty miles per hour on the road. She could feel his despair and his anger; his face was twisted in a snarl, and his eyes continued watching her every move.

"How did you find me anyway? How did you know I would be at my mother's place? Have you been following me?" she asked him.

He remained silent.

There was no need to follow her. Wacka knew her mother was important to her. He had been showing up at the house three or four times a day for weeks, waiting for Maxine to show up, going unnoticed by the neighbors and the old woman. He felt pity for the old lady. She was alone with no regular visitors. It seemed like Maxine had abandoned her.

"You're a selfish bitch," he growled.

"I'm not," she said.

"I coulda killed your mother weeks ago, and you would'na known she was dead."

Immediately she felt guilty. "I love my mother."

"You left her to grow old and die alone. I was willing to put her out of her misery," he said.

She frowned. It was a conversation she didn't want to have with him. He made her feel small and self-centered. Maxine wanted to change the subject. She glanced at him and then said, "Shiniquia was my best friend. I would never do anything to hurt her. She helped me out a lot."

The fast wallop from the butt of the gun to the side of her face came unexpectedly. It caused her to swerve on the highway, nearly creating a crash. She regrouped and took control over the car. Blood trickled from the side of her head. The pain was agonizing.

"Don't you ever say her fuckin' name again," Wacka shouted.

Maxine frowned. She would not be bullied or threatened. She felt he would kill her anyway. She would not go quietly.

"I didn't double cross her. I was her fuckin' friend," she said. "I can help you, Wacka. I can become a friend, and I can get you closer to Layla. She's the one you want to kill, not me. "

He scowled and thrust the gun to her temple. "Shut da fuck up!" he hollered.

None of it was getting through to him. His family was dead, and he was a wanted and hunted man in the city and most likely everywhere else. Scott was an influential man, and Wacka knew people like him wouldn't stop until the day he was dead. But Wacka wasn't going out without a fight, and his first victim would be Maxine.

"Keep fuckin' driving," he said.

She wasn't persuading him. He was dead set on killing her. She saw the signs on the Belt Parkway taking her to the Verrazano Bridge. How far was he taking her? Maxine guessed he was taking her to a desolate place to kill her. She had to do something. She was desperate to survive. She wanted to live, but if she did die, then she would take him with her, and that meant she had to do the extreme. So, she accelerated the car, and it went from fifty-five to seventy-five miles per hour in a heartbeat.

Wacka noticed the sudden speed. "What the fuck you doin'?"

Maxine turned the steering wheel abruptly, veering into a sharp right and deliberately sideswiping a van at high speed. The car flipped over several times on the highway, tumbling around like a bouncing ball and violently throwing her and Wacka around in the car before coming to stop in the middle of the road. Maxine could feel her ribs cracking and a few bones breaking before everything came to a halt. The chaos on the highway turned into a pile-up with three vehicles. Blood trickled from her face. She felt trapped, and she smelled smoke. Wacka was inside the crashed and twisted piece of metal, still. Was he still alive? She didn't know. But she knew that she was in bad shape. Her body felt mangled. She heard screaming and heard people surrounding the car.

"Someone call 911," she heard a woman shout.

It didn't take long before someone was pulling her out from the driver's seat, and every part of her body was in pain. Maxine could hear the emergency sirens getting louder as they neared the car crash. Her breathing was sparse, and she felt herself slipping into unconsciousness. A female kept shouting, "Stay awake! Ma'am, stay with us!"

Her eyes closed and everything went black.

The chair went smashing against the wall of the room and broke apart, and bottles and small objects went flying across the room, breaking either against the wall or the floor. Scott was going berserk. He put his fist through the wall, cursing and shouting. He was ready to take his guns and hunt for the man who kidnapped Maxine himself.

Bugsy had never seen his father so mad. It was a dangerous situation. He simply stood out of Scott's way, knowing that at the moment there was nothing he could say to him. Scott had been threatened, somehow outsmarted, and embarrassed in front of his goons and his woman. An unknown assailant had gotten the best of him and taken what he loved, and now there was no telling if Maxine was alive or dead.

Beneath all that seething anger and hatred was grave concern and worry for Maxine—and sadness. She could be anywhere by now. He had every one of his men searching throughout the city for Maxine. But New York was a huge place.

Finally, after his emotional temper tantrum, Scott collapsed into the one chair he hadn't broken apart and released a deep sigh. Now wasn't the time for him to fall apart. He had to be more focused and stronger than ever. He needed to finish what he'd started in Delaware and elsewhere, and, most importantly, he had to find Maxine.

Bugsy stood nearby and quietly watched his father's every movement. He knew it wasn't the right time to speak. He read his father's face and gave him his space, knowing that if they had taken Alicia, he probably would have acted the same way.

Why haven't we found and killed Deuce and DMC yet? Scott thought. Was Deuce and his crew that elusive? It had been too long now, and Deuce was that thorn in his side growing more painful. Scott didn't blame himself for trying to take over a town already occupied. The place had potential, and Lucky was right, it was a cash cow. It was a wise business decision, but it also came with significant casualties—his precious children could never be replaced.

Scott lit a cigar, still worried about Maxine. He blamed his men for her being taken and for his kids being murdered. They weren't doing their jobs. Scott felt they were lazy and incompetent. He wanted to kill one of them to release his anger. Any man would do. But he had to get a grip on himself and control the impulse. If he kept killing his people when something went wrong, it would become harder to recruit new soldiers. The last thing Scott needed was unrest among the troops or a revolt against him. Sure, he would rather be feared than loved; but if that fear consumes someone, then they will lash out and kill the one they fear most.

He took a pull from his cigar and continued to remain quiet with Bugsy close by. Scott knew that he needed to strategize. He felt he was holding back on Delaware and Deuce, and now it was time to break out the big guns and go in full throttle. The room was quiet with apprehension, and Bugsy stood like a statue near the wall. Why was his son so calm? Scott wondered. What was he thinking? Bugsy always had a game plan—some clever strategy. Was he now out of ideas?

Scott took a few more drags from his cigar and finally spoke. "I want you to gather everyone on our payroll for a meeting with me. We end this shit today."

Bugsy said, "Where do you want to meet them?"

"The farm upstate," he said.

Bugsy nodded. "I'll have them all up there within the day."

Bugsy left the room to arrange the meeting, while Scott went back to silence and his cigar. Bugsy had to bring over a hundred men in their organization to the farm in upstate New York. It was a giant task—like a massive recall, but he could do it. Why Scott wanted everyone to meet there was a mystery to him. To Bugsy, it seemed like a desperate move, and one thing Bugsy knew was that desperation brought on mistakes. They were in a position where they couldn't afford to make any mistakes.

Bugsy saw several things wrong with bringing gangsters into a rural area in upstate New York, namely the attention it would bring to the rednecks and the police. With that many men in one location, Bugsy saw problems already. But it was his father's call, and Scott was adamant he wanted all of his goons on the 100 acres of farmland he owned.

It was another cold day in January, and there were over fifty cars, vans, and SUVs parked on the West farmland. Droves of thugs and gangsters had traveled nearly two hours from the city to the luxury farm in Hillside, New York for the impromptu meeting with the boss. The men were bundled up in their winter coats, Timberland boots, and ski hats, shielding themselves from the bitter cold.

Winter had frozen the land and decorated the trees with ice as thick as cake frosting. There was a lake a half-mile away and trails throughout the property. The property also boasted a horse facility that included a ten-stall barn with tack room, feed room, wash rack, outdoor ring, and numerous paddocks with four-board fencing. Scott had a thing for horses and had invested hundreds of thousands of dollars into breeding thoroughbreds.

The main residence was a mansion placed in the middle of the farmland, at the end of a long driveway flanked by board fenced paddocks. The mansion overlooking the vast property was like a palace inside with the latest amenities. The interior was decorated with stone fireplaces and giant flat screens.

In the mansion's great room, the men were greeted with food and drinks, and they socialized like they were at a convention. The West goons were ready for war. They all had heard about the kidnapping of Scott's new love—or old flame—Maxine. They knew about Whistler and Lucky's affair, and now he was an enemy to them all, as was Deuce and his DMC soldiers. They all knew there was a civil war brewing inside the organization. Word on the street was that Layla West had broken off from the faction, stolen an abundance of money from her husband, and had started her own thing with Meyer and Lucky on her team.

It was the first time Scott had called all of them to one location. He had a lot on his plate, but he wasn't buckling or folding in defeat. If the king wanted a war, then the men were prepared to paint the city red with their enemies' blood.

Scott lingered in the master suite alone, contemplating his next move. It was time to galvanize his soldiers. The wolves were trying to knock down his door, believing he was weak from the gossip they'd heard. Whistler was gone, his wife was against him, Lucky and Meyer had defected, and Deuce was trying to make a mockery of his reputation and damage the organization. The wolves wanted to take his empire apart, but they all had another thing coming. He was a veteran of the streets and war. He knew how to survive and read his enemies.

Bugsy was there to oversee everything and everyone. He was respected and feared—the prince to the king. He stood tall among the dozens of goons on the farm. He was the second in command, but it was his father's show.

Scott loomed into the great room looking the part of a leader and a king, dressed in his black tailored suit on such a cold day and his diamond Rolex watch peeking from underneath his diamond cufflinks. His presence was intimidating and demanded respect. To many in the room, especially the younger goons, he was a myth. Finally, they were seeing the man in charge in person. Their leader was flanked by his son and three other armed goons.

Scott eyed the men crowded into the room and stood in quiet for a moment. He puffed on his cigar, and his silence was making a statement. Once he showed up, the room fell quiet, knowing he was about to speak. But he didn't. He only stood there smoking his cigar in silence, and it bewildered Bugsy and others.

Why were they there? Why did he invite everyone to the farm if he would not give them a speech, give those orders, or animate them with rage and hate?

But then he spoke. "I have a treat for y'all niggas," he finally said. "It's outside in the stall barn."

He walked away. His soldiers exited into the cold weather and walked toward the stall barn in droves. Bugsy walked with them. He was in the dark like everyone else.

Once there, several of Scott's lieutenants removed large wooden crates from the barns and pried them open with crowbars. Everyone looked on as the men removed several advanced and high-powered weapons from the crates. There were dozens of Heckler & Koch MP7A1s, over fifty TEC-9s, enough Uzis for an army, and a handful of Z-M LR-300s.

The soldiers were like kids in a toy store. The sight of the weapons generated a new level of enthusiasm among the troops. Bugsy stood there near his father and watched the men unload the weapons from the crates. *Where did they come from?* Bugsy thought. He knew they must have cost his father a small fortune, but they were worth the payment. Now he saw the reason Scott wanted all their goons on the farm. The excitement on everyone's faces was evident. Scott had galvanized his troops into taking action without saying a single word. Bugsy was impressed.

"Now, y'all niggas got your fuckin' toys, I wanna see results with them," Scott boomed out at them with authority. "I want to see every last one of Deuce's men gunned down and destroyed."

Scott didn't care about the fallout it would create on the streets. He'd had enough of the bullshit. His lawyers were on standby, and his peoples knew to keep their mouths shut if caught. Everyone was ready.

Half of the goons were dispatched to Delaware, and those remaining would stay in the city to hunt for the man who'd abducted Maxine.

Scott turned to Bugsy and said, "I want you in Delaware too. You're the only one I can trust to get things done right down there. You got the guns and the manpower to smoke that muthafucka out from his hole once and for all."

Bugsy was taken aback by the request. He didn't mind the order, but he was his father's right-hand man, and he felt he should be close by with everything going on. He didn't disobey the order. Bugsy understood that Deuce was their top priority. They couldn't underestimate their rival any longer. The mistake had cost them dearly. With him still breathing, no one would ever be safe.

Bugsy nodded. "I'm on it. I already got something conjured up to make him come out of hiding."

"Get it done."

Bugsy knew he would.

Mason received an urgent phone call and knew he had to deliver the news to Scott right away. He walked toward his boss and whispered in his ear, "It's Maxine. They found her—alive."

"Where is she?" he asked with apprehension in his voice.

"In the hospital," Mason said.

"The hospital?"

"She was in a terrible car accident on the Belt Parkway. She's in Brookdale."

42

The news made Scott pivot and hurry from the stall barn. He was on a mission to get back to the city quickly. He needed to see her. He needed to see if she was okay. He remained deadpan and marched toward the SUV. He wanted to be by her side. And he wanted answers. Where was the goon? How did she get into an accident? He climbed into the backseat of the Escalade, and his chauffeur whisked him away. He left Bugsy in charge.

8

The Learjet descended toward the private airfield in Miami. The pilot announced that they would be touching down in fifteen minutes. Layla downed the last of the champagne from her stemmed glass feeling ambivalent about being back in Florida. She was there for business, not pleasure. She had no access to her estate in the Keys and arranged to check into a hotel near the beach. The compound was a painful reminder of the grief and betrayal she'd been through. Fortunately, she had moved on to bigger and better things.

Layla stared out the window, observing the city below come closer and closer as her plane descended. It was mid-January, early afternoon, and it was a sunny and beautiful day in Miami—a complete contrast to the New York cold and snow. The plane touched down on the sun-drenched runway, and the pilots skillfully guided the Learjet onto the tarmac. The plane came to a complete stop near an idling black Maybach. The door opened, and the stairs came down. Layla, Lucky, and Meyer exited the plane and entered the Mercedes. The chauffeur exited the runway and drove toward the expressway. Immediately, Layla was on the phone conducting business, making big boy moves.

"We're in Miami. Our ETA is fifteen minutes," she said to someone over the phone.

"Who that?" Meyer asked brusquely.

"Insurance," Layla replied.

While the driver navigated the Maybach through the Miami traffic, Layla sat looking unbothered. If she was nervous about meeting with cartel kingpin Angel Morales, it didn't show on her face or actions. To her kids, she seemed as cool a cucumber.

"Where is this meeting at?" Meyer asked.

"In Coconut Grove," Layla said.

"I don't trust this fool, Ma. I don't trust the fuckin' cartel," Meyer voiced.

"He's willing to meet with me, so you keep your temperament cool and chill, Meyer. The last thing we need is any problems. I have enough of that with your father. We need a connect in these streets, so I'll do the talkin'. The two of y'all observe and watch my back," Layla said to her children.

"I am chill, and I got your back. I'm just sayin', this fool got a nasty reputation for making people disappear, even for the slightest disrespect. I heard these muthafuckas cut up bodies and dump 'em in barrels of acid— fuck a nigga up fo' real. No body, no murder, right?" Meyer said, almost sounding impressed by it.

"It's the cartel. What do you expect?" Lucky said.

"I expect them to treat us with respect once we're there. If not, then they ain't gonna be the only fools that will make a body disappear."

"Everything will be okay. Our reputation precedes us from the streets to business, and Angel is a businessman from my understanding. I'll make him an offer he can't refuse," Layla said.

"And if he does?" Meyer questioned her.

"He won't," she replied with confidence.

Meyer smiled and replied, "The ball's in your hands, Ma. Let's roll."

The Maybach traveled south on S. Dixie Highway and soon reached the affluent and lush neighborhood called Coconut Grove—a charming, bayside village within urban Miami. The sleek Maybach approached a sprawling estate at the end of Anchorage Way, and it came to a stop at the towering iron gates, where an armed Latino man stood guard. He gawked at the vehicle with suspicion. He approached the car with a scowl and leaned into the driver's seat. He asked, "Who you here to see?"

"Layla West to see Angel Morales," the chauffeur replied.

The guard got on his two-way radio and called it in to his superiors. It took less than twenty seconds for them to respond.

"She's expected. Let her through."

The guard nodded and waved them through. The gates slowly opened, and the chauffeur moved the vehicle through the gates and onto the property. Layla wasn't impressed with the extravagant estate. Her former estate was bigger and better. She eyed the trimmed shrubberies and the slim trees; everything was neatly manicured, and it made her think of her sexy gardener, Fabian. Oh, how she missed watching him work shirtless on her property. She wished she had fucked him.

The Maybach finally came to a stop outside the two-story home surrounded by privacy and opulence. Two armed guards were posted outside the double doors. Things were looking serious already.

The Maybach doors opened thanks to their chauffeur, and Layla was the last to exit the vehicle. Looking stunning in her open-back little black dress and high stilettos, she strutted toward the house with an air of confidence about her. Meyer and Lucky followed her inside. They were greeted by one of Angel's men, and he led them past lots of rooms and long hallways. Layla's stilettos clicked softly against the marble floors as she edged down the hall behind the henchmen. She strutted past rare paintings and cultural statues. She felt for a Mexican thug, the man had some taste in his decor.

The trio was led outside, and before they were to step any farther into the area, they were greeted by several security guards who all looked like they had swallowed something sour. Docked nearby was a 100-foot yacht.

"You all must be searched before meeting with the boss," the lead security guard said.

Meyer immediately let them know, "I'm strapped, nigga." He lifted his shirt to reveal the 9mm tucked in his waistband. He also had a pistol concealed in an ankle holster.

The guards looked at Meyer deadpan. They didn't see him as a threat, as he was outgunned and outnumbered, but he still had to surrender his weapons. He did so reluctantly. With that, the trio was led across the private 90-foot cement dock and boarded the lavish yacht.

Angel Morales sat at the stern with a bottle of Cristal champagne in an ice bucket in front of him. He was surrounded by several other yachts, the beautiful blue ocean, and a bright sun. Angel stood upon their arrival and smiled at them.

"Layla West, the wife of a street legend," he greeted them.

"Legends are usually dead, and my husband is very much alive," she replied quietly.

He smiled. "Yes, he is . . . and too bad he's playing for the wrong team," he said, referring to Scott's business relationship with Angel's rival, Javier Garcia.

"Well, I'm not here to talk about my husband. I'm here to talk business," Layla replied.

"I see. Sit. Let's talk."

Angel had a cigar shoved in the side of his mouth. *Men and their cigars. What is so special about them?* she thought. Layla and Lucky sat opposite Angel on the stern. Meyer stood. He wanted to be on his p's and q's. He didn't trust the man.

"Champagne?" Angel offered them.

Angel's male servant immediately loomed from the yacht's interior, ready to serve the guests with whatever they needed. Layla waved him off. She wanted to get straight to her reason for coming there.

Angel took a pull from the cigar and fixed his attention on Layla. She was a breathtaking woman—more beautiful than he'd imagined.

"You want to do business with me, this is what I hear," he said calmly.

"I didn't travel to Miami just to socialize and take in the view . . . been there and done that," Layla said candidly.

He chuckled. "I know that you're no stranger to my city."

His appearance didn't seem dangerous or threatening. Angel was mild-mannered, standing five-eight and 180 lbs. His wardrobe was neatly put together. He wore white shorts, a clean white shirt with white loafers, and a gold watch around his wrist. There was nothing gaudy about him. He was missing out on muscles, with slicked-back hair and a neat Freddie Prinze mustache. He didn't even have a two-pack under his white shirt. What he lacked in physical dominance, he made up for with his brutal temperament. He was a dangerous man with a hair-trigger temper. He'd collected enough bodies to fill a cemetery.

"Listen," Layla leaned forward in her seat, "I have the muscle and the means. All I need is a connect to help build my organization," she said.

"You see, my problem with you is you're a señora. And I always believed a señora is only good for two things—giving me pussy and giving birth," he said.

The insensitive comment made Meyer scowl. Lucky frowned too, but Layla didn't even flinch at the remark.

Angel then continued with, "And two, your *Scott's* señora, and do I need a war with him and Javier by jumping into bed with you? I hear there's a lot of discord in your camp."

"You wouldn't have taken this meeting with me if you weren't willing to hear me out," replied Layla.

He puffed on his cigar and wasn't quick to respond to her comment. He did everything leisurely. He was the boss, and he didn't have to hurry for anyone.

"How do I benefit from you?" asked Angel. "How can you guarantee that our business dealings will be worth the heat?"

Layla sat back and crossed her long legs in front of him. "I can handle Scott." She meant that. "I'm a dangerous woman with the heart of a warrior. I don't scare easily, if at all. Now, you might think señoras are only to be fucked, which is understandable. But I didn't come this far to debate antiquated ideologies. But to let you know how serious I am, I came with gifts."

She glanced at Meyer and nodded. He pivoted and left the boat.

"I like you already," said Angel.

"I don't want you to like me; I want you to respect me," she said.

Angel laughed. He reached forward and removed the champagne bottle from the ice bucket and poured himself a full glass. He took a sip and leaned back. His eyes were on Layla and her lovely figure in the tight, black dress.

"I assume you heard about my reputation," he said.

"I have. I vetted you, as I know you've vetted me," she said.

"So knowing what you know about me, does it scare you? Because believe me, I treat women as equals to men when it comes to punishment."

Layla didn't miss a beat. She locked eyes with him. "I'm a businesswoman, and I can hold my own in the streets and anywhere else. Do I look like I'm ready to fuck you over?"

Just then, Meyer arrived back on the yacht carrying a brown duffle bag. It caught Angel's attention. Meyer walked over to him with Angel's gun-toting goons watching his every move. Meyer placed the duffle bag on the table near Angel and slowly unzipped it. Angel took a peek and saw the abundance of cash inside. It was 1.5 million dollars to be exact.

Layla looked at him smugly and said, "Like I said, I'm about my business, and I'm ready to work with you. That's just a taste."

"And what's your network like?" Angel asked her.

"I learned from the best, and I have a team put together in New York City, Delaware, New Jersey, and upstate. You deliver the kilos to me in New York, and I'll take over from there. I can guarantee turnover in a week's time," she said.

"A bitch in your position and you still want to run and play in the mud with the dogs and get your cute shoes dirty. I find that puzzling. You have many legal businesses and you can step away from all of this, so why?"

"Because this shit—it's in my fuckin' blood. I love the hustle, and I love the power. It's the one thing that gets my pussy truly wet," Layla replied.

Angel laughed again. "I'll toast to that," he said, holding his glass up.

Meyer stood near his mother, still on edge. He felt he could never trust a man like Angel Morales, and he would protect his mother by any means necessary. Lucky remained silent and allowed her mother to work her magic with the cartel kingpin. She was nervous, but she didn't show it. She too wanted respect from men like Angel Morales and to gain that power—not just on the streets, but everywhere from the political world to the corporate. She didn't want to be in her parents' shadow forever. So, she watched her mother work, and she was taking notes.

Layla and Angel worked out the details in shipment, payment, and logistics. She was ready to flood the city with so many drugs, it would look like the blizzard of '96. She would show Scott and everyone else how she got down. It was her time, she felt, and she was ready to become the next Griselda Blanco, but even more powerful.

The trio left the house and climbed back into the Maybach. As the car drove away from the location, Layla felt proud of herself. She'd sealed the deal with Angel Morales, and this was only the beginning.

"What was your insurance that he wouldn't kill us right there?" Meyer asked her.

Layla replied, "I vetted him and knew that he likes to take his meetings on his yacht. My insurance was our goons on the adjacent yacht with their guns trained on Angel. All I had to do was give the signal, and Angel's brains would have blown out of his eye socket."

"And we still would have been fucked. I was unarmed," Meyer said.

"But our chauffeur wasn't," she said.

"So you had everything under control, huh?" Lucky said.

"I wasn't goin' in there blind," said Layla.

It was all a risk, but it had paid off. Layla felt she thought everything through, but Meyer and Lucky knew that they were still on shaky ground. Lucky knew that you don't betray or kill a man like Angel Morales and not have it blow back on you.

As the Maybach traveled to the hotel, a call from New York came in to Layla's cell phone. The juicy gossip about Maxine had reached her in Miami.

"What happened?" she said.

By the time Layla got news from a source that Maxine had been kidnapped, the next thing she heard was that she'd escaped death and was in the hospital.

"That bitch got nine lives," Layla exclaimed.

Layla was pissed off on so many levels. She couldn't revel and gloat that Maxine was most likely kidnapped because of Scott. Maxine had stepped into her shoes just in time. She was making major moves and felt that Maxine and Scott deserved each other. Their time would come.

Lucky was happy to be back in New York. Miami was beautiful and sunny, and their meeting with Angel Morales had gone well, but there was nothing like home—though it was asshole cold in the Big Apple. Lucky had personal and business affairs to tend to. Like her mother, Lucky was a hustler. She was smart enough to know how to make something happen for herself and not fall victim to the streets. She had learned from the best—her father, even though she hated his guts at the moment. Scott and Whistler were once her idols, and they knew the street game. Her father could hide behind a suit-and-tie and his companies all he wanted, but he was still a Brooklyn drug dealer deep in the game.

Lucky was a hundred percent behind her mother, though. She would follow Layla into hell. The trust was there, and Layla had a plan and a motive. Her mother was determined to outshine Scott and take complete control over the drug trade and build up her empire. Layla was setting up a system for herself that seemed foolproof, starting with winning over Angel Morales. Layla planned to forge a level of trust with Angel so strong, he would support her when push came to shove.

Lucky glanced at herself in the small mirror in the sun visor. Her look tonight was simple— long hair in a ponytail, a baseball cap, blue jeans, black Puma sneakers, and a winter coat. Her gaze lingered on her droopy eye for a moment, a harsh reminder of what she'd been through. Lucky felt Whistler was to blame that she was no longer flawless. She was still pretty, but she wasn't perfect anymore. *Why not kill me?* she thought. Why leave her alive to remember when they beat her and disfigured her? Why kill Gotti, Bonnie, and Clyde, but spare her life? Lucky had so many questions, and she wondered if she would ever get the answers. Would she ever run across the men again that brutally attacked her? She could remember the smell of one; his stench was strong of alcohol, cigarettes, and body odor.

Lucky snapped herself out of that nightmare and released a deep sigh. She sat parked outside the glass high-rise residential building on 57th Street in Hell's Kitchen. Instead of her G-Wagen, she drove a green Tahoe—the company car, as her mother would put it. The name of her mother's new empire was Boss Bitch, Inc. Layla had big plans, and they were being implemented skillfully. It was gonna be like Rome during its heyday.

She climbed out of the Tahoe and strutted toward the building in the middle of the night. Lucky was on a mission, one she hoped would benefit her. She needed tonight, especially with so much on her mind. She stepped into the lobby, moved past the night guard with ease, and headed toward the elevators. Moments later, she was on the fifteenth floor and knocking on the apartment door.

Carter answered with a smile, expecting the company at the late hour. He allowed her into the swanky apartment. It was something she was used to—the affluent lifestyle—her place being bigger than his. But as far as he knew, Lucky was a down-to-earth girl from humble beginnings. He did not understand who she was—that she was a West, and that her father was Scott West, major drug kingpin, real estate tycoon, and business mogul.

Dressed in a long, black robe and Nike slippers, looking like he had just stepped out of the shower, Carter looked at Lucky hungrily, like he just ordered takeout food. He was excited to see her. He was high yellow and clean shaven, but a solid looking man in his mid-forties with notable power. He wasn't as powerful as her father, but Carter was a major player in the game, and he controlled areas in Staten Island, Philly, B-more, and West Virginia. Over the years, he'd taken a lot of losses, longer stints of jail time, and was shot three times in different incidents. Yet, he was still in the game. He was a survivor, and he knew the game and the streets like the back of his hand. It was one reason Lucky was drawn to him.

"You look beautiful tonight," he said.

Do I?

She remained expressionless—no smile and no thank-you. What she was wearing seemed Salvation Army, but he liked her in the plain wardrobe. She wasn't pretentious like the other women he'd encountered, and he was itching to spoil her rotten. He stepped toward her and promptly grabbed her roughly into his arms. It wasn't a shock to her. He pushed her against the wall, pressed his body against hers, and locked his lips with hers. She didn't resist. They kissed passionately. He swiped his tongue across hers, tasting her, learning her, demanding a lot more from her. Her coat flew off, his hands went up her shirt, and he cupped her breast. It was an intense moment. He wanted her so badly that his penis grew hard like steel and concrete combined. His robe opened up, and he was naked underneath. Lucky was still pinned to the wall when she took his hard dick into her hand and gently jerked him off while they continued to kiss passionately. Their breathing became one.

"I want you to fuck me," she said into his ear.

He hurriedly undressed her. Her jeans dropped, her shirt ripped away, and her bra quickly unsnapped. Carter scooped Lucky up into his arms, urging her thighs apart so she could she straddle him. Still pinned to the wall with her legs wrapped around him, he thrust himself inside of her, not pausing to wrap up his dick. She grunted and felt him inside of her. What was it about older men she loved so much?

"Oh shit . . . Ooooh, you got that good pussy," he howled, plunging deep inside her.

He continued to fuck her vigorously against the wall, feeling a strong orgasm brewing. He was dangerously close to getting his first. Her nails clawed into his shoulders, her hips bobbed, and her legs tightened around him with her tits smashed against his chest. She squirmed against him, clinging. He squeezed her ass and pumped his hard dick in and out of her.

"Fuck me!" she cried out. "I'm 'bout to come!"

It was becoming harder for him to hold out. Her pussy was tight and too wet. Suddenly, he released inside of her, shuddering from the excitement and feeling his knees wobble, but he remained upright and firm, still holding Lucky in his arms. Immediately, her walls tightened around him, and she screeched with pleasure as she came. Finally, he released her from his passionate hold and stepped back.

Shit! Carter exhaled. He needed to collect himself. The sexual rendezvous was intense. It almost felt like he would never stop coming inside of her. He'd never had it so good—and it was *good*. He was ready to spoil her, take her on a shopping spree again, and flaunt his wealth.

"I needed that," she said.

"I did too," he said.

Lucky was never one to be subtle. They were only two weeks deep, and he was already whipped. He was throwing money at her she didn't need, taking her on shopping sprees that she could afford herself, and buying her diamonds she wouldn't wear. But she loved the attention from him. Carter seemed to overlook her droopy eye. He believed that Lucky was a college kid in a one-parent home. Her fake mother was a doctor, and she never knew her father. It was a lie well told to him, and he wanted to take care of her. Carter wanted to parade his young and sexy woman around town, but Lucky wasn't having any of it. She only wanted one thing from him, and that was dick. She was never giving her heart to another man again. It would strictly be sex and nothing else. Whistler had fucked her all the way up.

They'd met at a nightclub. He sat in VIP, and something about her transfixed him as she walked by. Carter knew sex when he saw it, and Lucky was sexy; he saw no flaws in her. Her body was to die for. The two exchanged numbers, and he'd been relentlessly pursuing her ever since.

The more Lucky shunned his romantic and sweet gestures, the more it made him want her. It turned him on, Lucky's aloofness toward his money and power. Usually, bitches wanted Carter to wife them, but not Lucky. She continued to carry an exceedingly nonchalant attitude toward the things he could do for her. She was nineteen years old, and on one hand that made Carter feel young and virile, but when she didn't want to be seen with him that made him feel unwanted and old, and sometimes used.

The one thing Lucky didn't like about him was the controlling attitude—and his mouth. Trying to impress Lucky, and also to show he trusted her, he did the one thing that no drug dealer should ever do—and that was talk a lot. He wouldn't stop running his mouth to her about his operation. He would tell Lucky everything about his business, his connect, his crimes, and his wealth. It was pillow talk. A hustler's enemy.

But after fucking, she wanted nothing to do with him. He wanted her to stay the night. She didn't want to.

"I want you to fly with me to Jamaica this weekend. I got a meeting with some peoples out there, and I'll be staying in a beautiful resort—five stars, the best food, spa, and everything. You can enjoy the beach and the spa, manicures, and massage. Everything's paid for. You don't have to worry about anything," he said.

She politely turned him down, saying, "I have class."

"I'll have you back Sunday night. You'll have fun, believe me."

"Maybe next time," she said.

He was disappointed. Carter wanted more than just quickies with her. He wanted to get to know her better. He wanted to spoil her with the things she liked. But she never told him what she wanted.

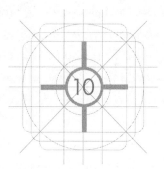

Whistler sat shotgun in the black Yukon watching the front entrance to the warehouse with Deuce and Jimmy. The men smoked cigarettes and made small talk while armed like soldiers in a Rambo movie. They were accompanied by a dozen henchmen in cargo vans who were ready to pop off and kill everyone inside.

The location was well known to Whistler; it was one of Scott's warehouses in Trenton, New Jersey. He told Deuce and Jimmy that the location was a large cash drop-off point—a hub between Delaware and New York—and five to ten million dollars could be inside.

Deuce wanted that money. He wanted to strike quickly and continue to wreak havoc on the West organization. With Whistler on their team—for now anyway, he felt it wouldn't be long before he brought the West organization to its knees. He would cut off the head and watch it all collapse. Deuce wanted this more than anything. He wanted bloodshed, and he wanted to crush everything his rivals had built. The bonus would be to murder Layla and Lucky in front of Scott and his two sons.

Deuce was thinking crazy thoughts. His latest was ruminating about burying the whole West family alive. He'd dig five deep holes and bury them in wooden coffins in unmarked graves. The thought of them clawing at the wood until they ripped their fingernails out—gasping for air and screaming to no avail—excited him.

Deuce sat in the backseat and looked through his binoculars at the two-story, brick-and-metal warehouse near the railroad with arched windows, pilasters, and other corbelled brickwork. He inspected the exterior from his distance and it appeared to be his for the taking. Everything seemed quiet in the industrial part of town in the late evening. The sun was gradually descending behind the horizon, and the cold wind was blowing. There was a brown van parked nearby, and one man dressed in a bubble coat was standing alone near the place, pacing back and forth. If he was security, then Deuce believed it was a joke.

"We hit them hard and kill everyone inside," said Deuce.

"I say we shouldn't—not yet anyway. Something isn't right," Whistler protested.

"Fuck that, nigga. You don't have a voice in this shit here. You're intel, nigga, and it's the only reason we kept you alive. If you correct wit' this information, then we good," said Deuce.

It was an uneasy relationship between them. Whistler had been caught slipping. He had been so worried about Scott and Lucky that he'd put Deuce on the back burner, and now he was paying for it. Deuce was smart, manipulative, and psychopathic. He had set the trap for Whistler and patiently waited for his capture.

Whistler griped about how the warehouse was oddly not guarded; one man standing outside didn't make sense to him. He wanted to hold back on the attack. He felt it was a trap, but Deuce wasn't listening. Deuce wanted to go into the place with his guns blazing, trap or no trap. It would be another knockdown on Scott.

Jimmy sat quietly for a moment in the driver's seat. He watched everything in the surrounding area. "You sure about this, Deuce? Maybe he's right . . . something ain't right," Jimmy said.

"Y'all niggas questioning me now? Huh, muthafuckas? You say it's some serious money in there—millions of dollars—and we gonna let that shit go by without checkin' it out? Y'all muthafuckas crazy. It's tax time, and they gotta pay. I say we hit these muthafuckas now and fuck shit up. I'm tired of playing wit' these niggas," Deuce shouted. He was the boss, and he gave the executive order to his men.

Whistler and Jimmy seemed to acquiesce. They locked and loaded their weapons and exited the Yukon. Behind them, the doors to the vans opened up and a gang of armed goons exited into the street. Winter coats, handguns, and assault rifles—they looked like overzealous thugs in a rap video. But this was the real deal; every man approaching the warehouse had a murderous resume, and there was no director on set to yell "cut" if there was a mistake. Whistler was among the men carrying Glocks. His heart raced, and he was watchful of everything. He knew Scott, and he wouldn't have made it so easy.

The man outside was taken out first and fast. He went down brutally with two bullets to his head. So far, so good. A dozen men were ready to storm the property. There was no turning back, trap or not. They kicked the door in and rushed into the building. Deuce's men were met with minimum resistance and gunfire from Scott's men. The gunfight was brief, and after the smoke cleared, three more of Scott's men lay dead. Deuce spit on their bodies and felt victorious.

The men inspected the entire building, and there was no one else inside—no other threats. Deuce noticed several black barrels on pallets, twelve in total. They were quickly opened, and what everyone saw inside elated them. Even Deuce grinned like a school child when he saw that the barrels were filled with money bundled in ten-thousand-dollar stacks. It was more than they could count at the moment.

"Shit! Now this is what the fuck I'm talkin' about," Deuce said.

Whistler stood in the background and was quiet. To him, it was still too easy. Did they not see it? Why were there only four men watching millions and millions of dollars? That uneasy feeling swam inside of him.

Could it be a booby-trap? Could there be hundreds of men on their way to the location to kill them all? Whistler didn't want to stick around and find out.

Deuce picked up a handful of stacks from the barrel and smiled at Whistler. "You did good, nigga. You were on point today."

Whistler didn't feel on point. He felt apprehensive. He gripped his gun tight, and said, "We need to leave quickly."

"Yo, y'all niggas start loading this money up into the vans," Deuce said. "We takin' it all."

They were all happy to oblige. The barrels were loaded into the white cargo vans for transportation.

Even Jimmy looked pleased with everything. Whatever apprehension he felt earlier flew out the door once he saw the money. He looked at Whistler and said, "Maybe your boy is getting sloppy."

Scott was never sloppy with his business, especially with the money. Even if Scott slipped, he had Bugsy to catch him—and Bugsy was just as diabolical. He was one to watch out for. He was smart and calculating.

With the last barrel loaded into the van, Deuce wanted to leave a thank-you note behind. He cut the throat of one dead man in the warehouse and scrawled onto the drywall of the building with blood: *Thanks for the gift! -DMC*

He smiled at his ruthless handiwork. The bloody message was displayed loud and clear. Whoever came in afterward would right away see the *Fuck-You* message from DMC.

"Let's get the fuck outta here," Deuce said.

Their exit from the warehouse was smooth. There was no surprise attack from the outside as Whistler had feared. No one was waiting to ambush them. The area was like a ghost town. Everyone got into the vehicles and drove off like bandits on horseback disappearing into the rugged terrain.

Alicia pressed her lips to Bugsy's chest and snuggled against him, slowly running her fingers across his chest, touching him tenderly and letting him touch back. The two had just made passionate love, and they were enjoying a quiet night together. Alicia's soft, naked frame was like heaven against Bugsy's skin as he held her in his arms lovingly. He relished moments like these. He looked into her eyes and saw an angel upon him. Alicia was everything he'd dreamed of. When she kissed him, it felt like she could wash away all his sins. What would he do without her? Their bodies touched beneath the sheets, and their kisses were passionate and lingering. He softly fondled her beautiful full breasts and ran his hands up and down her back and into her hair.

"I love you," Alicia whispered.

"I love you too," he said.

Their adoring and intimate moment was then curtly interrupted by Bugsy's cell phone ringing. At first, he didn't want to answer it. Running back and forth between New York and Delaware ate away at his quality time with Alicia. But it rang again, and he worried it was an important call. With Alicia smiling at him, he reluctantly got up from the bed naked and picked up the phone.

"What's up?"

The caller on the other end exclaimed, "Bugsy, the warehouse in Trenton got hit just now—four of our men dead! It was DMC. They left us a fuckin' message on the muthafuckin' wall!"

The news wasn't a shock to Bugsy. He was expecting it. He told the caller, "I'm on it."

He hung up. His intuition was right. Sooner or later their enemies would come for the money. He had a surprise for them, though. Though they had changed up everything in their organization, the one thing Bugsy kept the same was the warehouse in Trenton, New Jersey—one of their main hubs for money drop off and transport. He figured it would become one of their rivals' primary targets.

"Everything okay, baby?" Alicia asked him.

"Yeah, everything's cool. I'm just checking up on something," he said.

Bugsy went to his desk and logged on to his iPad. He went to a GPS tracking app and saw that the money was moving south on I-95. The trap had been set, and Deuce had taken the bait. Bugsy felt proud of what he had masterminded. Finally, they were one up, and when the money stopped moving, he would quickly pinpoint their location and send out the killing squad.

He got on his cell phone and called his father. They had a window of opportunity to strike, and Bugsy would not lose it. This was critical.

Interpolated cap: T

The realtor showed Layla the 15,000 sq. ft. warehouse space with a smile, bragging about the property and the location. It was once a printing factory, closed two years ago, and had been on the market since then. Located in the Bronx near the Cross Bronx Expressway, it was in the heart of an industrial area.

Layla walked around the large space nuzzled warmly in her long, brown mink coat and her Jimmy Choo leather boots, which echoed throughout the empty structure. Layla inspected the building, examining it from top to bottom. When she was satisfied, she turned to the female realtor and said with a blank look, "I'll take it. You can start the paperwork."

"Congratulations," the realtor said. Her commission this month would be large. "You've made a wise choice for the right price."

The warehouse was perfect for Layla. It was near the highway and nowhere near any residences. Her meeting with Angel Morales was several days ago, and she was expecting her first huge shipment of kilos from Miami within the month. Everything had to be on point, and Layla had to dot her i's and cross her t's. First off, she would sign nothing without her lawyer's review of it first. It had to be legit, and the money couldn't be dirty. The warehouse was for business, but it was also a personal gift to herself. Like her husband, or soon to be ex-husband, she saw investing into real estate a smart move and a way to wash money. On paper, she was a legit businesswoman, but behind closed doors, that location would become a hub for the tons of cocaine and heroin she would move throughout the Tri-State Area.

Layla walked out of the property with the cold wind hitting her like a ton of bricks. The idling Bentley and her driver were parked near the front entrance with a few goons she had on standby. Layla climbed into the car while on the phone with her lawyer. She would not waste any time. She had a very busy day, and she also wanted to rattle some cages.

"Where to?" her driver asked.

"Take me to Brookdale Hospital. I need to see an old friend and catch up on some lost time. I owe her," she said.

The driver merged onto the highway and headed toward Brooklyn via the FDR to the Brooklyn Bridge.

"I know she can't wait to see me," she added.

Scott sat by Maxine's bedside with his men posted outside the room and around the hospital. Seeing Maxine lying there in such a life-threatening condition brought Scott back to the time when Lucky was in the hospital. Unbeknownst to him, it was the same man, Wacka, who'd put both his loved ones in the hospital.

Scott was frantic, but he was relieved. She was alive. He had refused to believe she was dead, but never thought he would see Maxine alive again. And he was angry too. His woman was kidnapped and had gotten into a bad car accident on the Belt Parkway, but she was alone when the emergency vehicles arrived on the scene. Witnesses said that they saw a black male fleeing the scene of the accident on foot. He appeared to be hurt. Cops searched everywhere, but there was no sign of the perpetrator. He was gone like the wind.

"What's the verdict on this nigga? He caught yet?" Scott asked Mason.

"Nah, we haven't heard shit yet. We got peoples everywhere, from Jersey to Long Island, but the muthafucka is gone."

"What the fuck you mean *gone*? He dead? He out in space somewhere? If I don't see a body, he ain't gone. He's hiding, and I want him found!" Scott growled.

Mason nodded. "We on him twenty-four seven, boss. I got you."

The man left, leaving Scott alone in the room with Maxine. He took Maxine's hand into his. She was heavily medicated, and she was sleeping. Her mother was in the same hospital and she, too, was in bad shape. He had his men watching both rooms. Their safety wasn't threatened, but Scott would take no chances.

"You gonna be all right. I'm here, Maxine. I'm here," he said.

His cell phone rang. He didn't want to answer it, but it was his son calling. He picked up, hearing Bugsy say, "Pop, we got a problem down here in the lobby. She's here."

Bugsy sat in the lobby on his cell phone conducting business. His father was in a sad state—maybe distracted for a moment, but their business dealings had to go on. He was the man running everything, legitimate and illegitimate. He was already a busy man, and now with the murders in Trenton and DMC taking the bait, he was following the money. It wouldn't be long until he sent a squad of killers to the location DMC was holding up at with the money. It was an executive decision to sacrifice four of his men to make the trap believable. It was for the greater good. The men killed knew what they had signed up for, and their families would be handsomely compensated.

Then, another problem unexpectedly surfaced.

The sliding doors opened to the lobby, and Layla pranced into the hospital like the diva she was, flanked by thugs and looking like she belonged on *Keeping Up with the Kardashians* with her expensive jewelry, mink coat, and designer boots. She pretended to be grief-stricken. Bugsy spotted her and he knew his mother being there wasn't a good thing. He curtailed his phone conversation and called Scott before he marched Layla's way.

"You can't be here, Ma. This is a bad idea," Bugsy protested.

"My prodigal son, you telling me where I can and can't be? I'm here to see an old friend," Layla griped back.

"Pop is here, and he's not going to like it at all."

"You think I give a fuck about his feelings? And you have the audacity to side with him after he embarrassed me and went off with that bitch? I fuckin' gave birth to you, and you bend your knees for him and—"

"Just leave. Please, I'm begging you," Bugsy said.

She slapped him. Immediately, there was a minor scuffle in the lobby between her men and his. It was quickly broken up by the hospital security guards. Layla frowned at Bugsy. What a waste. He had so much potential, but he would rather help out his father than the woman who gave birth to him.

Suddenly, Scott loomed into view of everyone, and he was in no mood for Layla's bullshit. This was the first time they'd seen each other since he'd tossed her out on the street and she'd stolen his money.

"Why the fuck are you here!" he roared at her.

Layla stood her ground and glared at Scott. She looked intently at his face, and she could see he was visibly upset and saddened by Maxine's condition. It almost looked like he had been crying. Scott, crying? She felt it was impossible, but his face looked flushed, and his eyes were puffy. Seeing this made her even more upset. The audacity of him. Did he ever cry over her, or for her?

"I know you ain't crying over this bitch." She inched closer toward him. If looks could kill, then he would have been massacred.

"Fuck you, bitch!" he snapped back.

"No, fuck you!"

"Don't fuck with me, Layla," he said.

"You love that stupid bitch!"

Scott clenched his fist. "Leave, before I make you leave."

"I got the right to see my best friend. She's my friend, and she's hurt," Layla said, dabbing her eyes with a handkerchief and putting on a show for everyone.

"Friend? You're no friend of hers."

"And you think you're better? You fucked me while you were with her, lovin' this good pussy. You let that bitch rot in jail for over twenty years for me, Scott. Don't you forget that shit," she said, airing all their dirty laundry.

Scott wanted to murder Layla. The bitch had some nerve sashaying into the hospital after she'd stolen from him. Had Maxine not pleaded with him to spare her life, he would have killed her from his rage. He was tired of her, but the hospital wasn't the place, and this wasn't the time. Fifty million dollars she took from him. It made his blood boil.

He stood there with a hard scowl. "I want my money back."

Layla didn't take him seriously. It was her money too.

"Two weeks, bitch. And every penny better be there, or you'll be sharing a grave with Bonnie."

It was a low blow to Layla, for Scott to bring up their dead daughter. The look on her face transitioned from rage to full-blown crazy. She locked eyes with him and snarled, "Don't you dare threaten me and bring up Bonnie! My fucking baby girl! You sick, twisted, pussy-whipped bitch! Who the fuck you think you are? Bullets don't have names on them, and ya dumb ass ain't bulletproof, muthafucka!"

They went back and forth; their goons were on the sideline knowing things could go from bad to worse in a heartbeat. The look in Scott's eyes was murderous, and Layla mirrored the same reflection. She argued with him that legally half of that money was hers.

"You have no legal claim to any *illegal* money. Stop fucking with me. I promise you'll regret it if you keep this shit up."

More security guards emerged to defuse the argument and the growing tension between both groups. Layla was the aggressor. She wanted to slap him and snap his neck simultaneously. She was hurt. The thought of Scott sitting at Maxine's bedside was a lot for her to deal with.

"Get this bitch out of here," Scott shouted.

"Ma'am, you need to leave," a security guard said to Layla.

"You know who the fuck I am? Don't you dare fuckin' touch me!"

But he was adamant in doing his job and threatened to involve the police if she and her men didn't leave the premises immediately. Her goons were ready to pop off, but she didn't give them the green light. Reluctantly, she walked away, but she would remember faces and names. It was embarrassing. Scott had gotten her tossed out of the hospital.

Scott had become Maxine's guard dog, and Layla didn't like it. She'd gone there to rattle her husband's cage, but he shook hers.

Layla's skilled and very expensive lawyer, Jonathan Graham, was on top of things. It didn't take him long to sign a letter of intent and all the contracts for the Bronx warehouse. Layla was pleased. The faster the building was hers, the sooner her new business with Angel could start.

She left her lawyer's office and climbed into the Bentley. She sat back and lit a cigarette. Her driver, Manny, navigated the vehicle from downtown Manhattan to Brooklyn, where she was to meet with Lucky. Layla had a plan, and she was implementing it to the fullest effect.

The drive from Manhattan to Brooklyn took longer than she thought, with evening traffic crippling the roads, bridges, and highways. Layla sighed while caught in gridlock on the Brooklyn Bridge. Traffic seemed to have stopped. They were doing construction work a mile away, and they'd been sitting in idling traffic for almost an hour. She lit another cigarette. She had no choice but to be patient.

The traffic started moving, and her driver steered off the bridge and onto the local streets of Downtown Brooklyn. Two blocks into Brooklyn, and a black Suburban cut them off and brought the Bentley to a complete stop in the middle of the road. Manny cursed and immediately reached for the pistol under his seat.

Layla perked up with caution, knowing this wasn't a random incident on the road. The rear door to the Suburban opened, and a suited man climbed out and approached the Bentley. The man was tall and Latino, and he moved with coolness while car horns blew around them and drivers complained about the disruption on the road. This man had no concern for the traffic he was blocking. Layla and her driver didn't know if he was a threat to them or not. But Manny was ready to react.

"Manny, chill," Layla said, recognizing the face of the man. "He's cartel."

Manny nodded. He kept his grip on the pistol and unlocked the doors. The suited man quietly slid into the backseat with Layla and introduced himself. "I'm Gabriel, and Angel Morales sent me."

"Is there a problem?" she asked.

"No problem, but as you can see, we like to do business face-to-face. Mr. Morales gives his word on the shipment to arrive in a week. There was a simple hold up at the ports—nothing to worry about, everything is back on track. He just wanted to let you know."

Layla raised her eyebrows and blinked at him. "I guess he doesn't believe in phone calls," she said.

"In Mr. Morales's position, he rarely talks business over the phone. He sent me. I'm his voice."

Layla wasn't stupid. She knew what it was—it was a strong statement from the cartel to prove a serious point to her. They could find her and get to her wherever she was. Whether she was moving or not, they had eyes on her.

She smiled at him and replied, "Message received, clearly."

Gabriel looked at her expressionless, and then exited the Bentley like it was parked on the street. Car horns continued to blow around them, and they detoured around the two vehicles parked in the middle of the road. One man even cursed at Gabriel and flipped him the middle finger. "You fuckin' asshole, get the fuck out the road!"

Gabriel glared his way and was tempted to make another statement to rude drivers. But he declined. He was there for one thing only. He smirked at the slowly passing motorists before climbing back into the Suburban and driving off.

"Everything okay?" asked Manny.

"I'm fine. Just take me to see Lucky," she replied.

She was over an hour late to meet with Lucky. Layla wanted to fill her daughter in on the Maxine drama.

Once again, Wacka came to Tarsha's door in bad shape. With his left hand poorly bandaged and his face severely cut and bruised, he collapsed in the front room.

"What the fuck happened to you now?" she asked him.

"I need you," he cried out.

Wacka was in severe pain, but he was a tough son-of-a-bitch. The stolen car he used to get from New York to Maryland was left parked outside her home. Wacka had carjacked some fool with his severe injuries and made it back to Maryland, blowing through the tolls with the stolen E-ZPass. How did he make the long drive in his condition? It would always be a mystery to Tarsha. But he trusted her. He had no one else but her and their son.

It was the middle of the night, and, luckily, their son was sleeping, and so were her neighbors. Wacka cringed from the pain in his hands. From where Tarsha stood, it looked bad. She closed and locked her front door and went to tend to his injury. She undid the bandage around his left hand and saw the unthinkable.

"Ohmygod!" she uttered in shock.

Wacka was missing three fingers. He'd lost his thumb, trigger finger on his dominant left hand, and separated the pinky finger on his right hand from the horrific car accident that Maxine caused. With his adrenaline on high, he had found and picked up his fingers and run off. It took sheer willpower to carjack someone in his condition and drive the hours to Maryland.

"Wacka, what the fuck am I supposed to do wit' this?" Tarsha hollered.

"I need help, baby. I'm fucked up," he moaned.

"You need to go to the hospital. That's what you need."

Wacka looked reluctant. Not that long ago he had been in the hospital from his gunshot wounds. He had gone through days and days of therapeutic healing. But he didn't have a choice. He was in pain. His body felt mangled inside. Maxine did a number on him when she flipped the car. But he refused to die. The sheer hatred he felt for her and the West family kept his heart pumping with life.

"Fuck the hospital," he exclaimed.

"Wacka, don't be stupid! What can I do for you? Nothing! I'm no doctor."

He huffed in pain and agony. He was getting blood all over her floor. His body felt cold. The light in his eyes refused to fade out. He scowled and he cursed. Maxine had gotten the best of him again, and the thought of her still living gave him strength to stay alive.

Tarsha, however, was becoming tired of taking care of Wacka. He only came running her way when he was jammed up or tired of running through random pussy and wanted to bed her down. She was tired of trying to put him back together like he was Humpty Dumpty. He was broke, and her bills needed to be paid. She had a son to look after, but once again, he needed her attention too.

Wacka wasn't his old self; something had changed in him. Before it was about that money, and Tarsha received some of that money to help with their son. Although he was a monster on the streets, he still was taking care of his son.

Even though she didn't say it to his face, she strongly felt that his days as a career criminal were over. That meant they would most likely stay broke. She would need to get a real job, because public assistance wasn't enough to pay the bills.

She couldn't let him die. She couldn't let him suffer anymore. He was in pain and his hands were mangled. The hospital was their only choice. What she would tell them this time? What excuse could she give the doctors to keep the local police from investigating them?

"I'm takin' you to the hospital. You don't have a choice. You're not dying on my living room floor," she said as she hurried around her home collecting things and got ready to call her friend to come and watch their son.

Wacka propped himself against the wall, nursing his mangled hands and frowning heavily. Three fingers gone, and he was losing too much blood. His skin looked ashen.

Tarsha did her best to comfort him, but she carried a stink attitude. She was not happy about it. Wacka wasn't stupid. He knew what her attitude and disrespectful treatment were from. There he was again, bleeding and fucked up, but this time it was from a car accident instead of multiple gunshot wounds.

A half-hour later, Tarsha was helping Wacka into the emergency room. Unfortunately the doctors could do nothing for his fingers. They explained to him they should have been on ice, and they couldn't reattach them. His days of carrying a pistol were over, and guns were the foundation of Wacka's criminal operation. He was a handicap—a fuckin' cripple—to Tarsha. If he couldn't rob, steal, or kill—then what was he good for?

13

The bright red Bugatti Veyron was a beautiful vehicle. It stood out—almost an anomaly among the other cars crowding 125th Street in Harlem, New York. Heads swiveled toward the extravagant car as it parked in front of Sneaker Palace, a shoe store nestled among dozens of other businesses. People waited to see who would emerge from the vehicle, believing it would be a rap star. Two teens were already wide-eyed and itching to leap at the occupants of the car for a pic with whoever it was.

The doors opened, and Meyer and Luna emerged from the vehicle with all eyes on them. They weren't rap stars, a disappointment to many, but they looked like them with their platinum jewelry shining brightly, fresh Timberland boots, sharp jeans sagging, and designer bubble coats.

Meyer smirked at the onlookers and said, "What the fuck everyone lookin' at? Niggas ain't never seen a Bugatti before?"

With Luna watching his back, Meyer walked into the store looking to purchase high-end sneakers. They both had major money to spend. Once inside, they were immediately greeted by Lenny, the manager of the store. They were regulars, and Lenny would give them the royal treatment.

"Gentlemen, whatever you two need, I got you," he said with a smile.

"Lenny, you know what we like—the exclusive shit," Meyer said.

"Of course."

Eyes were on the two men as they walked around the store with the manager kissing their asses. Their personas screamed "drug dealers."

But people knew not to gaze too hard for too long; it would most likely provoke a confrontation they didn't want or weren't ready for. So the shoppers minded their business.

Meyer walked to the display wall of sneakers and observed their selections. He was a sneaker head, and he was very picky about his shoes.

Luna stood behind him, examining the dozens of sneakers on display and muttered to Meyer, "You know Gap talkin' that shit about us."

Meyer was listening, but his attention was on a pair of blue-and-white Jordans with a price tag of $198. "I like these. I might cop these too," he said. Then he glanced at Luna and said, "What that cocksucker sayin'?"

"He's talkin' 'bout we're weak now because you broke away from your father's operation. He talkin' shit about us, especially your mother—called her a cunt and everything. Plus, he ain't tryin' to pay what he owes," Luna whispered.

The information made Meyer fume inside, but he kept his cool in the sneaker store. He picked up one of the blue-and-white sneakers to get a closer look.

Gap had been in business with the Wests for nearly two years. A two-bit drug dealer from Brownsville, Brooklyn, he was moving one or two kilos a month for them. Gap had dreams of coming up large, but he was steadily falling on his face because of his gambling debts and mismanaged finances. Meyer had been forced to put him in check a few times.

Gap wasn't the brightest candle on the cake. He was a ruthless and mindless thug who caught a lucky break by meeting Meyer in the club. The two conversed, and Meyer saw he had some potential. Now Gap thought because of the split in the family, he could talk reckless and there would be no consequences.

"Yo, handle that shit fo' me. He's been dead weight for too long now. I thought the nigga had potential. Guess I was wrong," Meyer said, giving the code to Luna.

Luna nodded. "I got it. I never liked that muthafucka in the first place."

"Where the fuck is Lenny with these sneakers?" Meyer said.

As if on cue, Lenny emerged from the backroom of the store carrying two sneaker boxes, a size 11 for Meyer and a size 12 for Luna. He smiled at the two men and said, "Here they are . . . the exclusive shit."

"Open it up and let me see them shits," Meyer said.

Lenny crouched down in front of the two men as if they were kings and removed the lid to the sneaker box. Meyer and Luna gazed at the sneakers in admiration and excitement. The black and gold Nikes—the *Just Don*—were limited edition and so exclusive they were hard even for celebrities to get their hands on. But Lenny always knew to put the special shit aside just for Meyer and Luna.

"Yeah, that's what I'm talkin' about," said Luna.

"How much?" asked Meyer.

"For the two of you, six hundred apiece," he said.

It was pennies to them. Meyer looked at Luna and indicated to pay the man. Luna reached into his pocket and pulled out a wad of mostly hundreds and fifties totaling ten grand. The huge wad turned heads inside the store, but the customers and employees glanced cautiously, not wanting to be caught staring at a drug dealer's cash.

"Yo, throw in some Yankees fitteds and a few Nets caps while you at it," Meyer said to Lenny.

"I got you."

While Lenny and Luna were going through the transaction at the cash register, the door to the sneaker store chimed and opened, and in walked in a young girl who looked to be Puerto Rican. She immediately caught Meyer's attention. She was beautiful—exotic looking—and Meyer stared at her with awe.

"Damn," he muttered to himself.

She was tall with light skin and green eyes. Her hair was dark and rich, and it fell in waves to adorn her glowing peach skin. Her eyes were framed by beautiful long and dark lashes, and she had full lips and high cheekbones. Meyer was completely hypnotized by her.

The girl walked toward the toddler section in the store, and Meyer trekked her way, determined to get to know her better. He watched her as she picked up a pair of tiny sneakers and looked at them. He stood behind her and said, "Whatever you need, it's on me."

Her head swiveled in his direction and she looked him up and down. "No, thanks," she returned nonchalantly. "Do I look like I can't afford them myself?"

"You look exquisite, but I know you used to hearing that every day."

"I hear many things; it doesn't mean I'm used to it," she replied sharply.

He smiled and chuckled. She would be a challenge for him. "I know you do, but I wasn't tryin' to offend you. Just making conversation with you, that's all."

"It's a free country, you can talk all you want, and it doesn't mean that I have to listen."

"Wow, you're assertive, I like that," he said. "Boy or girl?"

"Excuse me?"

"The sneakers in your hands—are they for your son or daughter?"

"Neither. They're for my little brother. He'll be two next week."

She continued to look standoffish. So far, Meyer wasn't making any ground with her. But he wasn't giving up that easily. When he wanted something, he went after it wholeheartedly, and this one, she stood out. Already, he knew there was something different about her. While Meyer was trying to make a connection with the woman, Luna stood on the sidelines watching his friend work his charm on the young beauty.

"Let me introduce myself to you. I think I came off wrong. My name is Meyer." He extended his hand for her to shake.

She looked hesitant at first, eyeing Meyer with some uncertainty, but eventually, she shook his hand. "I'm Zoe."

"Beautiful name," he said.

"You're not gonna go away, are you?" she said.

He smiled. "I like you."

"You don't know me at all."

"We can change that right now," he said. "I can see it in your eyes, though."

"See what?"

"That you're already judging me without getting to know me."

"That's because I know your type," she said.

"My type?" he laughed. "I'm a businessman, beautiful."

"Yeah, my uncles are and were in the same kind of business too . . . and now they're either in jail or dead," she said.

"Beautiful, you simply got me mistaken. I own real estate, clubs, and I do promotion for rappers and celebrities. What is it that they always say? 'Never judge a book by its cover' . . . and you're reading me already and didn't even open me up. What's wrong, you don't like my cover?"

Meyer read her too, and he realized that she was used to dealing with legit men. Her speech was educated, and her mannerisms said that she expected the best. Meyer felt she was authentic and he would not let this one get away.

Zoe was different from the women Meyer usually dated. She was a beauty queen, and she was still competing in pageants and winning. She was the former Miss Puerto Rico. She was classy and stylish, and she had goals and ambition. She was a sophisticated girl, independent—not looking for someone to take her out the hood.

"How about dinner? Tonight or tomorrow night? You can pick the restaurant," he said.

She smiled. It was about time he got her to smile at him. "You serious?"

"Do I look like I'm joking?"

"I can have expensive taste."

His eyes never left hers. "Do I look broke to you?"

She simply stared at him, seeing the jewelry, the clothes and then there was the bright red Bugatti she saw parked outside.

"I assume that's your shiny new hot-wheel car outside."

He chuckled. "You're cute and funny—hot-wheel, I like that. But yes, that's me. You wanna go for a ride?"

"No thank you," she said. "But I'll take you up on your offer for that dinner. Why not? I'll give you a chance."

"See, how simple was that?" he said.

Mission accomplished, Meyer felt. But Zoe had more to say.

"I'll give you one chance to impress me. Tomorrow night, dinner. I'll call you with the restaurant that I'll pick. And I expect you to be on time. I don't do CP time, and I don't like to be embarrassed."

"I'm far from embarrassing," he said.

"I'll be the judge of that," she replied. "And wear something nice. I don't do hip-hop gear. And to let you know . . ." She leaned closer to his ear and said, "I'm not some easy-ass bitch that's gonna spread her legs for a few dollars and a nice meal. So don't think I'm an easy fuck! Okay?"

He grinned. "I hear you, beautiful." He was up for the challenge.

"And my name is Zoe, not beautiful."

"Zoe," he said. "I got you."

Meyer loved her poise and the boldness she carried. No woman had ever spoken to him like that. She took down his number and promised to call him. She pivoted and walked away, leaving her mark on him.

Luna walked over with the bags in his hands and asked, "What was that about?"

"Damn, my nigga. She a hard-ass bitch to break in, but she real. I like that. Her name is Zoe."

"You trust that?"

Meyer glanced her way, once again captivated by her beauty. "We'll see."

Just then, his cell phone rang, and it was Layla calling. He felt reluctant to answer, but knowing his mother, she would continue to call until he picked up.

"What is it?" he asked.

"I need to see you and Lucky," she said.

"Now? I'm kinda busy."

"I'm not asking, Meyer," she said. "In an hour, and don't be late." She hung up.

Meyer sighed and said to Luna, "Let's go."

Before leaving the sneaker store, Meyer glanced back at Zoe one last time and nodded his head. He couldn't wait to see her again.

14

Deuce, Jimmy, Whistler, and several DMC thugs sat in the VIP section of Club Pussy Cat, a prominent strip club in Baltimore. They were all in a celebratory mood. They all felt they'd come up in a smooth lick and made off with millions of dollars. They lounged in the extended booths in the extravagant VIP surrounded by beautiful and sexily dressed ladies, popping bottles of champagne and liquor, blowing through lots of cash, and having a good time. The DJ blared "Love Me" with Lil' Wayne, Drake, and Future through the club as the girls bounced, twerked, and grinded to the catchy song.

They were all balling and flaunting their wealth—each man was loud, vulgar, and fondling the girls in their company. Deuce sat in the center of it all, throwing his glass up, showcasing his diamond bracelet, pinky rings, and platinum chains. He was dressed to the nines in a mink coat and pristine Timberland boots and gripped a stack of hundred-dollar bills, making it rain on a few hoes.

Whistler sat right next to him, tossing back a bottle of Moët and watching the nude, big-breasted and big-booty stripper work the catwalk across the room. She had long platinum hair and worked the pole with a few guys on each side. She bent over and tried to pick up a dollar with her teeth while the guys behind her caught a full view of her goodies. Whistler was fixated on the stripper's activity. She pushed her tits in a man's face and made him suck on her nipples, and he laughed. Shit was crazy.

Deuce suddenly threw his arm around Whistler. The alcohol was working on him, jollying his temperament as his breath smelled of champagne. Deuce abruptly stood up, catching everyone's attention, and he looked at Whistler and raised his glass in the air to give an impromptu toast. "Everyone shut the fuck up and let me say this," he exclaimed.

Everyone knew to be quiet when Deuce had something to say. The music still blared, but it felt like the volume dimmed in their area. Deuce towered over everyone like he was the Statue of Liberty; his presence alone was commanding. His eyes shot down at Whistler like they were kindred spirits and said, "You did good, Whistler—really fuckin' good. That shit was lovely, and you were on point. This my nigga right here. You fuck wit' him, then you fuck wit' me."

All of Deuce's henchmen stood up and toasted with their boss.

Whistler remained nonchalant, knowing it could have gone the other way if they had come up empty. But it worked out in his favor. He was sure that Scott and Bugsy would be smart enough to move the money and not let it sit when their network had been corrupted. Deuce was happy about it, though, and so were his men. To take away that amount of cash— millions of dollars—would stir up the other side and create mayhem. Was this Whistler's home now? DMC—his crew? It wasn't too long ago that he was plotting against them, and now he was drinking and partying with them, and Deuce was toasting him and showing him love inside the club.

Whistler smiled and went with the flow. Damn it, it felt good taking that much money from Scott. The man tried to kill him, and his daughter was a cunning slut!

While everyone was all smiles, throwing back champagne and feeling on tits and pussy, there was one man among them who wasn't. Jimmy had this sour look about him, and it caught Whistler's attention. Jimmy was feeling a certain type of way about Whistler, and it showed. He and Deuce had roots that ran deep, while Whistler was a small plant in their jungle.

"My nigga, I got you tonight—pussy, drinks, whatever. We partying like rock stars today, cuz we take what we want and we don't give a fuck," hollered Deuce.

People cheered, and more champagne was ordered. The girls gave out lap dances and clarified to the men that anything was fair game with them.

However, Jimmy sat aloof from it all, and he was feeling insecure as if Whistler could be taking his place. He didn't like it, and he didn't trust him.

"Jimmy, stand up, nigga, and have some fun. What the fuck you moping for? All this pussy in the room and you lookin' like a nigga done slapped your moms," Deuce said.

"I'm good, Deuce," Jimmy replied.

Deuce was ready to drown himself in alcohol and pussy. The strippers were all over him, and he was all over them. He was happy. It was an enormous payday, and he felt that with Whistler's intel, there was much more to come. And when there was no more to take from Scott, then they'd go in for the kill and take no prisoners. It would be a bloodbath out there, and Deuce had his knives and swords already sharpened.

Whistler downed more champagne. He needed to free his mind from the reservation he felt. He was smarter than this, and he knew he was only good to these fools if the intel he provided was on point.

The enemy of my enemy is my friend, right? But in Whistler's line of business, there was no such thing as friends. Friends could easily turn on you, and friends got greedy and could become corrupt. For now, he was among the wolves and wearing the same skin they wore, but in reality, he was still behind enemy lines, and he needed an escape. He smiled, though, and partied with them, but how soon would it be before things weren't cool with DMC and they turned on him? He felt the way Jimmy looked at him was a sign of major trouble to come. But he would play along for now and provide them with the information they needed to bring down

Scott and his organization. The former friend was now his enemy, and he would do anything to survive.

Whistler guzzled down the Moët and stood up. He needed to free himself from the stress he felt, and he saw one way in doing that.

"Excuse me, fellows. I need to go handle some business," he said to them.

They encouraged him. There were plenty of bitches to choose from, but Whistler had his attention on the platinum haired girl that was butt naked and nasty with it on the stage. She looked to be no older than nineteen, and he had that penchant for young ladies. He excused himself from the VIP area and made his way toward the stage. With a fist full of money, he immediately captured her attention. She smiled his way, and he tossed two hundred-dollar bills at her and then said, "I like you. Let's go somewhere private."

She walked off with him. She knew what was expected of her.

In the bathroom stall, the young girl lowered herself in front of Whistler and undid his jeans. She reached into his pants and removed his big dick and didn't hesitate to place it into her mouth. She opened her mouth wide, relaxed her throat, and took him all the way in. Whistler leaned back against the stall and exhaled with gratification. Her head bobbed back and forth as he closed his eyes. He needed the blow job. The way she was sucking him off was about to make him come real quick. He wasn't complaining. Young girls like her were the best at helping him relax. There was nothing better than a good blowjob and some young pussy.

15

The cute whore with the slight, graceful figure and oval face held the dick upright with her hand and lowered herself onto the man's thin and fleshy shaft. Gap groaned with the sudden jolt of pleasure and felt cloud nine consume him. Her pussy was tight and wet, and he closed his eyes, grasped her moving hips against him, and enjoyed her from top to bottom. Her body was taking him to a place he didn't want to leave—not too soon anyway.

"Oh yeah, give me that pussy," he moaned.

She gyrated her naked hips against him, feeling him inside of her, and feeling his hands cup her tits and then smack her ass. He couldn't stop touching her. She was like gold to him. Her pussy pulsed nonstop around his hard dick, and it felt like his cock was being sucked on by a gulping throat.

"Shit . . . damn . . . oh damn, I'm 'bout to fuckin' come! Oh shit, oh shit," he hollered. Then, as quickly as it started, it ended. He came. The duration of their sexual experience was less than a minute.

She smirked and climbed off his soon-to-be limp dick and wiped between her legs with a towel. He was another satisfied customer. She lit a cigarette and inhaled. Gap removed himself from the bed and got dressed. He then left her payment on the dresser near the bed. It was three hundred dollars for her time. He had a knot of cash on him and had plenty more to go around.

She donned a robe and said, "You like it?"

"Yo, ma, your pussy is too good," he said.

She smiled. "I'm glad you enjoyed it."

She liked him. He was easy to please. He always came fast between her legs or into her mouth. It didn't matter how she serviced him, he was a minute man.

Gap finished dressing and tucked the .45 in his waistband. The gun was the testimony to the dangerous life he lived and the drugs he sold. He was an overweight man of average height, black skin, a bald head, and a lazy eye. He wasn't handsome, but he was a savage on the streets. The projects of Brownsville were his to control and run. He was a man who wasn't afraid to kill, and he wasn't afraid to speak his mind. He was blunt and fearless. And he was a bully. Gap was a tyrant in his own right.

She walked him to the apartment door, and he praised her pussy once again before his exit. "Keep that good pussy nice and wet for me. I'll be back."

"When I'm gonna see you again?" she asked.

"Yo, ma, maybe tomorrow night. I gotta handle some business and shit. You know a nigga moving up on the food chain. I got this new connect and we 'bout to pop off."

She cared nothing about his business in the streets, only the money he left her after they finished fucking. "Be safe," she said.

"I'm good. Ain't nobody fuckin' wit' me out there," he said haughtily. "I'm the fuckin' man on these streets."

She closed the door, and Gap turned and walked toward the elevator. So far, it had been a quiet night—good pussy and easy money. He was content, but he wanted more. He walked down the narrow ghetto hallway and stopped at the elevator, pushing the button impatiently. He had to meet up with his crew and handle his business. He glanced around at his surroundings, and everything was quiet and dim. He could smell urine and smirked at the nerve of someone using the bathroom in the hallway. But it was the ghetto for you—nastiness and people not giving a fuck! He pushed the elevator button again and muttered, "Shit is takin' forever!"

He adjusted the gun in his waistband and glanced around his surroundings again. A man in his position always had to be on-guard.

Finally, he heard the bell chime above, indicating the elevator had stopped on the eighth floor. The doors opened up, and before he stepped inside, he heard a sound. It was faint, and it sounded like the stairwell door had opened and closed, but he saw no one emerge from it. Gap thought it was his nerves getting the best of him.

He stepped into the elevator and pushed for the lobby. Everything seemed to move in slow motion, and the doors weren't closing fast enough for him. He repeatedly pushed the button for the lobby and was growing more impatient. But before the doors could close, a dark, hooded figure abruptly loomed into Gap's sight, standing a few feet opposite of him. The man outstretched his arm with a 9mm at the end. Gap was in utter shock and stumbled back against the wall. He desperately tried to remove his pistol to defend himself, but he wasn't quick enough.

He heard, "Meyer says to shut your fuckin' mouth!"

The gun discharged—*Bak! Bak! Bak! Bak! Bak!*

The muzzle flash lit up the dimness of the area briefly, and several bullets went into Gap's head, chest, and throat. He collapsed in the elevator in a pool of blood, dead. His gory frame was a mess for whoever would find him. Someone finally shut his mouth for good.

Luna quickly pivoted and fled the scene. He moved like a shadow in the night. He was unseen and quick. This was his nature, a killer. The shots noisily echoed throughout the narrow hallway and woke up the residents on the eighth floor. But by time the first person came out of their apartment to witness the horror, Luna was in the passenger seat of a black Charger speeding away from the scene.

Layla lit her Newport, took a few pulls from it, and then downed a shot of vodka on ice. It was a cold night, but her soul and heart were even more frigid. She was still worked up over seeing Scott fucking teary-eyed and upset over Maxine. Her cage had been rattled by it. Her husband looking after and caring for Maxine made her see red. It was a feeling she couldn't shake, and she didn't want to shake it to be truthful. She wanted revenge.

She pranced around her penthouse apartment chain-smoking and drinking. Maxine did over two decades in a woman's prison, and she was probably some carpet munching dyke. She probably didn't even like dick anymore. She probably was fucking Scott just to be spiteful toward her, Layla strongly felt. There was no way Maxine could fuck Scott better than she could. Could she? There was no way that Maxine could take her place. Had she? Layla gave that man the world and six kids. She was his true ride-or-die bitch, the one who would kill for him and had, and the one who stuck by him through thick and thin. But now, she had been rejected and humiliated. She should have seen it coming. It was a mistake inviting Maxine into her life and bringing her around her husband.

She finished the cigarette and the drink, lit another Newport, and poured herself another shot of vodka. Stress and anger had her worked up—the nerve of Scott to ask for the money back. Fuck him and his two-week deadline. It was laughable. He wanted to leave her penniless.

It wasn't happening! Layla was happy she thought ahead and did what she did. With all the legal businesses he owned, his assets worth in the hundreds of millions of dollars, he wanted to make a fuss over fifty million that belonged to her too. No fucking way!

The penthouse was dim and silent. The shades were drawn and the doors locked. She had an arsenal of guns hidden throughout the place. Her penthouse had become a minor fortress. Layla wasn't taking any chances. Her security was tight. They were everywhere in the building and ready to act—but there was nothing better than being armed yourself and killing the threat.

Being from the streets of Brooklyn, she was trained for this environment. She'd been through it all and had tumbled with the best of them and survived. Muthafuckas thought that the money, the beautiful clothes, the lavish homes, and lovely things made her soft like baby shit. But Layla was still a hardcore bitch, and she was ready to remind anyone who wanted to challenge her that she was nothing to play with.

She downed the vodka and made another glass. The cigarette between her fingers was burning nimbly. She continued to pace around her place and was becoming impatient. She'd called her kids over two hours ago, and neither Lucky nor Meyer had shown up yet. Her time was valuable, and she had moves to make.

The shipment from Angel had arrived via 18-wheeler, the kilos stashed in hidden compartments in the truck—one compartment being the gas tank. It was a polished operation, no errors. Now, nearly fifty kilos of cocaine and heroin were sitting in the Bronx warehouse, heavily guarded and ready to make her an even richer woman. It was time to get it out there and flood the streets. The Tri-State Area wasn't ready.

The doorbell sounded, and Layla looked at the security monitors to see who it was. Meyer and Lucky had arrived. The second she opened the door to let them inside, she cursed and scolded them for their tardiness.

Meyer waved her off; he wasn't in the mood to hear his mother bitch and moan about him being late. She didn't control him. "We here, right?"

"Over an hour late," she retorted.

"Hey, better late than never," he said.

"Then next time don't fuckin' come at all," she snapped.

He sighed and walked away from her. He had a life. Like his mother, he went to the bar and mixed himself a needed drink.

Lucky, too, was in no mood to bicker with her mother. She lit a cigarette and lowered herself into a comfortable chair.

Layla stood between her children wearing a long, flowing robe and had "boss bitch" written all over her. She would play no games. With Meyer lingering near the bar and Lucky quiet in the chair, she reached into a small bag and removed a kilo of cocaine and tossed it at Meyer and a kilo of heroin and threw it at Lucky.

"You know the game, Ma. You don't bring the shit to the crib—that's a violation right there," Meyer said.

"Boy, I got too much security and cameras in my place to worry about 5-0. I'm 'bout my business, like y'all two should be," she barked at them.

Her kids inspected the packages. It was high-grade product.

Then Layla hit them with the unexpected. "I want all of the Brooklyn territories first. I don't give a fuck how y'all do it, just make it happen."

"Brooklyn? You gonna be stepping on Pop's toes," Meyer said.

"Do I look fuckin' worried about that? I helped that muthafucka build that shit from scratch—from the bottom up—and I want it all."

"Ma, is that wise? I know you're hurt over what he did to you, but going to war with him and tryin' to take Brooklyn? I thought we were going to build our own shit," Lucky said.

"Y'all questioning me? Who the fuck y'all think y'all are? "

"Look, you got the connect, Ma, and we can spread anywhere outside the city with that product. But mixing it up with Pop and Bugsy? I don't think that's wise," said Meyer. "Fuck it. Get that money and just pay him back. And we ain't just talkin' about Pop here—you ready to piss off other players in the game?"

"Meyer's right," Lucky chimed. "Look, I easily found Delaware, and I can get another area to move in on. We got the muscle, but stirring it up with Scott—it's just crazy." After the verbal and physical abuse, Lucky refused to call her father by anything but his first name.

Layla wasn't having it, though. She didn't want just to build her own; she wanted to take her husband's shit too—by any means necessary. As long as he was comforting and supporting Maxine, then she would fuck his shit up. She would rock his world and attack him where it would hurt the most—his pockets and then his bitch.

Layla scowled at her kids. "Do I fuckin' smell pussy in this room? Y'all lookin' like two bitches ready to get fucked! And you, Meyer, I thought you weren't scared of anything—and now you wanna back away from your father and brother and pay him the money back? I'm fuckin' disgusted by you right now. And Lucky, that muthafucka put hands on you and violated this family, and you're fuckin' afraid of him! You wanna give him a fuckin' pass?"

"I'm not afraid of shit!" Meyer proclaimed.

"Then fuckin' prove it! I didn't raise my son a fuckin' pussy!"

Layla's unkind words angered her kids. Meyer pouted, and he was ready to bang his fists against his chest like an ape, charge violently, and declare that he wasn't afraid of anyone. Lucky wanted to make money and thrive, but be careful too. They tried to reason with their mother, but she was being stubborn. The most Meyer thought he'd be doing was shielding his mother from trouble with his father and using the fifty million as seed money to invest in drugs, broads, and mayhem.

But Layla was ready to amplify things. She was a woman scorned and saw one way for her to be happy, and that was creating the downfall of

Scott and Maxine. This was the war of roses. She wanted people to die. She wanted bloodshed, chaos, and Armageddon—all of it at one time. Her heart was broken, and she wanted no one to have a happy ending.

Meyer had a few words with his mother. Lucky too. But Layla was domineering. The look in her eyes said it all; there was no turning back. She was decisive, and she would set the city ablaze to get her revenge.

Layla refused to tell them where the location of the money was. "I'm keeping that the fifty million locked up in a safe place for rainy days."

"You don't trust us?" Meyer griped.

"It's just business," Layla replied.

"Just business," Lucky repeated. "We *are* the business!"

The choices she was making didn't sit well with either of her kids. They fussed, but Layla refused to listen. This was her show, and she would choose how she ran it. Some of the cash went to hiring hardcore killers with no consciences. Some of the money went to her new luxurious penthouse on the city's west side. The rent was $55,000 a month, and the place came with a panic room. She felt it was needed. It made her feel safe at night.

Meyer's gripe was that he wanted some fuck-you money too. But if his father ruled with an iron fist, Layla ruled with an iron heart. She was vengeful with no "off" button.

She gave the order. Meyer and his goons were to break backs and fuck shit up out there—bust open heads to take over the Brooklyn territories. They were to rob, steal, pillage, and kill.

"Do it quickly and stealthily, so that by the time Scott tries to come back at us, it will be too late."

She wanted Lucky to get her meth and the heroin out to Long Island. Layla wanted to wear the crown and become the queen of the city. Last on her list was Maxine. She wanted that bitch dead, dead, and more dead! And Meyer and Lucky would help her make that happen.

It had been over a week now, and Maxine was still in a coma. The hospital room was decorated with dozens of cards, balloons, and flowers. It was looking and smelling like a florist. Many people were wishing her to get well and have a healthy recovery.

Scott continued to sit by her bedside and observe her condition. He felt guilty.

He thought back to 1994 when they'd first met. The day he saw her coming off that train with her school friends looking too cute in her prep school outfit, he had to introduce himself. It was love at first sight. She had innocence and beauty, and she was smart and ambitious. Maxine was gonna be somebody in life. She was supposed to become a prominent lawyer, and they would be a power couple. She would be the businesswoman and Scott would be the streets—the thug with her back.

Maxine was always good to him—real good. She wouldn't even look at other guys. Scott was her everything. He took her virginity. He bought her whatever she wanted and needed. Scott didn't want his woman to want for anything. So what went wrong between them? How could he allow the woman he supposedly loved to do over twenty years in prison? How could he have forgotten about her? He did her wrong, and it pained him greatly. He'd allowed Layla to come between their loving relationship. Layla was great sex, but Maxine was the perfect woman for him. Layla knew his world while Maxine was sheltered. Maxine was the opposite of him, but she loved him dearly, and she was perfect for him, so why did he marry Layla?

When he first saw Maxine that day in their Florida home, he was taken aback. He was standoffish, even though he wanted to scoop her up into his arms and hug and kiss her passionately. Soon he charmed his way back into her life. Layla was foolish for bringing his ex-girlfriend back around. He did not understand what she was thinking.

Scott sighed as he took Maxine's still hand into his and felt guilt entirely consume him. He was a killer, but today he felt like putty, and his emotions were heightened. He'd been through a lot in the past months with the death of his kids, warring with a rival crew, Whistler's betrayal, and now Maxine being kidnapped and winding up in a coma.

Scott was determined to remain by her bedside until she woke up. He'd abandoned her a long time ago, but today, he was rooted by her side.

While Scott was deep in thought, it finally happened. Her eyes flickered, and her hand gradually moved in his. Scott perked up and watched her with anticipation. He immediately alerted the doctors. They hurried into the room to check her vitals and to make sure Maxine was okay. She was finally awake, and she was aware. She stared up at Scott watching her with concern. She was happy to see his handsome face. He leaned forward and kissed her forehead and gently squeezed her hand. It seemed like she would be okay, although she had a lot of pain medication in her system.

"You had me worried," he said. "You were in a coma for over a week."

She wondered if he'd been by her side the entire time.

A week . . . the last thing Maxine remembered was being held at gunpoint. She didn't even remember the car accident she'd caused to escape Wacka. Wacka would have killed her. His eyes didn't lie. The man was overtaken by rage and revenge. It was a miracle she even survived her escape. She had seen her life flashing before her eyes.

All she could do was lie there and recuperate slowly. Her legs felt numb and she felt some pain in her body. Scott continued to talk and comfort her. With him there, loving her and being her man, it felt like '94 again, when life was good and they were so young and had so many dreams.

The door opened and Bugsy entered the room. He smiled Maxine's way and he greeted her warmly. He kissed the side of her cheek and was genuinely happy to see she was out of her coma.

"You had us shook," he said to her.

Maxine stared into his face. The guilt consumed her, and she burst into tears. Looking at Bugsy, who showed concern for her well-being, made her feel like a monster.

What had her life become? What had she become? Arranging the death of Gotti, Bonnie, and Clyde brought forth no closure. She thought their murders would fill the void, remove her sadness, but it didn't. Maxine wasn't proud of what she had done. It was the past, but the guilt would stain her soul—it would forever corrupt her core.

Scott wiped away her tears and continued to comfort her. He believed she was crying because of the kidnapping. She had overcome a terrifying incident. Something like that could scar someone for life.

"Don't worry about that fool. I got every nigga on him and we'll find him. He's gonna pay for what he did to you," Scott told her with conviction.

She remained silent. In reality, she hoped that they never found him— alive anyway. Wacka had too many dark secrets that, if revealed, would turn her entire life upside down and most likely be her demise.

"Tell me anything you know about this nigga. Did he say anything about where he's from or who sent him at you?" he asked her.

Maxine shook her head. "He was just there at my mother's place. I don't know why."

"Don't stress yourself, baby. He won't bother you anymore. I promise you that."

Scott and Bugsy shared a quick look between themselves. It was something bad—something that they weren't telling her.

Maxine noticed it. "What is it?" she asked them.

They both looked reluctant to tell her. Scott took her hand into his again with his eyes locked on to hers. He would be the one to tell her. It was his right. Bugsy wanted his father to delay the news, since she'd just come out of a coma, but Scott felt it was better just to tell it—rip it off like a bandage.

He gently caressed her hand and said, "I have some bad news."

"What?" She felt her heart flutter and her stomach twist.

He heaved a sigh. "It's your mother . . . . She had a stroke . . . . She passed away while you were in a coma."

Maxine's chest tightened, and she began to sweat profusely. Large, round teardrops flowed down her cheeks.

"No! Ohmygod . . . no, please! Are you serious!" Her cries echoed from the hospital room.

"She died peacefully, Maxine," said Scott.

She sobbed in the hospital bed, the sorrow wracking her soul. She was inconsolable, but Scott was there to comfort her the best he could.

Bugsy had to leave the room. His cell phone was ringing and he stepped outside to take the call. He strolled down the hallway and could still hear Maxine wailing. He had to take care of business, though. It was AJ on the phone.

"What is it?" Bugsy asked.

"We got an exact location on where the money's at. It's been sitting for three days straight, unmoved," AJ said.

"A'ight, you know what I want," Bugsy said, choosing his words wisely while on the phone.

"I got you."

"Meet me tonight—you know where—and we'll discuss this further," said Bugsy.

"Got you," AJ said.

Bugsy hung up. He knew it was only a matter of time before their trap was discovered. He wanted to execute his plan immediately, and he wanted to handle it alone. His father was still distracted over Maxine's kidnapping and her condition. His nerves were rattled. But it would be unwise not to inform Scott of what was going on.

Bugsy turned and marched back to the room. He slowly opened the door to see his father holding Maxine in his arms.

Scott noticed his son looking in on them, and Bugsy's expression said there was something crucial that he needed to speak to him about. But he didn't want to leave Maxine.

"What is it?" Scott asked.

"It's about Deuce," Bugsy said.

The name made Scott's blood boil. Scott believed that Deuce had sent one of his henchmen to kidnap Maxine. He didn't want to depart her side, but this was important too.

"Baby, give me one minute. I need to handle something," he said to her.

He grudgingly left her side to talk to his son in private about their problem. They went into the stairwell to talk. Bugsy gave him the 411—told his father about the trap he deployed, the robbery and cash, and where it was.

"We have a beat on it right now, and the pigs are all lined up and ready for the slaughter," Bugsy said.

Besides Maxine waking up from her coma, this was the next best news for Scott to hear. He wanted to be there to see his enemy fall. He was itching to do it himself and finally put a bullet between Deuce's eyes.

However, Bugsy advised that he should stay in New York and remain by Maxine's side. She would need him.

Looking his father in the eyes, Bugsy said with confidence, "I got this, Pop. I'm on it."

"Bring him to me alive if you can. If you can't, then just bring me his fuckin' head," Scott said seriously.

Bugsy nodded. He had his father's blessing to raise hell. Bugsy turned and descended the stairwell while Scott went back to Maxine's side.

Several hours later, four vanloads of killers with heavy artillery were on the New Jersey Turnpike headed south. It was a three-hour drive to Delaware.

18

t was 3 a.m., the devil's hour as some call it. In Tarsha's case, the devil may be retired from the game. She sat shotgun next to her friend, Tammy, in Tammy's Cherokee after another night of partying with friends. The Jeep sat idling and parked outside her home. Tarsha released a deep sigh. She was a little tipsy and regretted coming back.

Tammy smoked her Newport and shared it with Tarsha, and then said, "Damn bitch, you act like you about to do a stint in prison and shit. What's up wit' you?"

"My baby daddy is gettin' on my damn nerves," Tarsha said.

"He stayin' wit' you now?"

"Yeah . . ."

"And I guess by the look on your face, it ain't goin' too well," said Tammy.

Tarsha took a pull from the cigarette and exhaled. "I wish he would leave! Broke-ass muthafucka!"

"Damn, girl. It's that bad?"

"Tammy, you don't even know the half of it. Nigga can't fuck, can't make any money, can't do shit. He's just a fuckin' cripple sittin' in my fuckin' house."

"Damn. Wacka? Fo' real?"

"Fo' real, girl. Nigga went to New York to take care of some bitch that did him dirty and ended up getting a few of his fingers cut the fuck off.

Like what the fuck, nigga? You supposed to be this big-time gangster, and you can't even handle some bitch?"

"Oh shit!"

"Yeah, and now he expects me to take care of him—like I'm fuckin' Molly Maids and shit," Tarsha griped.

Tarsha took a few more needed pulls of nicotine and exhaled. She stared at the entrance to her home, knowing Wacka was inside and probably sleeping or looking sorry.

"What you gonna do, girl?" Tammy asked her.

"I don't know, find me a new nigga," she joked, but was really dead-ass.

"Yo, you know that nigga Michael is feelin' you, and he moving up in the game too. He was all over you tonight, buying you drinks," said Tammy.

"Yeah, but I heard he got a small dick."

The girls laughed.

"Small dick, deep pockets, though." Tammy laughed.

"Bitch, you know I need the best of both worlds."

"I feel you, girl," Tammy agreed.

They continued to smoke and have their girl talk. Tarsha felt swallowed up in anger and unfairness. She hadn't signed up for this. What other options did she have besides taking care of a cripple and a has-been in the game?

She lingered in the Jeep for a few more minutes, then told Tammy goodbye and climbed out into the cold, late-January weather. She looked good in a pair of skinny jeans and stilettos, showing off her ample cleavage in a sexy leather corset she wore under her winter coat. Bright pearls adorned her neck, and she had on matching pearl earrings. The clothes and jewelry were perks she had received from Wacka in his heyday—when he actually got money.

She entered her home to see Wacka snoring on the couch with both his hands bandaged. He looked like a shell of himself. He'd lost weight and he looked weak. Weeks of trying to take care of him was sickening and tiring, and Tarsha no longer had the patience for him. So day in and day out, her acid tongue was emasculating him. She gave no fuck about his feelings. She wasn't happy. She wasn't satisfied. She wanted him gone so she could find a new man to take care of her and her son. What were they going to do for money with him not out there taking from others? He had no pot to piss in. The only thing he was good for was watching their son.

She frowned at the sight of him, disappointed by what he was becoming, and trotted off to bed.

The next morning, Tarsha woke up to the smell of someone cooking in the kitchen. The aroma of scrambled eggs and toast stirred her awake. She removed herself from the bed, donned a robe, and left the bedroom to investigate. She walked into the kitchen to see Wacka trying to prepare breakfast in his feeble condition.

"What the fuck you doing?" she barked at him.

"I'm makin' breakfast," he said.

The kitchen was a mess—eggshells everywhere, toast burning in the toaster. Their son was seated at the table, watching his daddy's attempt to scramble eggs with his hands bandaged. He could barely grip the spatula. It was pathetic. She didn't want breakfast, especially not from him.

"I'm not hungry for that shit," she said with an attitude.

"What you want then?"

She pouted and huffed. "You know what the fuck I want from your ass—you know what, never mind. I don't need shit from you. Just look at you, all fucked up and lookin' weak. I never thought I would see the day when my baby father would look this fuckin' pathetic. Nigga, you used to run these streets! Muthafuckas feared you out there! And you let some bitch fuck you up!"

Wacka simply stood there and listened. The eggs were burning in the frying pan. Their son cried. Tarsha went over to him and picked him up, continuing to glare at Wacka and put him down with harsh words.

"Nigga, we need shit for him like diapers and milk. He needs some clothes and shit, and money is fuckin' low. Muthafucka, you were the man in our lives, but I guess you ain't no more, right? Some bitch took your fingers and your fuckin' balls!"

Her words cut deep. Wacka no longer had the desire to finish making breakfast. He tossed the spatula across the room and marched out of the kitchen, feeling defeated by Tarsha's callous words.

Tarsha watched him leave the room and rolled her eyes and sighed. He couldn't even be a man and curse her out. The nigga just stood there and took the verbal abuse. It was a sad, sad thing to see. Wacka used to be that nigga who didn't play that shit, and it was like walking on eggshells around him. You didn't want to catch his attention and piss him off.

"I'm goin' out tonight, so you might as well watch your fuckin' son again. That's the least you can fuckin' do since you can't do shit else around here," she shouted.

I need a real nigga and some real dick, she said to herself.

She felt that her relationship with Wacka was over. A man who could do nothing for her—he didn't want to fuck, couldn't make money, couldn't cook, couldn't even eat her pussy right—was a man she needed to put behind her. They had history, but history would not help their situation and provide her with the life she was used to living.

She heard a door close. He was in the bathroom. She didn't care. Another sigh spewed from her mouth, and she carried her son into the next room.

Wacka took a hard look at himself in the bathroom mirror. He felt wrecked. What he saw, he didn't like. He stared miserably at himself and at the bandages that covered his hands. How could he be feared if he couldn't even hold a gun correctly? *That fuckin' bitch,* he thought. Maxine had destroyed him. He wanted to kill himself, but he couldn't even pull the trigger.

Such irony!

Instead, he angrily pushed his forehead against the mirror and shattered it. He bled, but he didn't care. He gazed at his warped reflection in the broken mirror. Like the mirror, Wacka felt broken, too. He repeated the same violent action again and again, until the mirror was gone completely with shards of glass scattered around and in the sink, and his face was coated with blood. He never thought he would see the day when his baby mama didn't respect him—and the day he felt helpless and defenseless.

The Victorian brownstone on Remsen Street was a quiet area near the Brooklyn/Queens Expressway. It was an unassuming three-story in the middle of the block where a few of Scott's men counted and protected millions of dollars brought in weekly from all over the city. Not too many people knew about the location. Two men could travel to the site and make the hefty cash drop. It was well guarded with steel doors in the front and back and security cameras craftily placed around the location. Inside the house, there were four men—three were muscle, and the fourth was the money man—the accountant, the money manager of the place. He was hood certified, and he made sure the count was always right.

There were several areas in Brooklyn that Scott controlled, which collectively brought in two to three million dollars a week. But this was the central hub, where all the cash went before it got shipped out of town, laundered, or invested overseas.

Meyer and Luna sat outside the property scoping the place. Meyer knew what buildings to hit and what time to hit them, and the intel was passed down to his minions. The orders were to kill Scott's men and take over everything. Layla wanted to leave a strong message. She wanted her husband to feel her wrath and know that the deaths of his men and the destruction of his organization were by her hands.

With it being nightfall in the beginning of February, it was so cold outside that Meyer farted snowflakes and pissed ice. The Dodge Charger they sat inside idled with the heat on blast. Parked behind them was a car full of hired killers. They were eager to strike and seize their opportunity as soon as Meyer gave them the word. The money made them hungry. And the time was now.

The block was empty and quiet. The cold kept everyone inside. It was an advantage for them. Meyer lit a cigarette and eyed the brownstone and waited. He looked at Luna and said, "You know that bitch I met at the sneaker store in Harlem the other day?"

"Yeah, shorty was fine," Luna said.

"The bitch finally called me."

"That's what's up. What she about?"

"She talks that smart and educated shit. I mean, she speaks three languages and done seen the world. She's in school, trying to get her bachelor's in business and communication," Meyer said.

"What, you intimidated by the bitch?" Luna said.

"Nah, I like her. She's different. We goin' out this Friday night. She picked this restaurant in the city—some shit called Eleven Madison Park. I checked it out, and you need a fuckin' suit and tie to eat there. Fuckin' place is high end and shit. I gotta come correct wit' this one, Luna."

"You can afford it," Luna teased.

"It ain't about the money. I don't know . . . shorty got me thinkin' about her and whatnot."

"Nigga, you pussy whipped before you even fucked?" Luna joked.

"Nigga, you saw her . . ."

"Yeah, I did. But I'm sayin, did you vet shorty? Is her shit legit like she says it is?"

"I don't feel no setup with her," Meyer replied.

"You never know, though. Beautiful woman like that happens to walk into the store and catch your attention, gives you her name and number. I don't want you walking into anything treacherous. We got enemies, yo."

Meyer understood where Luna was coming from. They could take no one for granted, no matter how sexy they looked. Trouble could come in any form or shape.

"I feel you. That's why I want you to be my eyes and ears while I'm on this date wit' shorty. Get a few goons together and watch my back. But I don't want her to know y'all there—be invisible. I don't wanna scare her off," said Meyer.

Luna nodded. "I got you."

They shared the last cigarette from the pack and waited. In mid conversation, a dark blue Escalade rolled by them and double parked outside the brownstone they were watching.

"This is it," Meyer said. He alerted his men. Everyone was on standby.

The passenger door to the truck opened, and a tall, well-dressed man in a long, black trench coat exited and made his way toward the brownstone. Meyer was very familiar with the man. His name was Nicholas. He was the man of the hour—the accountant—and he had been on the team for as long as Meyer could remember. The driver was security.

"Yo, let's do this!" Meyer said to his henchmen via cell phone.

The doors opened swiftly, and a gang of armed men flooded the cold streets. Tonight, Meyer chose the 9mm to do his dirty work. The confrontation toward Nicholas was quick. The gun was shoved into his back and Meyer spewed threats his way. "You fuckin' move and I'll blow your spine out." Nicholas's driver was also being held at gunpoint.

Nicholas remained calm. He didn't want to appear as a threat to them, but he had some words for Meyer. "This is how we're playing it now, Meyer? You want to go there with your father? He's not going to like this at all. You know what he'll do to you."

"I don't give a fuck about him," Meyer spat back at him.

He and Luna forced Nicholas into the building, through the steel doors, and into the brownstone. It was dark. Immediately, Meyer knew something was off. They were met with no resistance. There were no men inside, and even worse, there wasn't any money. The place was empty.

"What the fuck is this! Where the fuck is everything!" Meyer cursed.

Nicholas slowly turned to face Meyer with a mischievous smirk. "What did you expect? He knows you and her better than y'all know yourselves," Nicholas calmly said. "They expected this from y'all. It was cleared out weeks ago, and I was merely sent to give you a message."

Nicholas was cocky and arrogant. He didn't fear Meyer. He didn't fear Luna. He was one of Scott's top guys in the organization. He was good with numbers and he knew how to launder millions. He did wonders for Scott and the family's finances—a cash guru.

Meyer frowned with the gun aimed at Nicholas's head.

"He says it's not too late to come back where you belong. Your father wants you home, Meyer. He's giving you a second chance," Nicholas told him. "And the same goes for Lucky."

Meyer frowned even harder. The audacity of Nicholas trying to convince him to go back to his father—a man who disrespected and humiliated him. He wasn't taking the bait. He would rather starve than take anything from Scott West.

"Fuck him! I'm not goin' back! And fuck you too!"

"You're making a very bad choice, Meyer. Do you think you and your mother can go against him? It's suicide," said Nicholas calmly.

"I'll take my fuckin' chances. And I'll leave him my message for him— one that he'll clearly get."

Meyer's trigger finger squeezed back, and the outcome was fatal— *Bak!* A bullet tore through Nicholas's forehead. His body jerked from the impact of the bullet, and he collapsed facedown near Meyer's feet. A pool of blood collected around his head. He was a bleeder.

"Fuck him!" Meyer said. There was no turning back. He was on Team Layla.

Luna knew the blowback of this would be massive, but he was in this civil war between families at full throttle. He never liked Nicholas anyway.

The driver was hit with two shots to his head, leaving his body slumped over the steering wheel. They retreated from the area empty-handed and knowing there would be consequences. But they were ready.

It all was all a failure. His father and brother had changed everything up. Every stash house he knew of was empty. *Sneaky muthafuckas!* Worse than that, Meyer had to relay the news to his mother.

Two miles away from the bloodshed, Meyer finally called Layla.

"Tell me what I want to hear," she said.

"It was a bust. Ain't shit happen," he said.

"What the fuck are you talkin' about?"

"They changed up on us, Ma."

"What the fuck you mean *changed up?*"

"It's what the fuck I mean. They moved shit around and cleaned house. We came up empty on everything."

She was livid. Scott was one step ahead of her and she would not tolerate it. She refused to accept failure. The thought of her husband gloating and feeling victorious over her created some desperation inside of her to be triumphant, and there was a way to turn things around.

"Change of plans, then," Layla said.

Meyer was listening. Luna was driving. Layla didn't want to say too much over the phone, so she spoke carefully.

"I want you and Luna at the hospital," she said.

"To do what?"

"It's where Scott is spending his time, now, right? And he has men coming and going. I want you to follow one and find me something new. They'll lead you somewhere. And when they do, we fuck 'em up!"

It was a plan, but Meyer felt it wasn't perfect. They could be following these fools right into another setup.

"And don't fuck it up, Meyer. Don't get caught tailing anyone. I'm counting on you," she added.

The remark angered Meyer. "I'm no amateur in these streets, Ma. I know what the fuck I'm doin'!"

"You do, huh? Well tell me something. Is the bitch dead yet?" she said.

"What bitch?"

"Maxine. Did she die from complications? Is my husband still by her bedside, grieving over her trifling ass?" She didn't want to say too much, but she almost couldn't help herself. Her anger was getting the better of her. Maxine—fuckin' Maxine! And then she exploded. "Did you kill her yet, Meyer?! No! So don't tell me you know how to handle things when that bitch is still breathing!"

Meyer quickly hung up. His mother was losing it. The boldness and stupidity of her to speak about murder over the phone was insane. She should've known better than to talk reckless on an open line like that.

Whistler curved over from the bed and placed the tightly rolled-up hundred-dollar bill into his right nostril and inhaled a line of cocaine from the small mirror on the nightstand. It was a definite pick-me-up. He did another line and felt the white girl straddling his mental and physical being and riding him into greener pastures at full speed. The bitch was a beast!

"Damn," he muttered.

The drug hurled him into a euphoric state. The nigga almost felt like he was Superman! Cocaine was one hell of a drug. He was shirtless and clammy, and lying beside him was a naked, young whore. She cradled against him, and he felt her breasts against his back.

"Can I have some too?" she asked.

He eagerly welcomed her to the party. The pussy was better on cocaine, and the young girl was a freak. Whistler shimmied to the side to allow the girl access. She picked up the same C-note and inhaled a line of coke. It picked her up like a rocket taking off, and she giggled. It was high quality—some potent shit! She wasn't done yet. She did another line. She had a nose like a vacuum. Feeling the influence of the white girl made her pussy spark and her body light up like a Christmas tree. She turned to Whistler and opened her mouth for him, and the two kissed fervently. She slid her tongue into his mouth and cradled his balls in her palm and massaged them.

The party was about to start, and they were the main attraction—the only ones on the dance floor. She lowered her face into his lap and enveloped his erection between her lips. He tilted his head back and enjoyed the moment. A moan escaped his lips as her head bobbed up and down.

"Oh shit," he groaned.

"Relax . . . I got this," she said evenly.

It would be an all-night thing for them. Neither of them were tired or ready to call it quits after several hours of fucking and cocaine—the ultimate Viagra.

Whistler felt like he was living that DMX song . . . *I'm slipping, I'm falling, I can't get up.* He had been on a downward spiral since his abrupt departure from Scott and Lucky. His drug use was becoming more frequent, and he wasn't as sharp on the streets like he was in his heyday. He was getting sloppy. His association with Deuce was an illusion. He thought he had a plan to thaw out Deuce and Jimmy and get out from under their thumb, but things weren't working out as planned. They steadily had eyes on him.

It was after midnight, and Whistler and his chick were twisted in each other's arms and legs once again, after doing more drugs and having multiple orgasms. The muscles in Whistler's back, thighs, arms, and butt flexed repeatedly and he cried out into the night. "Oh shit . . . Ooooh God! Ooooh, right there!"

Their freak fest was interrupted by a hard and loud knock at the door. It brought a stop to everything and made Whistler climb out the pussy. He reached for his pants and his .45 and carefully approached the apartment door. The knocking didn't sound too welcoming. He looked through the peephole and saw it was two of Deuce's men. Seeing them at his apartment door at such an early hour had him worried.

He cocked back the gun and said, "What's up?"

"Deuce wants to see you," they said through the door.

"Now?"

"Right now, nigga," the young goon exclaimed.

"Give me a minute to get dressed."

"We ain't got all night," the goon responded.

Whistler went back into the bedroom and collected a few things, got dressed, and shoved the gun into his waistband. His young companion looked at him puzzled. "You leaving?" she said.

"I gotta go take care of something."

Whistler left the room and left the eight ball of cocaine for her to enjoy. She beamed. For her, it was still party time.

Whistler followed behind the young goons and got into a black Chevy. It drove off with him the backseat. During the ride, he couldn't help but to wonder how he'd gotten to this point. He was a god in New York and elsewhere. He was respected and feared, and now he was being summoned by someone he'd once considered inferior to him like some young boy on the block.

Crazy!

The drive to meet Deuce was on the other side of town. It was a warehouse near Browntown, and it was a stone's throw away from the I-95 expressway. Whistler ascended from the backseat of the Chevy and followed the two thugs into the building. The cold night had everyone wrapped up in winter coats and ski hands. At the door, he was immediately searched and his pistol was removed from his person.

"What's this all about?" he asked them.

They didn't answer him. They were just following orders. He was escorted farther into the warehouse and to another room. Deuce, Jimmy, and several other men waited inside. The congratulatory vibe Whistler had experienced the other day now seemed cold and aloof. He was met with scowling faces. It was a nerve wracking moment, and he feared for his life. But regardless of what was about to go down, Whistler wasn't going out without a fight. He was a man built for that life and had done seen it all and been through it all.

"What's this about?" he asked in a stern voice. There was no bitch in him.

Deuce, who was seated in an old chair, stood up swiftly. Whistler noticed the money in his hand. They were all hundred-dollar bills. Deuce stepped toward Whistler in an aggressive manner and threw the money at him. It sprinkled everywhere. Then Deuce shouted, "It's all fuckin' fake!"

"What the fuck you mean *fake*?" Whistler questioned.

Deuce, scowling heavily at Whistler, said, "Every last dollar of it! It's fake—fuckin' counterfeit!"

Whistler was taken aback. He didn't see that one coming. He marveled at the boldness of Scott, but he knew this was more Bugsy's doing. Bugsy was the real brains of the organization. To set them up to rob counterfeit money, it was a priceless scheme. But where was the backlash? Once again, Whistler was puzzled by it.

"You fuckin' knew about this, muthafucka?" Deuce hollered. He was livid.

"I didn't know shit! But I told you it was too easy! We should have waited!" he countered.

"Fuck him, Deuce!" Jimmy chimed. "I'll do him right now." Jimmy was itching to put a bullet in Whistler.

Whistler didn't flinch. He locked eyes with Jimmy and stood his ground.

"Fuckin' counterfeit!" Deuce screamed, kicking over a barrel of the fake money.

Whistler found himself in a sticky situation. He knew it was too good to be true. A lot was going through his mind. Why would Scott keep the bins there with the fake money? They weren't into counterfeiting or selling it. And it wasn't a trap because they would have been attacked at the warehouse. Whistler didn't know what was going on, but his situation with Deuce was looking bleak.

"Yo, I want y'all to burn it all—every last fuckin' dollar," Deuce instructed his men.

"And what about Whistler?" Jimmy asked him.

Deuce swiveled his head in Whistler's direction with a menacing scowl. "He's coming wit' us. We ain't done conversing yet. I need answers."

The three men left the building while DMC soldiers burned the fake cash.

Outside, they got into a Suburban truck and sped away. Unbeknownst to everyone, there was unwanted company approaching the building.

21

The van doors opened, and several men stepped out into the cold air. It was dark and cold with temperatures dropping below twenty degrees. It was game time, and things were about to go into overtime with some serious offense. Their target was several blocks away, and their foes had no clue what was about to come their way. The element of surprise was a beauty in the art of war, but they needed to prepare themselves for battle.

Each man with Bugsy was dressed in black military gear, and they all had tactical training. Many were ex-military—Marines, Navy, Special Forces—who had transitioned into cold-blooded mercenaries. Bugsy had the cash, and they were ready to slaughter for a good price. Along for the ride were AJ and Choppa, Bugsy's two right-hand goons.

The big-boy toys came out for the action. They all carried high-powered weaponry meant for complete chaos and total annihilation.

Bugsy briefly held court in the cold, saying to everyone, "Everything dies tonight!"

Each man nodded. Their weapons went hot—locked and loaded—and the night vision goggles adorned their heads. Bugsy armed himself with a machine gun.

The warehouse was a quarter of a mile away. They approached the location in two groups, one marching toward the front entrance and the second advancing from the rear. They looked like a SWAT team, but were delinquents of the law. They even brought their battering ram to break down the doors.

"On three," Bugsy said.

They were in position, and mayhem was only moments away. They stood poised near both doors with their assault rifles ready to burst out. The men swung the battering ram and the front door crashed open. Immediately, several flash grenades were thrown into the building and exploded.

Confusion and chaos ensued inside the warehouse. The blasts had temporarily disoriented the senses of the men inside, including their vision. They believed it was a police raid. The barrels with the counterfeit money were on fire, and there was screaming and yelling, and then intense gunfire.

Bratatatataataatatatatatat!

No warning shots!

"What the fuck!" someone screamed out.

Tchu-Tchu-Tchu-Tchu-Tchu-Tchu-Tchu!

"DMC for life!" a young goon yelled before opening fire.

"Aaaah, I'm hit! I'm hit!" another DMC soldier cried out.

Rat-a-tat-tat-tat-tat-tat-tat-tat!

Quickly, several DMC goons went down as the bullets tore into their frames. The remaining men scrambled in confusion, knowing it wasn't a police raid. It was a hit. They attempted to shoot back, but were at a grave disadvantage as Bugsy's henchmen came well equipped from both sides and could see through the smoke and darkness with their goggles and masks. Easily, they hunted down everyone inside the warehouse and gunned them down. The assault was swift and effortless. When the smoke cleared and the gunfire ceased, bullet-riddled bodies lay everywhere in a pool of blood.

"Too fuckin' easy," one of Bugsy's men exclaimed.

There was no remorse. They searched through the dead to check for survivors. If they found any, they quickly put a bullet into their heads. Bugsy scanned the sea of dead men to see if Deuce or Jimmy were among them, but he didn't see them. He only came across another man barely living. He was shot multiple times and sprawled on his back. There was a gurgle in his throat, and he was spitting up blood. His eyes were open, and he glared up at Bugsy. Bugsy towered over the dying man and pointed a pistol at him. Scowling down at him, he asked, "Where is he—Deuce?"

He could hardly speak, but his last words to Bugsy were, "Fuck you!"

"Fuck you too!" Bugsy rebuked and coldly shot the man between his eyes.

Bugsy didn't know it, but he'd only missed Deuce, Jimmy, and Whistler by a few minutes. They had slaughtered over a dozen men, and although Deuce wasn't among the dead, it was a good hit.

Meyer stepped out of his bright red Bugatti, fixed his tie, and walked toward the front entrance of the four-star restaurant called Eleven Madison Park. He looked sharp in a dark blue, two-thousand-dollar Tom Ford suit. Meyer knew that if he wanted to impress this girl, he had to become his twin brother.

He came unarmed and humble, but he didn't come alone. Luna sat in a Benz nearby, and a few of his goons patrolled the area subtly, making sure there weren't any nearby threats. Traffic on Madison Avenue was thick in the late evening, and it was a mild winter's day, where it wasn't bitter cold, but a moderate fifty degrees outside.

Zoe climbed out of a yellow cab and strutted toward him wearing a white embellished coat. Her long, luscious black hair was flowing, and her eyes dazzled like she had diamonds in them. He was new in her life, so she'd arranged to meet him at the restaurant. She wanted no one picking her up from her apartment. She didn't trust too many people.

"You're beautiful," he said.

He kissed her on the cheek, trying to be a gentleman, and she smiled.

"You look handsome yourself," she said.

They entered the crowded restaurant and approached the maître d', a lovely and well-dressed female who greeted Meyer with a smile. "How may I help you, sir?" she asked.

"I have reservations," he said.

"And what is your name?"

"Meyer West."

She searched for his name and quickly found it. "Table for two, right?"

"Yeah—I mean, yes."

They were escorted into the dining area, and Meyer took in the lavish décor. The high-ceiling art deco space had floor-to-ceiling windows with a picturesque view of Madison Square Park and a giant crystal chandelier suspended above. The dining room accommodated up to fifty people, and the patrons were all sophisticated and mostly white—high-end businessmen and Wall Street tycoons out on dates with their wives or mistresses. It was a place you brought someone you wanted to impress.

Zoe removed her coat to reveal her dress, and it was stunning. Her curvy figure was formed perfectly in the off-white turtleneck sweater dress she wore with a pair of black-tie back boots. Meyer had to remind himself to be a gentleman tonight, and he pulled out her chair to allow her to sit first. He then sat opposite of her and once again proclaimed, "You're beautiful."

She flashed a quick smile. "Thank you."

This wasn't Meyer's cup of tea—the décor, the people, and the scenery. It all made him nervous. He was a chicken-and-waffles type of nigga—a Popeye's and Burger King eating dude. Although he came from money and had plenty, he was a street thug at heart. Bugsy had tried to introduce his twin brother to the world of the classy and the elegant many times, but Meyer always shied away from it. Those weren't his peoples; the streets were. But tonight was an exception. He felt Zoe was worth doing something different.

"First time here?" she asked him.

"No, I came here with family once," he lied.

"Oh really? I like it here. The cuisine is exquisite," she said.

She was spoiled. He knew it. But the look in her eyes and her beauty overwhelmed Meyer. *Damn, she is fuckin' gorgeous*, he kept thinking.

The waiter made his way toward them. He stood erect with a smile at their table dressed in a white button-down shirt and black vest with a black bowtie. "Sir, madam, my name is Jonathan, and I am your servant tonight. Can I start your night off with our wine list?"

"Sure," Meyer said.

Jonathan handed him the wine menu. The prices were high, but it was change in the bucket for Meyer. He didn't know shit about wine. It was like a foreign language to him. Instead of choosing himself, he said, "Just give me a bottle of your best."

"Will do, sir," the waiter said before he pivoted to leave.

"What are you in the mood for?" Meyer asked Zoe.

"I'm famished," she said. "I'll start with a few appetizers."

She used words like *famished* and *cuisine*. She was not in his ballpark, but Meyer was determined to impress her. He had to think and act like his twin brother. There was no way he would mess this up.

They quickly looked through the menu, and she already knew what she wanted. Meyer could go for a cheeseburger or a large steak, but he didn't want to look ignorant or hood. So, he tried something new. For their appetizer, they ordered crab stuffed mushrooms and cucumber bites. The cucumber bites were an acquired taste, but Zoe loved them.

While munching on the appetizer, they talked. He got to learn a lot more about her. She had no children and no boyfriend. She was Puerto Rican born and raised but moved to the Bronx last year. She was twenty-two, and she had goals. Zoe had already accomplished a lot by being in beauty pageants and being the former Miss Puerto Rico.

Like her, he had no kids—well, not any he knew of. His child died when Penelope was killed. Thinking about it was still painful for him.

Meyer had to talk the talk to keep Zoe interested, so he mentioned his business portfolio. It was something he'd picked up from Bugsy. He talked about his investments in real estate and the clubs he owned.

"So, you're into real estate, I see," she said.

"I am . . ." It was the partial truth. "I'm a black man with a plan."

"It's always nice to hear about a man with a plan. I admire that."

"And I admire you, Miss Puerto Rico," he said playfully.

She smiled and chuckled.

They enjoyed a $500 bottle of rosé and talked freely. Meyer was leaving a small impression on her. He did everything opposite of his usual and tried to channel his twin brother. He remembered different wines that Bugsy used to drink and things he would say that made him look smart.

For dinner, she had the agnolotti, made with small pieces of flattened pasta dough folded over a roasted meat and vegetable filling. She also ordered the red wine braised octopus and bone marrow. It was a dish that made Meyer cringe. It reminded him of something out of *Indiana Jones and the Temple of Doom* movie. Meyer said "fuck it," and ordered a giant steak with some vegetables. It had been a long day, and he was hungry. But he made her laugh, and she liked to laugh.

Meyer saw no threat in her. She was a beautiful, smart, and educated woman, not to mention breathtaking. He had to have her, by any means necessary. He wanted to call off the goon squad, feeling they wouldn't be needed, but it was still better safe than sorry.

Meyer and Zoe spent nearly two hours in the restaurant. Dinner went great—better than they both expected. Zoe was somewhat shocked. They talked about everything from sports to history, and Meyer kept her intrigued. Some of his twin brother's knowledge had rubbed off on him, and he wasn't a drug dealing, cold-blooded savage high on the food chain that night. Meyer did his best to become somebody different.

When they walked out of the restaurant, Meyer noticed that Luna was still parked nearby in his Benz, watching everything. Meyer subtly nodded his way, giving the signal that everything was okay.

"I had a good time with you," Zoe said.

"I'm glad you did. I had a good time, too. When can I see you again?"

"I'll let you know."

He didn't want the date to end. Every time he would look at her, he was in awe. He couldn't remember a time when he smiled and laughed so many times. Zoe brought something out of him that contradicted who he was. He wasn't a monster tonight. He was a gentleman.

"It's late. Let me drive you home?" he offered.

"I'm okay. I can take a cab," she said.

"Ridiculous. You can trust me. I don't bite."

"You probably do," she joked.

He chuckled. "I'm serious. What kind of man would I be if I allow you to take a cab home? It's late and it's cold."

"Meyer, I'm a big girl. I'll be okay. Besides, we're still getting to know each other, and trust—that has to be earned. You're doing an okay job so far, but I'd prefer to take a cab."

"I respect that. Well, at least let me hail you a cab then." He stepped out into the street and lifted his arm into the air to hail a cab. He did it with authority, and right away, a yellow cab slowed near him and pulled to the side. He opened the back door to allow Zoe to slide inside. It was hard to watch her go.

"Thank you," she said.

"You're welcome, Zoe."

Their eyes were fixed on each other for a moment. Her grace and beauty hypnotized him. God, he wanted to kiss her so badly—and fuck her, too. But he didn't want to seem too forward. She wasn't that type of lady. She simply kissed him on the cheek and said "Goodnight."

"Goodnight."

The cab drove off. Meyer was left standing in the road watching it disappear into the city traffic and the sea of other yellow cabs that swallowed the road. He felt something that he'd never felt before. *Shit!* he thought. He couldn't stop thinking about her.

It was back to business. Luna approached him. He was curious to know how everything went.

"So, what's the 411 on that bitch?" he asked.

Immediately, Meyer turned his way with anger and exclaimed, "Watch your fuckin' mouth, nigga! She's no bitch!"

"My bad . . . I guess she's legit then?"

"Yeah, she's something different, Luna. I like this one. I do."

"I see it on your face."

"It's that obvious, huh?"

"She got you glowing like the Christmas tree at Rockefeller Center." Meyer chuckled.

"What you wanna do now? The night is still early," asked Luna.

"Fuck it, let's go to the club. I need a drink and some head. I gotta get my mind off shorty."

Luna laughed. "Yeah, I bet you do."

Maxine was making good progress, but her recovery was bittersweet with her mother's passing. She cried and cried, but she knew she had to be strong to make funeral arrangements. Maxine wanted her mother to go out in style, and with Scott's help, she would get her wish. So she prepared herself for a hardship moment of healing and grieving. At least she had Scott by her side to comfort her and help her with everything.

Before the funeral, Scott stood her before her mother's casket, got down on one knee, and asked for Maxine's hand in marriage. The huge engagement ring was an exquisite piece of jewelry, a glimmer of joy amid Maxine's heartbreaking grief. Maxine accepted, but not before Scott could promise her mother that she could rest in peace knowing that he would always take care of her daughter.

The funeral was held at Southern Baptist Church on Stanley Avenue in East New York. Maxine remembered when her parents used to take her to church there every Sunday morning. Her mother used to sing in the choir and was active in the church activities and numerous community programs. Her mother steadily preached the gospel and salvation to her, but Maxine strayed away from the church and fell in love with a drug dealer and the lavish lifestyle he provided. She knew the choices she'd made in her life broke her parents' hearts—especially her mother's. Their little girl was supposed to be somebody in life, but instead, she became a convicted felon.

A few tears trickled from Maxine's eyes as she gazed at her mother's body in the solid walnut hardwood casket dressed beautifully in a blue-and-white dress. She looked so peaceful. Finally, her mother was reunited with her father, resting in peace.

Maxine felt guilt too. She didn't get to spend enough time with her parents—over twenty years was lost. What was worse was to be in a coma while her mother was dying. More tears trickled from her eyes, and the hurt she felt in her heart and her soul was becoming overwhelming.

She touched her mother's body gently and sulked. Maxine wanted to show her mother the good life. The cruise was only the beginning. There just wasn't enough time. It wasn't supposed to be like this.

It was a beautiful service. The choir sang and the pastor gave a lovely eulogy. There were flowers and pictures of her mother everywhere.

Mrs. Shirley, her mother's best friend, hugged Maxine, gave her condolences, and said to her, "Your mother was a good woman, and she loved you so much. I'm gonna miss her. But you be strong, Maxine."

Maxine nodded and wiped the tears from her eyes. Mrs. Shirley was good peoples. She gave Maxine a lingering hug. It was comforting.

"God bless you, and I'll be praying for you," said Mrs. Shirley.

The slow church hymns made everyone emotional, and there wasn't a dry eye in the place, except for Scott. He sat in the front pew stoic. He was there for emotional support. He'd seen his fair share of funerals and had shed his tears for loved ones.

After the service, the hearse led the line of cars north of the church toward The Evergreens Cemetery. It was a bright, blue-sky day and windy, but not too cold. Maxine climbed out of the limousine looking immaculate in her classic black dress, black shoes, a large black hat, and dark shades. Scott walked with her toward the burial site. It too was bedecked with lots of flowers and pictures, and there was a seating area under a tent canopy for the family and close friends.

As a precaution, Scott had a few of his henchmen scattered around the cemetery for security. They was dressed in black, armed, and moved around covertly.

The pastor stood near the casket with his bible, prepared to send the woman off in good measure. Each mourner held a red or white rose to toss onto the casket when it would descend into the ground. They stood around the burial site in silence. So far, everything seemed at peace, until it wasn't.

The black Maybach came to a stop inside the cemetery, and it immediately caught the attention of Scott and a few others. Scott's head turned toward the lustrous vehicle in the distance, and he stood on high alert. He was armed and ready for anything. The doors to the Maybach opened, and out stepped Layla and Lucky. Scott scowled at mother and daughter, and he felt his blood pressure rising.

Why is she here?

"This fuckin' bitch," he muttered. He knew his soon to be ex-wife wasn't there to give her condolences to Maxine. She was there to stir something up.

Maxine noticed the bitch too. The nerve of Layla to show up to her mother's funeral. The anger Maxine felt was murderous, and she was ready to confront Layla, but Scott stopped her.

"I'll handle it."

Layla was dressed to the nines, wearing a long, white mink coat, matching mink hat, and shiny white pearls that contradicted the black and gloomy mood at the cemetery. She strutted in a pair of white heels with red bottoms and was smiling with Lucky in tow. Besides the driver, she and Lucky had come alone, no goons—or so it seemed. Right away, Scott's men intervened before Layla could step any closer to the tent. They stood in her way like a closing gate, frowning and on their jobs. She wasn't invited or allowed there.

"Excuse me!" Layla barked at them.

"You're not welcome here," said one man.

"Don't tell me where I'm not fuckin' welcome. I came here to pay my respects to a friend," Layla exclaimed.

"There's no trouble here—not today!"

Layla and Lucky were defiant; they weren't going anywhere. Layla threatened the men, but they weren't backing down. Then Scott approached.

Scott exclaimed, "Leave here now!"

"Fuck you, Scott!" Layla cursed.

Scott gritted his teeth and scowled. "This is a funeral. Show some damn respect!"

"Respect? You have the nerve to talk about showing some fuckin' respect. You and that bitch don't know shit about respect!" Layla retorted.

Scott was so sick and tired of her over-the-top antics. She had no reason to show up. His goons kept her away, but a commotion was ensuing. Layla loved the attention. It's what she wanted—a disturbance—and Scott was falling right into her trap.

"Fuck that bitch and her dead mother!" Layla shouted.

The obscenity was harsh and highly disrespectful. Scott got close to her with his fists clenched. He wanted her gone.

When she threatened him with, "They gonna be burying you and that bitch next," he lost it. The punch to her face came rapidly, and it hit Layla so hard her legs buckled and she went down like Joe Frazier. The pain was unlike anything she had felt before. It shot through her whole body and knocked off her mink hat. She'd threatened him, and he didn't like to be threatened.

The scream she released was ear-piercing. She was lucky he hadn't broken her jaw. But Scott wasn't done with her yet. As Layla shouted, "You fuckin' bastard! I'll kill you!" Scott charged at her and grabbed her roughly into a strong chokehold. This was a funeral, and Layla was making an absolute mockery of it.

"Get the fuck off me! Get off me, you sonofabitch!" she screamed as she struggled in his chokehold.

Everyone was shocked, including Lucky. How could he treat Layla like that—his wife and mother of his kids? He punched her like she was a man and a stranger to him. Lucky was still salty from the slap he gave her over Penelope, and she didn't like the way he was manhandling her mother. She just couldn't stand aside and watch. She shouted, "You fuckin' bastard!" and went to aid her mother. She attacked him from behind; she bit his forearm, punched him, and scratched his face repeatedly to pull him off her mother. A violent spectacle developed at the funeral, and everyone was watching and looking stunned. Maxine wanted to jump up and stop the spectacle, but her feet felt like stone. She was unmovable. Her eyes darted as Scott sent blows from Layla to Lucky, all in her honor.

"You ungrateful little bitch!" Scott howled at Lucky.

If Lucky thought her slap was sobering, or the face shot Scott had given Layla was embarrassing, then she wasn't prepared for the ass kicking he was about to dole out. Scott was to be respected and feared, but his wife and daughter were treating him like he was Mickey Mouse. These two bitches were spoiled. He released his frustration on them both, tired of Layla's bullshit—the fifty million she'd stolen from him, the stunt at the hospital, the disrespect she showed to him on the streets, and now at Maxine's mom's funeral.

Something snapped inside of Scott, and an ugly and snarling beast manifested in front of everyone. He attacked Lucky too. She was no match for her father. He punched her and she folded over like a chair. His fist tightened around Lucky's long and curly hair, and he yanked it so tight that pieces ripped away from her scalp. He hit his only living daughter like she was a punching bag in the gym. The violence that erupted at the burial service had all eyes on the fight. Layla jumped to her feet desperately and tried to attack Scott, but his men held her back.

"Get off her like that, you muthafucka! You're gonna kill her! You're gonna kill your own child!" Layla yelled.

"This bitch wanna be grown and come at me like a fuckin' nigga!" Scott shouted. He gripped his daughter into a tight chokehold and could feel her gagging from lack of air.

Maxine and others finally ran toward the conflict.

Layla's driver, Manny, emerged from the Maybach and charged toward the incident with his gun in hand. The driver aimed his gun at Scott, ready to shoot and kill the man to protect the two ladies. Scott's goons pulled out too and aimed their guns back at the driver, and a Mexican standoff quickly ensued. Maxine ran toward Scott, and although she hated Layla and Lucky and wanted both bitches to suffer, she wanted no bloodshed or killing at her mother's funeral.

Scott still squeezed Lucky in a strong chokehold, and the light was gradually fading from her eyes. Her struggle against him was useless. He would kill her.

Layla helplessly watched as she couldn't free herself from the men that held her. Their strength was crippling her from charging and aiding Lucky. Her eyes shot over at Maxine and they pleaded—she pleaded, "Maxine, please stop him! He's gonna kill her!"

"Scott, please! Not here! Not at my mother's funeral," Maxine shouted at him.

It seemed Maxine's voice and words were pulling him away from the rage he felt. Maxine was right. Today wasn't the day. He finally released Lucky from the chokehold and she fell forward, collapsing on her knees and gasping for air while clutching her neck.

Scott was breathing hard. Where he'd come from, it was a very dark and ugly place. He'd almost killed Lucky. He could have snapped her neck like a twig, and it would have been another child of his dead—but by his own hands.

Layla and Lucky stood near each other, breathing hard, their outfits and hair in complete disarray. They were traumatized. Scott had taken things too far. Layla locked eyes with him. She wanted to fuck him up real good. She growled, "You fuckin' bastard!"

He stood there in silence for a moment, collecting himself and collecting his sanity. Finally, he spoke. "Take my daughter to the hospital," he told his men.

Lucky looked terrible. Her hair was everywhere, and her lip was bleeding. It was a damn shame. Scott's goons walked over to help her, but she resisted. She could kill her father right now. She wanted to so badly. She spit a mixture of blood and saliva at Scott and cursed, "Get the fuck away from me! Fuck you, nigga! I hate you! I fuckin' hate you!"

Scott didn't flinch. He showed no regret for what he'd done to her. They wanted to test him, and he passed with flying colors.

Layla was on fire like the pit of hell. "You do this to your daughter! You're a damn coward, you fuckin' bastard and woman beater! I hope you rot in hell, you bitch-ass nigga!"

Layla helped her daughter back to the car with Manny's help. They were soon long gone, and the burial resumed.

24

t felt like the longest drive of Whistler's life. He was nervous, but he refused to show it. Deuce was behind the wheel of the Suburban and Whistler sat shotgun. Jimmy sat behind him with a gun aimed at the back of his head. Everything felt tense. Whistler didn't know if he would live or die tonight. The counterfeit money had pissed them off, but he had nothing to do with it. He didn't see that one coming.

They were on I-95, going south toward Maryland. It was late and cold. Whistler couldn't help but to think that at any moment, his brains and blood could be splattered all over the front seat. But they wouldn't be so stupid to commit a murder in public like that, while driving. But they were taking him somewhere—maybe to be interrogated. Wherever it was, it would not be nice.

An hour later, they were in a rural area in Maryland, about thirty-five minutes away from Baltimore. It was nothing but farmland, trees, and back roads. Whistler couldn't help but to think that they'd brought him out there to be killed and buried where no one would find him. Anyway, who would even come looking? He had no one.

There was a house on the property a half-mile from the main road. The place had history; it was a former plantation home built in the early 1800's. It was haunted by the countless slaves who had lost their lives on the land. The two-story house was well maintained and had two floors and a wraparound porch, and it seemed vacant.

Deuce brought the truck to a stop near the house and climbed out.

Jimmy forced Whistler out of the vehicle by gunpoint. "Get the fuck out, muthafucka!"

"Just take it easy, Jimmy," Whistler replied calmly.

"Nigga, I'll shoot you dead right here. You're lucky Deuce still wants you alive."

At Jimmy's forceful behest, Whistler exited the Suburban and looked around. The darkness of the area surrounded them. For miles there was nothingness. The cold was crippling, but neither Deuce nor Jimmy looked chilly. The anger they felt had them heated.

Deuce walked ahead. Jimmy pointed the gun at Whistler's head and said, "Walk, nigga!"

Whistler ambled toward the front entrance. He ascended the stairs one by one and stepped onto the large porch. He could hear every one of his footsteps loudly—like they were signaling that they would be his last.

Inside, there was nothing—no furniture, no remnants of a cozy home. It was dark and even colder than outside. Whistler saw a folding chair in the middle of the room atop some clear tarp covering the floors. He already knew what it was. It was a killing zone. It was a place where people were brought to be questioned and tortured. Whistler knew his chances of leaving the place alive were zero. He turned back to look at Jimmy, and Jimmy had a smirk on his face. He had done this plenty of times. Like him, Jimmy was a calculated and cold-blooded killer. Whistler knew if the shoe were on the other foot, Jimmy wouldn't survive either. But the shoe wasn't on the other foot, and Whistler was in a sad predicament that seemed inescapable.

The door closed, and Deuce turned and looked at him. "You know I bought this place five years ago? It used to be a plantation during slavery times. Imagine the stories this place could tell, from the slaves that died here to the people we killed," Deuce said.

Whistler stood there quietly. He wasn't in the mood to hear stories, but Deuce didn't care.

"You know, my ancestors used to be slaves on this plantation. Imagine that—the shit they went through—what their masters did to them. My grandmother told me about this place, and I remember sayin' to myself, 'I could kill those white masters with my bare hands.'"

Deuce paced around Whistler while Jimmy looked on.

"A white family used to own this land—the land my family slaved over and were killed on. I offered to buy it from them, but they wouldn't sell it to me. They looked at me like I had some audacity to make them an offer. The husband—I saw it in his eyes—no matter how much money I had, I would always be a fuckin' nigger to him! Here we are, a hundred and sumthin' years after slavery, and this white muthafucka is still lookin' at me like he's better than me. So one night, I had my boys pay them a visit, and it wasn't a friendly one. The husband, he had a beautiful family— three daughters and a pretty wife too. We beat the fuck out of him, and I made him sign over the deed to me. I mean, with a gun to his head and his family's lives in danger, the muthafucka didn't have a choice."

Deuce continued to pace around the barren room telling his story. Whistler wanted to know where this was going.

Deuce moved closer to Whistler and continued with, "Oh, my goons had some fun that night. They raped all three of his daughters right there in front of him—tore those white snowflakes up with big, black dicks. And the sound that man made, seeing his daughters' pussies being spread open and enjoyed by niggers and nothing he could do about it—that muthafucka cried like I never heard anyone cry before. I just stood there and watched it all play out. It was like watching *Roots* in reverse. And his wife? Oh, she was saved for last. My goons ran a train on her—beating and fucking her at the same time. You see, all night we fucked these white people up, and I remember thinking about the pain my ancestors felt from their family—the feeling of helplessness and not being able to protect their families—their wives. So I made this white muthafucka feel the same way. I took sumthin' from him, and I enjoyed it. And when my men were done wit' those white bitches, I cut their throats and watched them bleed out like gutted pigs. All night that man cried and begged. I watched his soul being ripped away, and it made him want to die. And I gave him his wish. The payback felt good."

Whistler didn't care for the story. It wasn't how he got down. It was an old slave house—who gave a fuck?

"You see, this is a very special place to me, Whistler. And I only bring special people here. And you, muthafucka, are special," Deuce said. "That family is buried right here on this sacred land as trophies, and you, nigga, are about to be added to my collection."

They forced Whistler to sit in the folding chair. Jimmy still held him at gunpoint. Deuce stood over him and removed his coat and shirt, showing off his large muscles in a wifebeater. Whistler frowned. He had nothing to say. Was this his fate—dying on some old farm with family history? Even if he could run, where would he go? It seemed like they were in the middle of nowhere.

Before Deuce could get started with the interrogation, his cell phone rang. He answered the call. Jimmy stood on the side, frowning at Whistler. He couldn't wait to kill this man.

"What the fuck you talkin' about!" they both heard Deuce scream into his cell phone.

"How many?" Deuce yelled. "How the fuck they find it?"

Deuce's hand was clenched so tightly around the cell phone he nearly broke the thing into pieces. He curtailed the phone call and charged toward Whistler in a heated rage. He punched Whistler, knocking him off the chair and crashing onto the floor. Whistler spit out blood.

"Hold that nigga down!" Deuce shouted.

Jimmy didn't miss a beat. He grabbed Whistler into a tight chokehold. "What the fuck going on, Deuce? What happened?"

"Everyone's dead!"

"What the fuck you mean?"

"There was surprise attack at the warehouse we just left. It's a bloodbath over there."

It was shocking news to Jimmy. There was only one person to blame, and they had him right in their grasp. But Whistler was taken aback, too. He had nothing to do with it. But they wouldn't believe him.

Right away, Deuce hammered his fists into Whistler with head shots and body shots. His face bruised heavily, and he spit and coughed out more blood. His body felt like it had gone through a grinder.

"You set us up, muthafucka!" Deuce howled at Whistler. "Jimmy, kill this fool!"

Jimmy stepped toward Whistler with the gun and was ready to blast away.

Whistler turned and looked defeated. This was it! But he wasn't going out without pleading his case.

"I didn't set you up, Deuce. It wasn't me!" he shouted.

They didn't believe him.

"Look, you like trophies right? I can get you that bitch for your trophy case," Whistler said.

The words caught Deuce's attention, and he halted Jimmy from executing Whistler. "What bitch you talkin' about?"

"Lucky West—and Layla. I can bring them both to you alive—mother and daughter," Whistler said.

"You lying to live. Why would they trust you?"

"Look, I know everything about Lucky. You take her hostage, and then I can get you her mother, and you can have them both and hold them in exchange for Scott."

Deuce glared at him and said, "Why should I fuckin' trust you?"

"Because that wasn't me at the warehouse. I didn't kill your men. Scott and Bugsy set that up somehow—the fake cash. Just think . . . maybe we were followed. Tracked somehow? They knew you would come for it. Scott's smart, and believe me, he'll keep coming for you no matter what. You gonna need me to figure him out. I know him. I know his family."

Deuce was listening. Maybe Whistler was still better off alive than dead. Could he still be useful?

Jimmy wanted to shoot him, but he could tell Deuce was changing his mind. "You gonna believe this muthafucka, Deuce? He can't be trusted."

"We lost a lot of men tonight, Jimmy," said Deuce.

"And? I don't fuckin' trust this nigga!"

"He'll have his day, Jimmy, but for now, I need him alive. I want payback on that entire family. The rules have changed. We keep him on a tight leash. We lure in them bitches and take out the rest."

Deuce crouched near a beaten and defeated Whistler. "Look at you, nigga. You went from a king to a fuckin' peasant. I did this to you! And don't you forget it. You bring me those bitches. You make this right, and maybe we'll kill you fast."

"You have my word. I'll bring you Lucky and Layla," Whistler said with assurance.

"Punk muthafucka," Jimmy uttered with contempt. "Your nine lives are running out fast, and I'm gonna be the one to skin the fuckin' cat."

Whistler ignored him. He had been reprieved for now. His gift of gab had saved his life. Now, he had to get in contact with Lucky and get back into her life somehow. It was easier said than done.

B ugsy felt that his family was dysfunctional with a capital D. The drama was worse than a fuckin' reality show on VH1. Word had gotten back to him about what'd happened at the funeral. The thought of his father beating Lucky and his mother was sickening. But why would those two show up, knowing what the outcome would be? If he were there, he would've stopped it.

Bugsy knew that his mother was pushing her luck. She was stubborn—a fuckin' bitch mostly, and Lucky was following right in her footsteps. Layla sent him pictures with a text saying: HE'S A DEAD MAN! They were disturbing. Lucky was black and blue, bruised and swollen everywhere, eye puffy with her hair ripped out. Layla was beaten too, but not as bad as Lucky. The pictures were hard to look at. It was his family. Had the transgression been carried out by anyone else, they would already be dead. But how could he go against his father? And Layla was the one steadily provoking him. It was civil war inside the family, and it needed to end.

The hit in Delaware succeeded, but it wasn't a game changer. Deuce and Jimmy were still alive. The bloodshed they'd created, it was a bloody message—but Deuce would be too ignorant to get the hint. They'd killed over a dozen men at the warehouse, and Bugsy would lose no sleep over it. But he needed something comforting. He needed to be somewhere else at the moment, and that somewhere else was with Alicia.

His black Beamer traveled up her driveway and into the garage, and he climbed out of the car holding a bouquet of roses. The cold night made him look forward to a warm evening with his woman. It was a full moon and a quiet neighborhood. Westchester was a distant safe haven away from the madness in the city. Bugsy was the only one who knew about the house. After the last incident, where a sniper shot at him, he took extra precautions in securing the safety for his woman and her home. They had to move. There were security cameras and motion lights, and the house was purchased under an alias. Bugsy carried a 9mm for his protection.

The garage was well lit, and there were no blind spots for anyone to catch him off guard. The door closed, each step he took was a careful one. Being shot made him wary of everything. Seeing that everything was okay, he went into the home to greet Alicia.

Don't bring it home with you; Alicia had told him. She didn't want to hear about his lifestyle. She knew about it, but she didn't want it brought into her new home. The attempt on his life at her old place had spooked her. She was a nurse, and she saw it all at the hospital where she worked.

She was lounging on the couch in a pair of blue camisole pajamas, watching one of her favorite shows on Showtime, *Shameless.* He presented the bouquet of roses to her, and she loved them. He joined her on the couch, pressing close to her and wrapping his arms around her. It felt so right. They hugged and kissed.

She didn't ask him how his day was because it might have involved something disturbing. So, she asked him, "You okay?"

He answered the same as always. "I'm fine now that I'm home with you."

Bugsy had fallen hard for her. The quiet evenings with Alicia were something he always looked forward to. They sat nestled on the couch, eating popcorn and watching TV. Bugsy laughed at *Shameless,* and said, "Damn, and I thought my family was dysfunctional and fucked up."

"Oh, y'all up there," Alicia joked.

He laughed. He couldn't argue with her.

He held her snugly against him and gazed at her. She smiled at his tenderness. He caressed her cheek. She touched him invitingly. What he felt, it was real. He wanted to be with Alicia forever. With her, everything felt normal. After what happened at the warehouse in Delaware, her touch made him human again, and her smile quieted the monster he had to become out there. She stirred in his arms and felt protected by him. There was no way Bugsy would allow anything to happen to her.

"I love you so much," he said, gazing into her eyes.

"I love you too."

He saw a future with her. He saw her becoming his wife. He wanted no one but Alicia. She was everything he dreamed of. So he asked her, "Do you see yourself having a family with me . . . kids?"

She smiled. "Do you want a family with me?"

"I do."

"I do too," she replied.

It made him happy to hear that.

"I think you would make a great father," she said.

"I would, right?" He laughed.

There was one dilemma with that dream, and that was Bugsy's family. He wanted normalcy in his children's lives. He would teach them better than his parents taught him. He wouldn't bring his street life anywhere around his kids like Scott and Layla had.

Eventually, they stopped watching TV and focused on each other, kissing fervently and slowly undressing each other while sprawled on the couch. Alicia's long legs were spread and straddled his lean frame. Her nakedness was beautiful, and she felt like paradise as he thrust his erection between her wet pink folds and groaned from the sudden jolt of pleasure. Their mouths hungrily devoured each other's lips. She tightened both her legs together around his thighs, and Bugsy could feel the heat of her lust rising against him. Her eyes were bright with a lustful hunger for more; they glistened with a deeply devoted love for him.

"Ooooh, Bugsy . . . oh God," she moaned.

With each deep penetration, he felt her convulse around his dick. He quickly pulled her up and made her ride him against the couch. Alicia bounced on his lap, crowding him with her passion while her tight walls compressed around his dick. The sensation was nearly mind blowing as her legs squeezed and she arched her back, feeling every bit of him inside of her.

"I'm gonna come, baby!" she announced.

His eyes closed and there was no place like home. Every bit of him invaded her. When she came, her body shuddered lightly against him. Their sex was the best, and when he finally came, it was like all the pieces to the puzzle were finally put into place.

They collapsed against each other; her face was on his chest, her body warmly held in his arms. They exhaled.

"I think we just got started on our family."

She laughed. "You so silly."

He looked at her intently. There was never any hesitation with it. "I love you."

"I love you too."

26

Another tailored suit and hard bottoms, another night out with Zoe. Once again, Meyer was looking more like Bugsy than himself. His time with Zoe was always uplifting and fun. He took her wherever she wanted to go, on his dime. Together, they toured the city like two kids, and she took Meyer places he would never go himself. They went to the top floor of the Empire State Building and walked around the observation deck. The view was breathtaking. She took him to the American Museum of Natural History, and they went skating at Rockefeller Center and saw a concert at Radio City Music Hall. Then there was the occasional dinner and a movie.

It was a timeout from the thug life. When Meyer was around Zoe, he was someone different. She still believed he was into real estate and a businessman with the occasional club promoting.

It'd been a while now, and she still had him waiting on the goodies. Usually, it only took a day to break in a new bitch and fuck, but Zoe had a ninety-day rule. She was adamant not to break it. If it were a lesser female, Meyer would have already told her to suck his dick, but this one was special. She was wifey material.

The two walked in the cold, hand-in-hand in Central Park, and conversed naturally. With Zoe, Meyer became a romantic. They had just finished a horse and carriage ride in the park. It was dreamy, and it impressed Zoe. He presented her with flowers and candy. He also gave her diamond earrings and a diamond tennis bracelet. It was the best money could buy. She loved it, but she loved the horse and carriage ride and the flowers more.

"So, why no boyfriend? I mean, a beautiful woman like yourself, I would think a nigga would have wifed you up by now," Meyer said. "You sure I don't have to look over my shoulder for some stalking-ass nigga? I'm sure you have plenty of those."

She chuckled. "I'm a very picky person," she replied. "And besides, I'm a busy woman, and some men just can't keep up with me."

"Picky, huh? I'm a picky man too. It's the reason I don't have a girlfriend," he said.

"What, no string of young girls to play with?" she joked. "Handsome, rich, and romantic—you probably got females lined around the corner waiting to get with you."

"Nah, I'm busy with my career, and besides, when I meet a girl, I don't know if she loves me for me or my money."

"So what about me? You think I'm with you because of your money? You think I'm a gold-digger too?"

"Nah, you're different. I saw that the very first day I met you."

"I'm different, huh? So what makes me different?" she challenged.

"It was your conversation and your attitude. You were just different."

"You can't elaborate more?"

"See? There you go, using cute words like *elaborate* . . . and taking me to museums and Broadway shows. You have culture, Zoe, and that's a turn on."

"Thank you."

They walked and talked more. The cold weather wasn't bothersome to them. Their chemistry was keeping them warm. Holding hands, especially in a public place, was never Meyer's thing. He was surprised he was doing it. It was like he was living a double life. But no matter what kind of image he presented for Zoe, the streets never rested, and the streets never forgot. Life went on, and he was a murderous drug kingpin, and his business was in the millions. The phone call he got from Layla was a reminder.

Meyer wanted to ignore it, but she was trying to reach him a second time. The caller ID said that it was Layla, and Zoe looked at him with suspicion and said, "You might want to get that. It could be important."

It could be important, and, knowing his mother, it was something majorly important.

"It's my mother," he said.

"Oh."

"Give me a minute," he said.

He reluctantly answered her call, and immediately he heard Layla's rage. "I want that muthafucka dead!" she hollered. "I want you to kill that nigga, Meyer! I hate his fuckin' guts!"

"Ma, hold on . . . calm down," he said. "What's going on?"

Meyer felt that now wasn't the time, but his mother was making it the time.

"It's your father. What he did to Lucky and me—he needs to die! Right fuckin' now! I need you here, Meyer." she hollered.

"I'm busy right now, Ma."

"I don't a give a fuck what you're doing. We need to meet now! I'm not asking you."

Meyer sighed. Zoe was standing right there, and he didn't want to come out of his character. He knew if he denied Layla, she would keep calling him. He could turn off his phone, but he would never hear the end of it.

"I'll be there in an hour." He hung up. He was vexed.

Zoe asked him, "Is everything okay?"

"It's my mother. She's upset about something, I think her and my father went at it again," he told her. It was the partial truth.

"Well, go see if she's okay."

"I'm sorry."

"Don't be sorry. It's your mother. I understand."

He smiled. "Thanks."

And just like that, their lovely night together ended.

Meyer was becoming tired of Layla's bullshit. He had a life too, and it didn't revolve around her. He hated being summoned like he was some dog.

27

Whistler pulled back the blinds and carefully looked outside. The black Dodge Charger with tinted windows was still parked nearby. He knew they were watching him. It was Jimmy following his every move. Deuce had him on a tight leash. He knew he didn't have long to lure Lucky into his web and tangle her up so Deuce could sink his fangs into her. He was at Deuce's mercy.

Deuce was right; he had gone from a king to a peasant. Day by day, Whistler was spiraling downward and losing more and more of himself. The cocaine he snorted daily expedited his collapse. The nose candy was his escape from his troubles, but looking out his window and seeing that black Dodge Charger parked outside, he knew there was no escape. They distrusted him and didn't hesitate to let him feel the animosity. But tonight, it was now or never. He couldn't prolong it. He had to take care of business.

He donned a leather jacket, snatched up his pack of cigarettes from the nightstand, and exited the room. He climbed into his Lexus and drove off. As predicted, the Charger followed right behind him. Jimmy was becoming a headache to him. He was on Whistler tighter than white on rice. And if it wasn't Jimmy, then it was one of his henchmen. For two days straight, Whistler couldn't take a piss without someone watching him. It was time to execute. He'd promised them Lucky and her mother, and he had to deliver or he was a dead man.

The midnight hour and the winter cold made the streets sparse of traffic. Calmly, Whistler drove into the night knowing time was ticking. He got on the highway and drove a mile and then exited at the gas station/ rest stop. The Charger followed. Whistler stopped at a gas pump behind a brown jeep Cherokee, scanned the area, and saw an opportunity. Walking toward the station, he saw Jimmy sitting behind the wheel of the Charger and idling close by. They frowned at each other.

Whistler walked into the station and followed a man into the bathroom. The man was average height, middle-aged, and not put together neatly. Once they were in the restroom, Whistler made his move. The man didn't even see him coming. The hit was swift and to the back of his head. The man dropped. Whistler hit him again, knocking him unconscious. Whistler rummaged through his pockets, grabbed his car key with the Jeep emblem, wallet, his jacket, and hat. He removed his clothing and put on the stranger's garb. He dragged the man into a stall and closed the door. One look in the mirror and Whistler was confident he could pull it off.

He exited the bathroom looking like someone else. Composedly, he walked out of the gas station and glanced at the Charger. Jimmy was climbing out of the Dodge and walking toward the station to check in on him. But Whistler was walking right by him with his head lowered and moving toward a different car. Jimmy glanced his way, but there was no recognition. Keep cool, keep moving!

He got into the man's brown Jeep, the only other car besides his and Jimmy's, and drove away. He'd finally ditched his babysitter. He got onto the highway and drove north from Maryland. New York was a few hours away. He was free, but he had some work to do. He lit a cigarette and accelerated to 70mph. He wanted to get as far away from the area possible. Jimmy would not be fooled for long. He would figure it out—the brown Cherokee was already marked and maybe Jimmy remembered the plates. The man was good, and there was a reason he was Deuce's right-hand.

Jimmy reminded Whistler of himself—they both took nothing for granted and trusted nothing. They both paid attention to the details and were good at killing and tracking people down.

An hour went by, and Whistler's cell phone rang. He glanced at the caller ID, and it was Deuce calling. He refused to take the call. What was he going to say? He'd ditched Jimmy and he was on his own. But they would come looking for him, so he had to be ready. He had to give them what he had promised. He'd get to Lucky, and then he'd get to Layla. But he had to be smart about this. He was making enemies everywhere, and one wrong move would wreck everything.

The sunrise over the city was alluring. Whistler had been sitting outside of Lucky's building for over two hours. He watched everything—people's comings and goings, the traffic going by, the employees entering and exiting. When he felt he'd inspected the area long enough, Whistler exited the car and approached the towering brick building. He thought back to the last time he was there. It wasn't a fond memory.

Being back in New York was dangerous. Scott had people everywhere—eyes watching and alerting him from every corner of the city. Whistler knew a bounty was on his head, and all it took was one phone call and his former friend would send out the killing squad.

Whistler walked into the grand lobby of the building and swiveled his head in every direction. The doorman was new. Whistler knew the doorman watched everyone come and go. He would know Lucky's face; she was hard to miss. Whistler approached him with extreme caution, got his attention with three hundred-dollar bills, and asked, "Have you seen this woman in the building lately?"

The doorman's job was supposed to come with discretion, but for a few extra hundred dollars, he was easily swayed. "No, she moved out a while back," the doorman said.

It was all the information Whistler needed. There was no use in prying further. The man wouldn't know Lucky's new address. He slipped the man the three-hundred and headed out.

Fuck! Whistler thought. It was a wise move. They were at war, and he was now their rival, so he knew they would change anything old. But he was a tracker, and he was on the clock.

Think, think, think, he told himself. He had to think fast and find her. But what if she was no longer in New York? Could she be in Delaware? Or Florida? It would be easy for him to keep on driving, maybe go far out west and start a new life there. But then what? He would spend the rest of his life looking over his shoulder, and Whistler wasn't the type to run. It would end someway and somehow. Even if it meant by *bang, bang.*

He knew everything about Lucky—her likes and dislikes, her taste in clothing and men, and the foods she loved. Lucky didn't cook. She ordered out and loved fine dining. But her favorite type of food was Thai, and she only liked the best. His next step was a tedious one, but it had to be done. He looked up all the best Thai food places. He remembered her favorite place was Tue Thai Food near Central Park. She'd moved away from the area, but chances were, she would still be ordering from her favorite restaurant.

Whistler was familiar with the delivery boy; he'd delivered food to Lucky's old address plenty of times, and Whistler was sure he remembered her well. It took some time, but he finally cornered the delivery boy outside of the restaurant. Whistler held the man's bicycle hostage and showed him Lucky's picture and demanded her new address. At first, the delivery boy was reluctant, but for five hundred dollars, he spewed the information out faster than he could breathe.

"I know you. You boyfriend. Why you don't know?" he asked Whistler.

"It's best that you just mind your business," Whistler warned him.

He took the advice and left.

Lucky felt like her life was unraveling, but she would not let her father win. She would not go off the deep end. The rift was widening more and more between them. Lucky wanted to shoot her father right between the eyes for what he did to her and her mother. The disrespect was insane, and she wanted to put a stop to it. The man she had once looked up to and adored was now enemy number-one.

Lucky arrived home to her luxurious apartment on the upper west side. Things were quiet and dark, like usual. Inside the bedroom, she dropped her handbag and pistol on the bed and turned on her stereo system to listen to some Sade. She undressed down to her bra and panties and lounged on the tufted chaise near her bed, as "The Sweetest Taboo" began playing.

Whistler hid in her closet, submerged in the dark. He was still and patient, watching her from the small opening in the door. He had to make sure that she was alone. He watched Lucky for a moment, noted the pistol on the bed, and saw his opportunity. He abruptly emerged from the closet and pointed his gun at her.

Lucky's eyes widened. She wanted to reach for her gun, but Whistler stepped closer in a threatening manner and warned her, "Don't do it, Lucky!"

She was staring down the barrel of a Glock 19, and the bang from it could easily make a mess of her.

"Why are you here?" she exclaimed.

"I'm not here to hurt you," he said.

"You could have fooled me. How did you find me? How the fuck did you get into my place?"

"You know I have my ways, Lucky," he replied.

She glared at him. He stared at her, and she didn't look too good. Her face still showed the bruises from Scott's attack. It looked like she had gone five rounds with Mayweather in his prime. It also looked like she was wearing a wig. This wasn't the Lucky he knew—she looked like she had been through hell and back. He tried not to stare too long at her, knowing how sensitive she had become about her looks.

"Look, we need to talk," he said.

"Fuck you!" she shouted. She was still itching to reach for her gun and kill him—if she could.

Whistler read her movements, and he knew her like a book. "You won't get the shot off, Lucky. I have the advantage. I didn't come here to kill you. I could have been done that. I came here to talk."

She scowled. Talking was no longer relevant to her. All she wanted was revenge. She wanted to fuck him and Scott up. The two men she once trusted had both betrayed her and had let her down. If they were on fire, she wouldn't piss on them to put them out.

"I came to make amends. I know I hurt you, and what I did to you, it was wrong. I'm sorry," he said.

"My father is gonna fuck you up!" she replied. "Fuck your 'sorry!'"

Coming there, Whistler knew he was risking his life, but he had to try. He had to get through to Lucky somehow. So far, it was a very rocky start, which he expected. And as much as he thought he hated and despised her, he didn't want to see her dead. Whistler knew that once Deuce got his hands on her, he would slowly tear Lucky apart physically and mentally. He would torture her in cruel ways. The man was a sadist, and he knew Lucky and Layla would be the ultimate prize in Deuce's hands.

"I'm working with Deuce now," he blurted out. There was no sugarcoating it, no going around it.

"What?" She was shocked to hear that. "You're workin' with that monster? The man who had my brothers and sister killed?"

"Your father left me no choice."

"So you go and side with the fuckin' enemy? You fuckin' coward!"

"I tried talking to you and your father. I wanted to reason with him, but he went crazy. He tried to have me killed."

"I wish he would have succeeded."

Whistler shook his head. A woman scorned, huh? But he would not give up. He'd come this far. She would hear him out one way or another. He was a serious man, and maybe he needed to remind her of that. But she quickly spoke again, exclaiming, "I loved you! I always loved you! You took advantage of me. You started to care more about your whores than you did me! I wanted to be your fuckin' woman. I didn't want anyone else but you. What the fuck did you want, huh? What did you want from me? I gave you the best sex, and I woulda died for you, but that wasn't enough, was it!" A few tears trickled from her eyes.

"I can't change the past, Lucky. I can't change the things that I've done. But I can make it right."

"How can you make it right?"

"Look, you're in danger," he uttered.

"You think that's something new to me?"

"Deuce is out for blood, and he won't stop until he has you and your mother in his clutches. He wants you dead, but not before he has his thugs exploit you and then bury you on his plantation as a trophy from his drug war with Scott. And believe me; you'd rather be dead than to have him take you hostage."

"So, you're here to kill me? Save me the pain?"

"I have a plan."

"And I'm supposed to just trust you?"

"I know it's hard, after everything that's happened, but I'm not gonna let him hurt you," he said with conviction.

Lucky stared into his eyes, and they were filled with fervor and some sincerity. He lowered the gun. Gradually, he was getting through to her, he felt. He said, "He wants you alive, but my plan is to kill you first."

Lucky was confused. "Kill me?"

Whistler detailed his plan to her, but first, he warned her through clenched teeth not to double-cross him.

"You double-crossed me, nigga," she retorted.

"It was my mistake."

It was a thin line between love and hate between them. But they needed each other. They had to survive.

"I need a female to die in your place, Lucky. I will make it look like an accident off the LIE in your truck. A fiery blaze leaving the body charred beyond recognition."

"Say what now?"

"You heard me. It's either gonna be the real you or a fake you, but you're marked for death. Deuce is gunning for you, and this could buy us a few days."

He would need her truck and some of her accessories. Jewelry would be perfect, especially her diamond nameplate. She was upset about her G-Wagen and the jewelry, but wasn't bothered that an innocent girl would probably die in her place.

Whistler continued, "Word will get back to Deuce that you were killed in an accident before I had a chance to get at you, and he'll be furious and want to kill me on the spot. But I'm putting my life on the line and betting that I can still convince him that a captured, grieving Layla is still worth keeping me alive. Jimmy will object, and this time Deuce will insist on having Jimmy not shadow me but ride shotgun when I drive 95-North to kidnap Layla. And this is where you come in."

"Me? Why should I help ya sorry ass?"

He exploded. "Got-damn it, Lucky, can't you grow the fuck up? Our fuckin' lives are on the line. This nigga done killed half your family, and your father can't seem to stop him and neither can I . . . I can't do it alone."

She rolled her eyes, not willing to park her childishness on a shelf.

"What else can I do to help you besides allowing you to burn up my beloved truck and liquefy my favorite necklace?"

There wasn't an "off" button with her, even in the face of danger. Whistler ignored her sarcasm and wondered, briefly, if he should just tie this bitch up and hand deliver her to his oppressor. Was she even worth the headache? From day one, their affair had cost him. Now it could cost him his life.

"You have access to something I don't. Shooters. Do you have a couple goons that are loyal to you?"

She nodded.

"Good. Then I am going to set up a trap for Jimmy. After Deuce hears of your death and sends me after your mother, I am going to bring Jimmy to the lake house in Albany that your parents own. Do you remember it?"

She nodded.

"When we get there, your shooters better be on point and take Jimmy out. And, Lucky, don't get cute and have them take me out too. If you keep up your end of the bargain, then I will hand deliver Deuce to you on a silver platter. So think long and hard on how you want to play this. Is it more important to see me dead, a man who's loved you until this very day, or the man who murdered Gotti, Bonnie, and Clyde and had you beaten?"

But Lucky didn't understand it. "Why not just kill Deuce?"

He planned on doing so. Whistler wanted his life back. With Deuce and Scott dead, he could show his face without looking over his shoulders and start up his organization. Once he got Deuce to put his guard down, he would have Lucky's soldiers kill Jimmy and make it look like Scott's crew were the culprits. With Jimmy gone, Deuce would become a much easier target to wipe out.

Scott had to die too. He couldn't fill Lucky in on that part of his plan, though. Whistler realized that Scott would never forgive him, and their friendship and partnership was long gone. The extreme was all Whistler had. Scott would never believe that Lucky was killed accidentally on the LIE and would finally snap and go ham on locating Deuce. Scott would be certain that just as his other kids' murders were made to look like accidents, so was this. He would feel like less than a man to have four children murdered by one man and would move heaven and earth to exact revenge. And Layla wouldn't rest until they got at Deuce. Deuce, too, would come out swinging and looking for payback for Jimmy. Lucky would help implement this plan whether she liked it or not. She was the catalyst to ignite the fire to burn it all down.

The key to this plan would be that Scott would believe that Lucky had been murdered. It didn't matter who took whom out; whoever survived would die by Whistler's hand. It was a long shot, like winning the lottery, but Whistler felt he had to be in it to win.

"If he were that easy to kill, don't you think Scott with all his muscle and millions would have done it already? Huh? Think, Lucky. This is the only way."

Lucky pondered the bizarre plan. She was pissed at Scott anyway, so the idea of making him grieve and suffer almost made her smile. But to have the rest of her family think she was dead?

"I hear you, Whistler, but to have my mother, Meyer, and Bugsy think I was killed in a car crash is just cruel."

Whistler did a lot more explaining and ended with, "It's the only way."

It was a lot to swallow, but Whistler knew how to be persuasive. She was up for it. She explained that she wanted revenge on her father anyway. Who did she hate the most, her father or Whistler? Each time she looked into the mirror and saw the bruises on her face and felt the pain and betrayal, her rage toward her father surfaced. Whistler had broken her heart, but he never physically beat her. Her father struck her and damaged her soul. She looked ugly, and she felt it too. She had bald spots in her head from her father's violence, and her face was still healing. She wanted some payback. Whistler came at the right time with his plan.

But what about her mother? Would she be safe? Layla could handle herself, but Lucky had to be there for her. Whistler assured her that Layla was safe, but she couldn't know about their plan. It was between them. Everyone had to be in the dark. They couldn't know that her death was a ruse. They had to feel the emotions, and it had to look and feel real for everyone to see—including Deuce and Jimmy.

"I'm putting my life on the line to save you."

She understood. And for a moment, they'd reconciled.

Their conversation went from the bedroom to the living room. Lucky picked up a bottle of red wine and drank it out of the bottle. Whistler watched her. The way she was drinking, it seemed harmful.

"Maybe you need to cut back some on the alcohol," he suggested.

She shot a hard stare at him and barked, "Muthafucka, don't tell me what to do! You don't fuckin' own me. And after what I been through, I need to relax."

He left it alone. He watched her walk around the room in her panties and bra. She didn't care to become decent in front of him. Though her looks had changed with her bruises, wig, and her droopy eye, her body was still curvy, thick, and in shape.

Whistler talked about his master plan. He wanted to map it out accurately, to where there would be no mistakes. This was life or death.

Lucky, however, continued to drink. She approached him with a wicked smile, pushed her body against his, and touched the side of his face. "Do you miss me?" she asked him.

Whistler stood there straight-faced. He didn't answer her.

Her hand went from the side of his face, traveled down his torso, and landed on his crotch. She squeezed his dick and said, "I do miss you. Damn, I do miss him."

He knew that she wanted to fuck. She tried to kiss him, but he gently resisted. "Now is not the time," he said.

"What's the matter? You don't find me attractive anymore?"

"It's not that. I just want to take care of business."

"I am your business, and you owe me," she said.

"Not like this. I'm trying to save your life."

She huffed and pouted. She drank more. She was becoming frustrated. The hostility she had toward him earlier had transitioned into yearning with lust for him. He was still fine, and he still had a big dick.

Whistler looked her directly in her eyes and undoubtedly proclaimed, "I still love you, Lucky. I always will. But I just can't right now. We both have too much going on in our lives to continue something that got me in hot water with your father in the first place. Before we even think about going there, we have to figure out this mess and stay alive."

She had no words. Strangely, she understood him. It was just that seeing him again, those old feelings crept back and she wanted to be touched and loved once more. She needed the affection—some affection, it didn't matter from who.

He handed her a burner phone. "We need to keep in touch." And with that, he exited the apartment.

Lucky stood in the center of her living room and watched him go. Just as easily as he'd come, he was gone. She looked at the phone and wondered if she'd made the right choice by allowing Whistler back into her life. Could she trust him again? What if it was all a ploy to take her and Layla down? Whistler was the master of manipulation. He had a way with words—ways of making people listen to him and believe him. His gift of gab was a superpower.

Was she thinking more with her heart than her mind? There was no telling what Whistler was up to.

28

Whistler avoided the brown Cherokee and stole a dark Toyota Camry. He started the ignition and peeled out. He glanced up at Lucky's towering brick building and felt he had worked his way back into her life again. The look in Lucky's eyes was inviting; he could easily have had his way with her. She was young and naïve, and that worked to his advantage, as did the history they had together. The extreme measures he was taking were risky, but Whistler's life had always been unsteady, and he was no stranger to taking it to the extreme.

He navigated his way out of the city and toward the west side highway, and from there, moving toward the Verrazano Bridge. He was on his way back to Maryland. But he made the phone call first, and Deuce answered.

"You muthafucka!" Deuce growled.

"I know you're upset with me for ditching Jimmy, but let me explain. The trap has been set. I'm back in Lucky's life," he quickly explained. "I'm sending you proof."

Before Deuce could rant and throw threats, Whistler sent a picture of Lucky from behind in her bra and panties to Deuce's phone. Once again, and somehow, Whistler was able to persuade Deuce to trust him.

"When can I have her?" he asked.

"In a week," Whistler replied.

"You have one week, muthafucka, and not a day more. But I have other business for you take care of."

"Like what?"

"Not over the phone. I expect to see you back in Maryland within twenty-four hours."

"I'll be back in town in five hours," Whistler replied.

"Don't fuck with me, Whistler."

Whistler sat shirtless in the room and did a long line of cocaine. The white girl was a boost—a stimulus. It was his escape, temporary though. He was alone, and he was under a lot of pressure. It had been two days since his reunion with Lucky. Time was winding down. Deuce expected to have Lucky and Layla chained inside his dungeon.

The TV was on, but it was muted. Whistler did another line of cocaine and felt that leash around his neck again, and it was tightening quickly. He wiped the powder residue from his nose and looked for his cell phone. He needed to call Lucky and get an update. He dialed her number, and her cell rang four times before she answered.

"What?" she said roughly.

"What you mean 'what?' You know why I'm calling. What's the verdict on what we talked about? Did you find someone?"

"I need some time."

"We don't have time, Lucky. This is life or death. If we don't get this shit right, we're both dead," he griped.

"Nigga, don't fuckin' rush me. You never gave me a fuckin' deadline!"

"Lucky, this is not a fuckin' game. You need to find someone and fast. This is my life you're playing with too, and before I take a bullet for you, I'll see you dead first. You have seventy-two hours."

He hung up on her. He was frustrated. He tried not to panic, so he did another line of cocaine. The predicament Whistler found himself in was disturbing. His fall from grace was hard, and it was ugly. He was becoming a drug addict and depending on a nineteen-year-old girl to save him. Going from a king to a peasant felt surreal. He had five days left to do what he'd promised Deuce—and those five days were winding down fast.

Whistler flicked the lit cigarette out the passenger window of the Maxima and sighed. Henny, one of Deuce's lieutenants, was driving, and a soldier rode in the back. They were headed north on I-95 to Delaware with five kilos of cocaine—packaged and concealed for street distribution. Traffic on the highway was light, and it was about to get dark soon.

Whistler had two days left to deliver Lucky, but until then, he had become a drug mule for Deuce. It was something he'd never had to do in his position with Scott. He had slid down to the bottom of the totem pole.

While doing the speed limit on the highway, Henny turned to Whistler. "How the fuck you go from something to nothing? Yeah, I heard about you—you were supposed to be this big shot muthafucka from New York, fucking Frank Lucas and shit. More like *Fred* Lucas."

It was said as an insult to him.

The soldier in the back laughed.

Whistler turned and looked at Henny. Muthafuckas were looking at him as a zero. Whistler was a regular guy to them—today, a drug mule just like him.

"You got a problem with me, nigga?" Whistler asked sternly.

"I'm just talkin', that's all . . . making conversation," Henny replied.

"I prefer if you keep your comments to yourself. You don't know me, and you don't have shit to say to me. I'm old school, nigga, and I'll cut your nuts off fast and shove 'em down your throat. We do this job and we go our separate ways," Whistler exclaimed. "Don't say another fuckin' word to me."

Henny frowned. He didn't like being talked to recklessly, but he'd heard the stories about Whistler. But that was back in the day—who was he now? Deuce's old school errand boy. He chose not to test the waters with Whistler and kept his mouth shut and kept driving. Whistler had nothing to lose, but Henny had three kids.

Whistler lit another cigarette and took some needed drags. It felt like a long trip on the road although Maryland and Delaware weren't that far from each other. Whistler was antsy. There'd been no word from Lucky yet, and he was ready to drive back to New York and confront her. Chances were, she was gone, and he would be fucked. He inhaled the nicotine from the Newport, but he was yearning for something much stronger. That cocaine was calling his name. He needed that extra lift.

New Castle, Delaware was six miles south of Wilmington on the Delaware River. Like almost all of Delaware, it was a blue-collar town. Unemployment was high, poverty was rampant, and drug use was prevalent. Deuce had been making a fortune in New Castle for the past year. It was untapped territory, and his foothold on the town was fierce. One of his stash houses was an abandoned market perched near the river. It was quiet, inconspicuous, and well fortified.

The plan was to meet with Deuce's New Castle drug dealers and simply drop off the re-up.

The Maxima drove toward the old marketplace and came to a stop. Whistler got out of the car first, followed by Henny and the soldier. He looked around and noticed an old van parked nearby. It wasn't unusual for owners to abandon their cars in the area, but something about it made his street instincts buzz. He was the only one eyeing the vehicle. He looked at the marketplace, and to anyone passing by, it was an old, decaying building, but inside, there some serious money being made.

Henny glanced around and proceeded toward the building. The third man removed the rear car bumper, where the kilos were concealed. But

Whistler still had a bad feeling about it. Then, the door to the van slid back, and Whistler's instincts were proven right. Four armed men quickly emerged from the vehicle and opened fire with assault rifles. Henny was immediately gunned down by machine gun fire. He got dead quick.

"Muthafuckas!" Whistler hollered. He took evasive action and ducked behind the car as bullets whizzed by him. He snatched his pistol from his waistband and opened fire.

Boom! Boom! Boom!

The young soldier did the same. They were pinned down by the gunfire. Bullets ripped through the car and shattered glass. Whistler returned fire. It was a hit—or they'd been set up. Quickly, Whistler pivoted toward the opposite direction of the car, crouching and positioning himself into a defensive stance. He rapidly took aim and caught one shooter by firing two slugs into his chest as he tried to creep their way. In an uncontrolled fever, he pumped two more slugs into the dead man.

One down and three to go.

They were outgunned, but Whistler wasn't going down without taking more enemies with him. He and his ally exchanged hot bullets with their assailants. The area lit up with gunfire louder than fireworks on the 4th of July. He spun around from the car one more time and fired—*Boom! Boom!*

Budda-budda-budda-budda-budda! It was returned fire—shredding almost everything in the surrounding area.

"Fuck!" Whistler shouted.

Still crouched, Whistler spun around and fired, this time hitting another assailant three times and dropping him dead. But now he was alone in the gun battle. A slug had punched a serious hole in the DMC soldier's abdomen, and Whistler found him collapsed nearby.

There were two enemies left. Whistler was breathing heavy, his ammo was running low, and time was running out. It was now or never, and he thrust himself into the now. He spun around to return fire, but in that moment he saw something. They both saw each other from a distance, and they made steady eye contact—him and Bugsy. But the recognition didn't stop them from trying to kill each other. Bugsy opened fire with the Uzi in his hands. He wanted to take Whistler's head off. But Whistler was adept with a pistol, and he was pushing both men back.

For a moment, Whistler stayed low and hidden behind the bullet-riddled Maxima and quickly checked his ammo. He had three rounds left. He was caught between a rock and a hard place. It was his time to die; there was no escaping it. But then everything unexpectedly became too silent—no more gunfire. He heard the van start up and the wheels screeched before it went speeding away.

"What the fuck?" he mouthed.

The smoke cleared, and he was the last man standing. He looked around him, and the place was a war zone littered with bullet holes and bodies. He was still alive—but why and how? Had Bugsy spared his life?

He couldn't linger in the area too long, so he fled on foot. Maybe Jimmy was right—maybe he did have nine lives.

29

Bugsy sat slumped against the door, trying to relax. He held his side and could feel the blood oozing from his small injury. It was only a flesh wound, but it hurt like hell. The bullet had torn pieces of his right side off. He would live, but he missed his chance at Whistler, and two of his men were killed. He knew it was best to retreat and come back fighting another day.

His driver, Bruce, hurried him away from the scene. He sped toward the highway, but Bugsy needed medical attention.

"I need to call your father, tell him what happened," Bruce said with fret in his tone.

"I'm all right. I just need a quick patch-up," said Bugsy. "Fuckin' Whistler. Ooooh, that fuckin' traitor."

Bugsy had a hunch what Whistler was up to—that he may have been the one to give up the organization's secrets to rivals. He wasn't shocked to see Whistler working for the other team. Bugsy had sources everywhere, and it was alleged on the streets. But it was a sad sight for Bugsy to see with his own eyes. Whistler and DMC working together. He had to tell Scott about it. It would not be easy news to relay. Knowing his father, the man would hit the roof.

"I just need a doctor to patch me up. I'll be okay," Bugsy said. "Find me a doctor; I don't care how you do it."

Bruce nodded. This was Scott's son, and he didn't need the boss's son dying on his watch—although Bugsy appeared to be fine.

Bugsy sighed. The last person he wanted to find out he'd been shot was Alicia. He feared it would be too much for her and he would lose her. He couldn't lose Alicia, and he couldn't go back to her bandaged up from a gunshot wound. She was a nurse, and it would be difficult to hide it. He'd promised Alicia he would never lie to her or hide anything from her.

Bruce pulled into a hospital staff lot and waited a few minutes. It wasn't long before he saw the man headed to his car.

Dr. Knight had just worked fifteen hours and simply wanted to go home and get some rest. But his plans would change. The unexpected assailant came from behind, the barrel of his pistol pressed to the back of his head.

"If you wanna live till your next shift, I suggest you get your kit and come with me," Bruce said.

Dr. Knight had no choice but to oblige the gunman. It was late and it was dark, and they were alone. There was no help on the way.

Dr. Knight treated Bugsy's wound in the back of the van. He was lucky it was a through-and-through—no bullet to remove from the flesh. The doctor put in a few stitches and bandaged to the wound.

"He's fine," said the doctor. "Can I go now?"

Bugsy nodded. The van door opened. Before Dr. Knight left, Bugsy tossed the man a ten thousand dollar stack—for his time and trouble. The doctor looked reluctant in taking the cash; he was just doing his job, helping a man in need.

"Don't think about it, just take it. You helped me out," Bugsy said.

Dr. Knight exhaled and walked away with the cash.

Bugsy looked at Bruce and said, "Now, take me back to New York."

The next day, Bugsy drove his Benz into his father's Brooklyn scrap yard and climbed out of the car. He was alone and in a serious mood. He was feeling much better from the shooting, knowing he was lucky to be alive after being shot a second time. His black shoes crunched against the gravel as he trekked toward the building, and his injuries were concealed by the overcoat he wore. The place was busy with workers and a few of Scott's goons loitering nearby. They greeted Bugsy, showing their respect, and kept on with their labor. The boss's son was back in New York.

Bugsy entered the building and went straight to his father's office. He knocked before he entered and opened the door to see his father seated behind his desk, going over some paperwork and smoking his cigar. It was the first time since Maxine's accident Bugsy had seen him somewhere other than at the hospital watching over her.

Bugsy closed the door and looked at his father. "Pop, we need to talk."

Scott took a pull from the cigar and leaned back in his high-back leather chair. It was an expensive piece of furniture that appeared to be an anomaly in the ordinary looking office. The boss had to be comfortable.

"What happened in Delaware?" he asked.

Bugsy approached closer. The look on his face indicated to Scott he would receive no good news.

"Whistler is working with Deuce. We got into a shootout. He escaped."

Scott stared at Bugsy. It was hard news to swallow, but his son wouldn't lie to him. Whistler, working with Deuce. The audacity of that muthafucka. His teeth chomped down on the cigar in his mouth, almost breaking it in half. He jumped up from his chair and in one rapid and angry motion, he swept everything off his desk. Everything scattered across the floor.

Bugsy just stood there. He'd expected this type of reaction.

Scott remembered when Lucky had told him that Whistler was the mastermind behind his children's murders. It was true. All along, Whistler and Deuce were working against him. His right-hand man was fucking his daughter and killing his children. The fury that Scott felt was biblical—he wanted to shake the earth to destroy these two men.

"I won't rest until we find them, Pop. I promise you that. I'll fuck up that traitor for good," Bugsy said.

Scott looked at his son. He was proud of Bugsy. He represented him, the family, and the organization well.

"You burn that fuckin' city to the ground if you have to, to smoke out that muthafucka," Scott growled.

Bugsy nodded. "I have my ways."

"I know you do. That's why you're my favorite, Bugsy. You never let me down."

Bugsy stood expressionless from the comment. He was sharp in his black suit and gray tie. His shoes were neatly polished, and his posture was more businessman than thug—but he was a gangster—a smart muthafucka who got shit done.

Scott, however, was still unraveling. It looked like he hadn't slept in days, and his clothing wasn't as neatly put together as his son's—a wrinkled and unbuttoned shirt and a five o' clock shadow. Scott knew he needed to put more boots to the ground and defeat his foes once and for all. Even though he'd placed a bounty on both of their heads, they were still breathing, and to find out that they had joined forces was an intolerable feeling. Layla's words were the extra bonus to his anger—her taunts about how he allowed Deuce to kill their kids and how he'd beaten his daughter nagged him.

Scott's irrational thinking made him believe that killing Deuce and Whistler would absolve him of any guilt.

Whistler had almost lost his life, but it wasn't the first time. Whistler was a survivor by any means necessary—a Brooklyn-born thug who pulled himself up by his bootstraps to become a productive, respected, and feared man. Time was winding down—tick-tock-tick-tock—and Deuce wasn't a kind man. There would be no extensions, only consequences. It would be war or appeasement with Deuce—no gray area.

During his drive north, Whistler thought about a question he had for Deuce once he got back on his good side. He wanted to know why he had Lucky beaten within an inch of her life only to let her go. Why the games? It seemed too personal for a drug beef. These were his thoughts as his car hugged the highway toward what he had hoped was a means to an end.

The trip to New York was fast, and Whistler chose the meeting ground. It was a day before the deadline, and Lucky had called him with the good news that she'd found someone to match her description and she had the bitch tied up in the trunk of her G-Wagen. Whistler told her to meet him near the Brooklyn Navy yard.

It was late and dark when Lucky showed up at the chosen spot, the perfect place to meet because traffic and people were few and far between. It was somewhat shady looking, but she wasn't afraid. It was cold, and a full moon glowed from above. She sat in the idling car and called Whistler.

"I'm here," she said.

"Change of plans," he said, throwing a wrench into everything.

"What the fuck? Why?"

"Because I said so. I want you to meet me near the Brooklyn Bridge in a half-hour," he said.

She sighed. She had no choice. She drove off and headed toward the bridge. She came armed with a .45, but it was in the glove box. She didn't trust Whistler and she had to protect herself just in case. He had proven himself before to be a snake. But who was worse—him or her father?

Lucky lit a cigarette and traveled to the Brooklyn Bridge. The area he chose was a restricted parking lot right near the bridge. It was quiet and empty of cars. There was no parking attendant and no residents. It was another shady looking location. Lucky parked and swiveled her head—no Whistler. She called him again. He answered, more bad news—change of location. *What the fuck?* She was becoming frustrated.

"You're fuckin' with me, Whistler!" she exclaimed.

"I'm just being cautious."

He told her the new location, and she left. When she got to the third location, she called, and he changed shit up on her again.

"Last time," he promised.

Lucky wanted to kill him herself. He was wasting her time. Why didn't she just leave? He needed her. She didn't need him even though he kept saying she did. He was supposedly protecting her from Deuce. The monster was coming for her.

The fourth location was farther from the others. It was in another parking lot off of Sullivan Street, near the Red Hook projects. The area was industrial—warehouses, large parking lots with broken down trucks, buses, and trailers, and old factories from block to block. On one side of the location, abandoned trailers were left overnight, maybe longer. They were cluttered together.

Lucky made the call. She was heated. Whistler was giving her the runaround. She didn't abandon the plan, although she felt like it.

When Whistler answered, he replied, "I'm already here." He flashed his headlights, catching her attention. He was parked subtly nearby, behind her. "I apologize for the runaround; I just had to make sure that you were alone—that you weren't followed. Get out the car."

He had to make sure she wasn't setting him up. Lucky's truck was the only other car in the parking lot. Whistler looked around; there was no approaching traffic, and her silhouette was the only one inside the car. He climbed out of his vehicle, and she got out of her Benz. He approached her carefully. He was still cautious. Immediately, he patted her down, making sure she wasn't armed.

"Seriously?" she uttered.

"I'm just watching my back."

"Fuck you!"

Once he saw she was free from any weapons, he looked at her and said, "So, the bitch in the back, she's alive or dead?"

"She's alive."

"And she's in the trunk, right?"

"Muthafucka, would I be here if I didn't have her?" she shouted.

"Don't get touchy, Lucky. I got enemies, you know."

"I know, me and my father included," she said gruffly.

"Let's just get this over with," he said.

They walked to the back of the G-Wagen and he peered into the vehicle, seeing someone who appeared to be bound and gagged. Whistler had to respect Lucky's gangster. She was a cold-hearted bitch. She had no trouble in having some regular Jane Doe killed for her benefit.

"Open it up," he said.

"What? No! Are you gonna do it here?"

"No, I just need to see for myself who you chose to take your place—if she can pass for you. I know you better than anyone," he said with a leer and touched her hip slightly. "You are still sexy, you know that right?"

She stepped back. What happened to the man who just last week got on his moral high horse and didn't want to fuck her? Now it seemed like he was throwing sexual advances her way. But it was who he was—one minute he was into her, and the next he would behave like they'd never met. She wasn't in the mood for his game or his bullshit. She was there for business.

"I want you to open it," he repeated.

"You don't trust me?"

"Let's say that we don't trust each other," he replied.

Lucky didn't argue with him. She went to pull open the rear door to her truck. Whistler watched her every move intently. He was armed with a Glock 17, but it was stuffed in his waistband. He had no reason to suspect any treachery from Lucky, not at the moment.

Lucky stepped aside to allow Whistler to view the female. He approached slowly. His eyes were fixed on the girl in the fetal position. After a closer look at her, he saw who it was—but before he could react, Layla popped up like a Jack-in-the-box and aimed the pistol at his head and fired—*Bak!* He dropped. Layla climbed from out the back and stood over the body. She fired one more time into him—*Bak!*—to ensure he was dead.

"Good fuckin' riddance," Layla said with distaste.

Lucky looked down at him, blood pooling beneath him, and she felt nothing—no remorse. Whistler had dug his own grave, and she betrayed him before he could betray her.

Damn, how far you've fallen, she thought.

"What you wanna do with the body?" Lucky asked Layla.

"Leave him there to fuckin' rot, and let the rats chew on his ass," Layla said. She then kicked his lifeless body. She hated Whistler.

"Let's go," said Layla. "One down and one to go."

Tarsha let the warm water cascade down her brown skin and sighed. She lingered in the shower trying to collect her thoughts. Wacka was still injured and useless, and his situation wasn't changing soon. She had to strip to make money to support her son. Even though the money was sometimes good, she wanted more of it. She wanted the finer things in life, and she was used to getting it from Wacka. He'd taken care of her, now she was taking care of him, and it was a strange feeling.

Her time in the shower spawned an epiphany. She let the soap rinse away and then stepped out of the shower and toweled off.

After finishing in the bathroom, Tarsha went into her bedroom to put on something decent. She opened the curtain and rays of sunshine touched her face.

Her son was sleeping on the bed, and Wacka was sleeping on the couch. Lately, that's all he'd been doing—sleeping. The last thing Tarsha wanted to see was her baby's father withering away slowly and dying.

She kicked the couch and stirred him awake. "Nigga, wake up. We need to talk," she said to him.

He picked himself up from the couch and looked at her. Damn, that fire he had in his eyes, it was burnt out—extinguished! He needed to get it back, and she felt she had a way. There was a way to get back at Maxine, and it would make them rich.

"Let me get a cigarette," he said.

Wacka sat on the couch, slouching. The doctors were working on getting him some prosthetic fingers. It was expensive, but he needed some dexterity in his hand again. He needed to grip a gun—being handicapped wasn't an option.

Tarsha gave him a cigarette and he needed help to light it. He did his best. He took a few pulls and sat back. "What you wanna talk about?"

"This bitch Maxine," she said.

Tarsha wanted to know everything about Maxine. She wanted to blackmail that bitch. If everything Wacka told her was true, then they had an advantage.

Wacka knew quite a bit about Maxine. He had information that stood between her and her fiancé, Scott. Her life was perfect now, because Scott made it perfect. But what if a little birdie suddenly told him something he would want to know about the death of his kids and who the real culprit behind it all was? It would destroy Maxine. It would ruin her life. But Wacka had to be careful too. Even though Maxine gave the order, Wacka was still the one who pulled the trigger and killed those kids. Also, Maxine was a conniving bitch with a lot to lose, so it would be easier to have Wacka killed than to shut him up.

"We just need to be careful wit' this bitch," Tarsha said. "She's smart, and we need to be smarter. We need to find a way to get to her."

Wacka needed to be feared by Maxine and everyone else. If the streets knew that Wacka was weak and injured, there would be no mercy for him, and his power would be nil.

"I'm ready to do whatever—fuck that bitch," Wacka grumbled. "I'll find a way."

Tarsha saw that fire in his eyes again. This was the nigga she loved and got pregnant by. It just took that one spark of a plan, and there he was, looking like a pit bull ready to be released from its leash.

"Now that's my nigga," she said.

Wacka knew that Maxine was capable of anything. If this psycho bitch had him kill her fiancé's kids for revenge and caused a car accident to escape from him, there was no telling what else she was capable of if backed into a corner and threatened. So they had to expect the unexpected when dealing with an evil like Maxine. They could trust nothing this ho would tell them.

Tarsha stared at Wacka with empathy and said to him, "I don't want you dying out there."

Wacka looked at her and replied, "I'm good, Tarsha. Best believe that. We gonna hunt that bitch down and do what we need to do—kill that bitch and get paid too."

She smiled. It was somewhat turning her on to see him speak that thug shit and get things popping again. She kissed him and he returned her kiss. She undid his pants and removed her clothes and quickly straddled his lap on the couch, facing him and feeling his hard erection sinking inside of her. They both moaned, as she bounced up and down on his dick, her knees sinking into the cushion and her body pressed against his.

"Fuck me!" she cooed.

He teased her nipples with his lips and tongue and she moaned.

She arched her back, placed her hands on his knees, closed her eyes, and relished the moment between them. It felt good to have Wacka somewhat back. When he made her come, she gripped him tightly, and she knew that she loved Wacka.

Bugsy did his best to hide his wound from Alicia. Lucky for him, she was doing extra shifts at the hospital, and it gave him some time alone to come up with a plan to smoke out the rats once and for all.

He spent some time in the bathtub—in the dark, soaking in hot water and pondering. But he wasn't thinking about the streets, or Whistler, or Deuce. He was thinking about Alicia. He thought about her night and day. It felt like she couldn't do any wrong. When he was down, she was there to lift him up. Love, it was a beautiful thing. The funny thing was, Bugsy saw that same love more with his father and Maxine than he ever had with his parents together. Bugsy was happy for his father. Maxine did something to him.

Maxine reminded him of Alicia, and he'd caught that love bug. Lingering in the tub for a long time, he said to himself, *Fuck it, just do it!* He smiled at the idea.

Finished bathing, he removed himself from the tub and toweled off. He glanced at himself in the mirror and went to get dressed in the bedroom. It was then he made the call. Maxine picked up, and he asked her for a favor. He didn't ask too many people for favors, but this was important.

Maxine agreed. She liked Bugsy; he was there for her at the hospital, and she would be there for him when he needed her. The man had class, but there was more than meets the eye. He was an intriguing guy.

Bugsy didn't choose this life; it chose him. So much was expected from him and his siblings. But Bugsy immediately stood out from the other children because of his smarts. He was educated—a high school graduate. Meyer wanted to be the chip off the old block—become just like his hardcore father and rule the streets. Bugsy was a voracious reader, and he finished one year in college. He liked to box, and he loved sports. He even thought about getting his masters degree in business and dabbling in politics.

But when his father came home after doing a bid, things drastically changed for Bugsy. His parents encouraged the street life on him, and he simply adapted to it.

His first murder was committed at the behest of his mother. It was a young local drug dealer named Mitch. He was a man with a lot of pride, attitude and mouth. Mitch wanted to intrude his business on family territory. He'd been warned plenty of times but still insisted on selling drugs in areas where he didn't belong. Mitch had big dreams of becoming the next Nino Brown of Brooklyn. He thought he was a gangster—a hardcore thug who could step on toes and not get touched back, but Layla wanted to show him there was severe penalty for not listening.

Bugsy was only sixteen years old when Layla put the gun in his hand and told him what to do. "Don't let me down, Bugsy . . . make your bones tonight," she'd said to him.

He'd nodded. There was a tinge of nervousness inside of him, but he knew he had to go through with it. This was the family business—and everyone got their hands dirty.

Bugsy set out with a crew of five to have his back—tonight, he was the trigger man. The location on Mitch had been received. He was predictable. He loved his whores and his weed. LG's in Flatbush was the spot to go for pussy and a good time. Mitch frequented the place almost every other day. The trap had been set. A girl got his attention. Mitch liked them young and light skinned with that pretty, long hair and pretty eyes. She was down—for the right price.

She took Mitch to the VIP room of the club, off limits for many. The right people got Bugsy inside and led him to the room, and from there, he was on his own. The gun he gripped was a silver Beretta with a silencer at the end. The door was unlocked, the club music blared, and Bugsy crept calmly toward his victim. He could see Mitch in action, fucking the young girl from the back with his pants down and his back to Bugsy, completely oblivious to the threat. Mitch was a muscular dude, and if it came to hand-to-hand combat, it would be a challenge for Bugsy, so he had to be accurate and fast.

Bugsy didn't want to shoot the man in the back. He felt it was a cowardly thing to do. So he said to get Mitch's attention, "Ay yo!"

Mitch spun around and glimpsed his killer, and then Bugsy shot twice—*Phewt—Phewt!*

Mitch went down with two bullets to his chest. The girl stood there, her eyes displaying a hint of concern. *Would he kill her too?* She didn't scream. She stood there frozen and exposed.

Bugsy wasn't there for her. He vanished quickly from her sight.

He wasn't sure what he felt when he killed that man—it was quick and it was a rush, but he was uneasy for a moment. His first murder . . . he would always remember. He had made his bones—popped his cherry—and the veterans in the game told him it would come easier after that.

The next day, Layla had scolded him for leaving behind a witness to the murder. Bugsy felt he did nothing wrong, but she'd schooled him that leaving the stripper behind was a mistake. She could prove that he was there. A week later, they found the girl's body in a park. She had been shot in the head.

Bugsy climbed into his Escalade and left the suburban neighborhood. Today was a special day for him. He called Maxine to confirm their meeting. Since her release from the hospital, she had been doing well. Scott provided her with the best care that money could buy, and she was a strong woman.

He pulled up to the swanky, thirty-story building in Midtown Manhattan, and Maxine was already waiting for him downstairs with security. Where she went, two bodyguards went for her protection. Maxine got into his truck, and security got into their vehicle and carefully followed them. Bugsy wanted to talk to Maxine privately—no prying ears around.

"What's this about, Bugsy?" she said.

"I wanna marry Alicia. I love her, and I want things to be perfect. I want the perfect ring, and I need a woman's advice," he said.

She smiled. "Wow, that is beautiful," she said. "She's gonna be so happy."

"I hope so."

"She will. A wonderful and handsome man like yourself, what woman wouldn't be happy?"

"I'm nervous about this, though. I'm never nervous about much."

"When I think about love—true love that can survive almost anything," she began, "I think about this movie I saw, *The Notebook*. Great film. That's the love I know you're going to give her."

Bugsy smiled. He'd never seen the movie. He noted to himself to check it out with Alicia when they got the chance. They enjoyed watching movies together.

"I've seen the two of you together, and y'all are perfect. The chemistry between you and her, it's real. And everybody wants real."

He nodded. It was real, and he'd felt nothing like it before. He thought about his woman night and day, and he couldn't imagine life without her.

177

The conversation with Maxine felt natural. He liked her. He knew that he couldn't have this conversation with Layla. His mother was different. She didn't say the right things, and sometimes it felt like Layla threw her kids into the lion's den. She was about her business, not much about family, but she loved them in her own way. Maxine seemed more family oriented. The look in Maxine's eyes showed him she cared more about his relationship with Alicia than Layla ever had.

He continued to fight the midtown traffic. Their security was right behind them, playing them close and making sure not to lose them.

"She's simple, you know. She doesn't like flashy things, so I want this ring to be perfect."

"It will be, no matter what, Bugsy, because it came from you. She'll like it, believe me," she said.

They finally arrived at Tiffany & Co. on the corner of 5th Avenue and 57th Street. The flagship store with its polished granite exterior was an iconic sight representing wealth, jewelry, and longevity. They say that only the elite shop at Tiffany's, and an engagement ring from there speaks volumes to the fiancée. Bugsy wanted to give Alicia only the best, so it had to come from a place like Tiffany's.

Inside was a grand display of opulence and riches and some of the finest and stylish jewelry in the world. Upon entry, they received help from a female employee who greeted Bugsy and Maxine with a polite smile and asked if she could assist them with anything.

"I'm looking for an engagement ring for my girlfriend," Bugsy said.

"Congratulations! Is there a particular ring you're looking for? Cut, setting?"

"Just a beautiful ring," he said.

"I'm happy to assist you," she said.

He and Maxine went through numerous choices. Bugsy wanted the perfect ring, even though they all seemed perfect and expensive—but money wasn't an issue for him. He wanted a ring that would fit his girl's personality and style. He noticed Maxine's engagement ring, and it stood out brighter than the North Star. Maxine felt proud to wear it. She loved Scott, and her huge rock on her finger showed how much he loved her. But like Alicia, Maxine didn't care for the big ring on her finger; it was more Scott's taste. She'd told him she would have been happy with a gold band.

Bugsy wasn't looking to pay a million dollars for a ring; Alicia would probably curse him out if he spent that much.

He finally saw the one. It caught his attention like Alicia had when they first met. It was a vintage one-carat diamond engagement ring. The price tag was seventy thousand dollars. He knew she would love it.

Maxine loved the ring too. "That's perfect."

"Yes, it is," the saleswoman agreed.

"I'll take it," he said.

Everyone smiled.

Bugsy was looking for the right moment to pop the question to Alicia. He would have loved to do it in front of family, but his family was a mess right now.

Layla's business with Angel Morales was going well. Cocaine and heroin was moving night and day with no trouble, and word on the street was the purity of the product was high. Fiends couldn't get enough.

She invited her children for a mandatory dinner under the guise of keeping the family together. She stated that they could bring no one—no plus-ones. She wanted to talk business, and there was a lot to discuss.

Sweet Basil Catering on West 77ᵗʰ Street prepared the large spread of food in the penthouse dining room. They specialized in seasonal cuisine with top-notch service and beautiful presentation. The dishes today included a creamy foie gras terrine with chilled quince marmalade and sweet concord grapes, sweetbread and lobster, sea scallops with an aromatic black truffle condiment, and roasted saddle of lamb.

Lucky was the first to arrive at Layla's penthouse suite. She came dressed in dark shades, jeans, and a sweater with her hair covered with a wig. She looked more like she was hanging out at a bar or on the streets than having a nice dinner with her family. She and Layla shared a secret— they'd killed Whistler. One problem was gone, but there were more problems out there.

Meyer showed up next, looking like he was ready to attend a rap concert. Weighed down in jewelry and urban wear, his Yankees fitted was skewed atop his head, and he was carrying two guns. He looked like he didn't want to be there, but Layla called and he came running.

The last to show up was Bugsy. He arrived handsomely dressed in a long overcoat over a black three-piece suit and hard bottom shoes. Everything about him was meticulous—from head to toe, he shined. He wasn't happy to see Layla, but no matter what she did, she was still his mother, and he respected her because of that. But if it was anyone else, God help them.

He went straight to the point, knowing there had to be motive behind it all. "Why the special occasion—all the food and the get-together?"

"What, I can't do anything special for my children? It's the reason why I only wanted y'all to come—no outsiders—so we can talk and catch up on lost time," Layla replied.

Bugsy knew his mother's sudden hospitality was bullshit. "You did all this for us?" Bugsy questioned with a raised eyebrow.

"No matter what is goin' on between your father and me, I'm still your mother and I still love you, Bugsy. You're my oldest."

"Only by ten minutes," Meyer chimed.

Bugsy glanced his brother's way. They still had their differences, but tonight, it was peace and respect.

"I know you love seafood; it's why I got the lobster and the sea scallops."

Meyer went for the food, and with no manners or class he picked everything apart, chewing like a cow. Though he couldn't pronounce some of the food correctly, he had a healthy appetite and shoved the good shit in his mouth.

Lucky remained nonchalant toward everyone. Her life had been one big rollercoaster—up and down, up and down, and she didn't know where she was going. Now that Whistler was dead, she felt no contrition—just some unneeded weight lifted off her shoulders. She didn't think about him. She'd moved on and knew he was only a con artist.

Layla pranced around the place in riding pants and some fuzzy slippers. She was in complete relax mode. She drank champagne heavily and put on this motherly show for her kids—smiles and kisses. Life was good. She was making lots of money, she had some good dick in her life, and all three of her kids had come tonight. For sure, she was a boss bitch in the game and becoming a powerful woman. Her only gripe was Scott and Maxine—the sooner they were dead, the happier she would be.

Lucky joined Meyer at the large spread of food. Bugsy, however, still looked skeptical. His father would disapprove of him being there—Layla was enemy number-one.

"You don't trust me, Bugsy?" Layla said.

"There's just a lot going on," he said.

"Yeah, there is, and your father and that bitch are the cause of it."

"Pop's got his life, and you got yours. You gotta move on and let it be."

"And what? Just forget about how they embarrassed me? Huh? How that bitch betrayed me and fucked your father behind my back, after everything I did for her?"

Bugsy knew the story of Maxine and his mother in full detail. Maxine had broken it down to him to where there was no other way of seeing it. Layla had betrayed her, and Bugsy believed Maxine. But he didn't bring it up. He knew mentioning the past would only add more fuel to the massive fire already raging out of control.

"I'm just saying, Mom, everyone is making money, and we're living the good life. You've got your thing going, and we've got ours."

"It won't fully be the good life until that bitch pays with her life, and if your father keeps choosing to protect her, then God help him too!"

There was no getting through to her—she was stubborn and ignorant. Bugsy saw where the conversation was going. He needed to change it.

"Well, I've got some good news," he announced.

Layla downed the champagne and went to pour herself more.

"Good news, I wish you would tell me that bitch is finally dead," Layla said, walking toward the mini bar.

Bugsy sighed. She would never stop.

"I'm going to propose to Alicia," he said.

The news made Layla spin around and shoot an objectionable look at her son.

"You're gonna do what?" she said, almost in disbelief.

"I said, I'm gonna propose to Alicia—ask her to marry me," he repeated.

"Wow, pussy that good and it got you whipped, huh?" Meyer said and then shoved more food in his mouth. "Hey, I'm happy for you bro. Do you, nigga! If that pussy makes you happy, fuck it, marry it, and have kids—make me a muthafuckin' uncle."

Meyer's way of congratulating him was both abrasive and warming simultaneously. Bugsy took no offense to his words.

"I'm happy for you too, Bugsy. Alicia's cool peoples," Lucky said. "I ain't got no beef wit' her."

It was her brother's life, and he would live it the way he wanted to. Lucky didn't see marriage in her future.

"Well, I think you're making a damn mistake marrying that girl," Layla announced. "I take it that you already bought the girl a ring."

"Yes, I did," he said.

"You know what kind of life you gonna give that girl?" Layla spewed with disapproval. "She's not us! That girl is not cut from the same cloth we come from. You think she's gonna be a ride-or-die bitch when shit hits the fan? You think she's loyal to you? God forbid you have to do jail time. I'm telling you, a bitch like that won't hold you down. Her educated ass will be gone!"

Layla was going in, and there was no stopping her.

"She's perfect for me," Bugsy defended.

"Perfect? Boy, there's no such thing as perfect. I think she's a fuckin' gold-digger, that's what I think."

Layla downed the champagne and screwed her face with anger about the engagement. She wanted to slap some sense into Bugsy. First, he goes against her and joins with his father, when she gave birth to him, and now he intends to marry some off-brand bitch.

"She's no gold-digger," Bugsy said calmly.

"Nigga, that bitch saw you coming from a mile away," Layla retorted. "You payin' her fuckin' bills, buying her a new house, and now you wanna marry her. Is the bitch pregnant?"

"You need to stop disrespecting my woman by calling her a bitch," Bugsy said to her.

"Muthafucka, you're my son, and if I feel the need to call your bitch a bitch, then so be it. This is my fuckin' home, and I do and say whatever the fuck I want!"

She was getting drunk. Everyone saw it. Her words were becoming more and more reckless.

"Ma, just chill," Lucky tried to intervene. "We came here to talk and try and be a family, right?"

"No, don't tell me to chill. I got my son about to marry some goodie fuckin' gold-digger bitch and she gonna take all his money, and I got Scott and Maxine laughing at me . . ."

"Nobody laughing at you," Meyer said.

"They won't be when they're dead!" Layla said. "A bitch takes from me and I'll take something from her. I don't give a fuck if she's a nurse or not—these are my fuckin' children!"

Bugsy took a deep breath and unclenched his fist. He was trying to defend his woman, but his blood pressure was going up. His mother was a vile woman and she needed help. Her drinking was getting out of control. The champagne bottle she was sipping on was nearly empty, and she always had a full glass in her hand.

Meyer stood between his mother and brother. He looked at Bugsy and said, "Don't let her get to you, she drunk. Believe me, I know how you feel."

Layla heard the comment and her eyes narrowed with anger and she huffed with contempt. "Meyer, fuck you too! You ain't no better, nigga. Both y'all bitches came out my pussy and y'all have the audacity to disrespect me?"

"You know what? I don't need this shit. I'm out," Bugsy said.

He went for his coat, threw it on, and pivoted to leave the place. It was a mistake showing up. He knew it would not be a lovely dinner with his family. They were never a family. He could make his family with Alicia. Maxine had been more of a mother to him lately than his own biological. Layla was hell.

"Fuck you, Bugsy! You're my fuckin' son! Don't turn your back on me, nigga!" Layla hollered.

Bugsy kept on walking out the door and let it slam behind him.

Layla's chest heaved with fury, and her face was hot with rage. She stared at Bugsy's sudden exit with scorn, her eyes narrowed. All she wanted from Bugsy was information about Scott and Maxine. She'd heard through the grapevine that Maxine and Bugsy were chatting and getting close, and that burned Layla's heart. Maxine had already stolen her husband. There was no way she would steal her son too and turn him against her.

The night didn't end well.

Several counting machines went off inside the room, and the sound of money adding up was music to Bugsy's ears. There was nearly seventeen million dollars to be counted, packaged, and transferred to one of their fortified safe houses to be laundered. Hundreds, fifties, and twenties were being sorted into ten-thousand-dollar stacks, and the stacks were placed in boxes, suitcases, laundry bags, and duffle bags.

It was a blizzard of dead presidents that overwhelmed the room. Two guys sat at a brown oval table and went through bill after bill—moistening the crumpled bills with a little water, then ironing them slowly and sorting the hundreds from the fifties and the fifties from the twenties. It was all about tallying the intake of cash and the neatness in it. The young men were gifted in mathematics and patient with the tedious task.

The location was private and remote. Twenty minutes from Queens, the two-story brick building was on Long Island, near the Long Island Expressway. It was guarded by the best, but Bugsy didn't want to attract too much attention, so he kept the guns and goons at a minimum.

With Choppa and AJ by Bugsy's side, he felt it would be another smooth operation tonight. Things were moving like clockwork so far, and they had only a few hours before the large amounts of cash would be transferred via U-haul vans to the safe house in New Jersey to be laundered.

It would be another two hours before everything was completed. Bugsy looked around the room and nodded. He looked at Choppa and

AJ and said, "I need to go take a piss. I'll be right back."

Both men nodded.

Bugsy left the room and went down the hallway. He stepped into the tiny bathroom to pee.

A few moments in the bathroom, and he heard the gunshots—they sounded distant and muffled, but there was no mistaking it. He hurried to make himself decent and pulled out his 9mm and cautiously exited the bathroom. Before he could take three steps, a gun was put to the back of his head.

"Move and I'll blow your fuckin' brains out," the assailant growled.

He was manhandled and brought to the counting room where he was held hostage like the others. Everything in the room had stopped—the money machines stopped counting, and every worker in the room was on their knees with their fingers locked behind their heads.

The masked gunmen came heavily armed with assault rifles and pistols.

How did they get in? And how did they know about the building and when to strike it?

Bugsy counted five of them. Each man's eyes glared from their ski masks as they tied everyone in the room with zip ties to their wrists, arms folded behind them. They were dressed in all black, and he could tell they were no amateurs to this. The way they moved around the room and shouted orders, they meant business.

A lone assailant stood near the door and kept quiet. Something about him caught Bugsy's attention.

"Yo, get that money—get all that shit!" one of the more vocal attackers shouted.

They were going for it all—the duffle bags, the boxes, and the suitcases. Seventeen million dollars would be a serious payday for these robbers.

Bugsy cringed at the thought of losing it all. He kept his eyes fixed on the silent robber, though, watching his movement astutely. That's when

Bugsy noticed his footwear—the sneakers. They were expensive—limited edition Jordans. The nigga was a sneaker head.

"Muthafucka," Bugsy grumbled quietly.

The masked robbers were violent. They didn't hesitate to pistol-whip one of Bugsy's men in the room. AJ and Choppa were on their knees, tied up and looking fiercely at the robbers. Bugsy had been slightly knocked around.

"Y'all niggas know who the fuck you robbing?" AJ growled their way.

"Nigga, who fuckin' told you to speak?" The butt of the AK-47 was smashed into AJ's face and he immediately spewed blood from his nose and mouth and it felt like his jaw had been broken. He hollered from the pain. His blood trickled to the floor. Choppa wanted to react, but he was held at gunpoint with his wrists tied behind him, and he knew if he moved wrong, he was dead.

The violent blow from the AK-47 didn't discourage AJ. He was angrier.

"You're a dead man," AJ threatened. "I'm gonna kill you myself. Fuck you, nigga!"

"Fuck me, nigga?" the masked man shouted back. He marched toward AJ and thrust the barrel of the assault rifle to AJ's forehead.

AJ didn't flinch. He glared up at the man and through daring and hard eyes, he shouted, "You know who the fuck I am?"

"Yeah, a fuckin' dead man," the masked man uttered and then he fired.

Rat-a-tat-tat!

AJ's brains were ejected through the back of his head and he collapsed, sprawled facedown at the triggerman's feet with pieces of his head everywhere. It was a gruesome sight. The thick blood pooled beneath the body, and it was spreading fast. Bugsy and Choppa could only frown at the murder. They were helpless.

"Fuck you lookin' at, huh?" another masked man shouted at Bugsy.

"I'm cool, yo," Bugsy softly replied.

The man marched closer to Bugsy and shouted, "You cool, nigga? You lookin' at us kinda funny and shit! I don't like that shit."

"You ain't have to kill him," said Bugsy.

"Nigga, you wanna die too?"

"You kill me and there will be hell to pay."

"Yo, you threatening me, nigga? I don't think you in a position to throw threats at a nigga."

"Just take the money. We'll meet later," Bugsy said.

"Nigga what?" The attacker put the barrel of his gun to Bugsy's head.

The masked sneaker head across the room shouted, "Nigga, chill!"

"He got mouth on him, son!"

"I said, chill." It was a strong command, but the man harassing Bugsy didn't seem fazed by it.

A split-second later, Bugsy found himself on the receiving end of a pistol whipping. The butt of the Glock crashed against his face repeatedly. He could feel his face breaking apart. The man with the expensive Jordans ran over and attempted to pull the guy off Bugsy, but he was pushed away and a few more hard and violent blows rained down on a defenseless Bugsy. He felt his jaw breaking and his ribs cracking. He was in the fetal position with his hands tied, and he couldn't defend himself. He was at the mercy of his attacker. It took the other masked goons to finally pull the dude off and stop him from killing Bugsy. They all ran out of the room with bags and boxes of cash, leaving everyone tied up and AJ dead.

Bugsy was in bad shape. He knew he needed to go to the hospital and quickly.

35

The masked gunmen made it to their getaway SUV, and the driver sped away like a bat out of hell, the tires screeching into the night. The mood was mostly jubilation. They made off with millions of dollars, and it was a successful lick. But the passenger riding shotgun wasn't too jubilant, although everything had gone as planned.

When it was safe, the masks finally came off. Luna was driving the truck and Meyer glared his way.

"We did it, nigga!" Luna exclaimed.

Meyer suddenly punched Luna in the face, nearly causing an accident on the freeway. The truck swerved and then came to a stop on the shoulder. Meyer snatched the gun from Luna's waist and put it to his temple. The men riding in the back were shocked. Why was Meyer attacking his right-hand man?

"Meyer, what's good, man? What the fuck?" Luna exclaimed with his hands up in the air in surrender.

"You almost killed him back there," Meyer shouted. "I told you, we don't touch Bugsy."

"I had to make it look good. The way he was lookin' at you, I think he knew it was you," Luna said. "I did what I did to throw him off. I was trying to help."

"Muthafucka, that's my brother!"

"I was lookin' out for you, Meyer!"

Meyer was breathing hard. The fact that Luna had assaulted his brother put him in a difficult situation. He didn't know what to do. Bugsy was his blood—his twin brother at that, and he wasn't supposed to be harmed. Luna was his right-hand man—his brother from another mother. They both were family. But their orders were explicit—get the money and leave Bugsy alone.

"I got mad love for Bugsy," Luna proclaimed. "I didn't want to hurt him, but we had to make it look legit. He's gonna be ayyite."

"Just drive, nigga," Meyer said.

Luna sighed.

Meyer removed the gun from Luna's head and seemed to calm down. The other passengers in the back looked relieved. They had just executed a nearly perfect robbery, and there was no telling how much money they'd gotten away with. The last thing they needed was a violent incident on the freeway and attracting unwanted attention on themselves. They weren't in the clear yet. They'd completed the job with one dead, and what they needed to do next was get the money to the boss bitch, Layla. It was the name she'd chosen for herself—boss bitch.

Meyer and his men walked into Layla's Bronx warehouse with the cash goodies to present to her. Every man carried a suitcase, a duffle bag, or a box or two. They walked into the boss bitch's back office, where she was behind her L-shaped desk conversing on her cell phone in her pricey reclining leather chair. Meyer emptied one of the duffle bags onto her desk, and the cash went everywhere. Layla curtailed her phone call. She was too happy with the score. It was like taking candy from a baby. Once again, she'd hit Scott where it would hurt a lot, his pockets.

Layla's eyes gleamed and she was ready to bathe herself in the cash. She rubbed her hands with a greedy gesture.

"How much is it?" she asked.

"We didn't count it yet," Meyer said.

"You did good, Meyer—real good."

Meyer didn't look too enthusiastic. He was expressionless. It had been a long night, and there was more to tell his mother. He wanted to wait for the right moment—for the others to leave.

"I wish I could see the look on your father's face when he finds out about this."

All the surveillance she'd had Meyer do had paid off big time. Also, their little birdie was on the money—a reliable snitch was worth more than gold. It would be another crippling blow to Scott's ego. She was winning, and it felt good. She couldn't believe that Scott was so far in his bitch's pussy he was letting his business go down the drain. It was too bad Bugsy was following right behind him.

When the goons left, including Luna, Meyer said, "Ma, some shit went down—" But as he was about to confess, her cell phone rang.

"Hold on for one minute," she said. "Who's this?"

It was Choppa on the cell phone. "Bugsy's in the hospital, Ms. Layla. He's hurt bad. We couldn't stay cuz we were riding dirty, but you need to go see him."

Layla couldn't believe what she was hearing. Immediately her eyes shot at Meyer and they were burning with anger. Choppa went into details about the robbery and the assault, and Layla seethed more and more.

"I'm on my way," she told him.

She hung up, and her joy toward Meyer pivoted.

"What the fuck happened? I told you, not one hair was supposed to be touched on my son's head!" she shouted.

"Shit just got out of control."

Layla stormed from around her desk, marched to her son, and slapped him.

"You let someone assault your brother and you didn't do a damn thing about it? Who did it? Who had the nerve to attack my muthafuckin' son?"

Her eyes were on fire. She wanted an answer from him.

Meyer frowned. He didn't want to give Luna up.

"Answer me, nigga!" she screamed.

Reluctantly, he mumbled, "It was Luna."

"That muthafucka put my son in the hospital and you let him do it!" She slapped him again. Meyer stood there taking the hits. He diverted his eyes away from her.

She shouted, "Look at me, nigga! What the fuck happened?"

"He had to make it look good," he said.

"Look good—by putting Bugsy in the fuckin' hospital! Are you stupid?"

"I already confronted him about it."

"Oh, you confronted him, huh? So he's dead, right?" She was being sarcastic.

"You just saw him walk out the door."

"Muthafucka, that nigga attacked your brother and he's still living. I want him dead."

Meyer frowned. "You want me to kill him?"

"Muthafucka, did I hesitate? I want him dead within twenty-four hours."

Despite Bugsy's defiance toward her, he was still her son—her flesh and blood, her oldest. And no one fucked with a West except a West.

Meyer stood there somberly quiet. The thought of killing his best friend was sickening to him. Luna was the only man he could trust. He was his right-hand man. They'd been through thick and thin together. How was he supposed to eliminate him?

"I want it done, Meyer. Luna fucked up, so he needs go. Family comes first," she said. "Today Bugsy, tomorrow he could easily attack you."

She was trying to get in his head. Luna always had his back. He wanted to make the robbery tonight look legit—make it look like it came from another crew—Deuce's crew. But he'd gone too far, and Bugsy was in bad shape—maybe in critical condition.

Layla readied herself to see her son in the hospital. But first, they needed to conceal the money. It was all put into two massive safes and left inside the secured warehouse. There was no time to count it, and no time to gloat. She needed to see her baby.

Now that Bugsy was in the hospital—she knew Scott would see that a line had been crossed. It was his favorite son. If word ever got back to Scott that it wasn't DMC and Meyer was involved, he would most likely come after Meyer and kill him. Layla was sure of it. She had to think of a way to spin it.

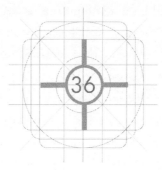

36

Scott heard the news about his son and went insane. Then, hearing about the millions of dollars that were stolen from him, he became unhinged. He manifested his rage with destruction, breaking things around him and firing his pistol at a few of his men. Luckily, no one was hurt or killed. He screamed. He hollered. Many people would die.

Choppa called him. He cursed out Choppa.

"Where the fuck was you?" he roared at him.

"They came out of nowhere. I was there, Scott!"

"Don't leave town. We need to talk," Scott said before hanging up.

Scott didn't want to hear any more news. His primary concern was his son and finding his money. It was another devastating blow to his organization. How did those fuckers find the location? It was a brand new spot, so Deuce finding it so quickly didn't add up, even if he did have Whistler on his side. Scott wasn't swallowing that logic easily. It was either Deuce and Whistler, or it was an inside job. Whatever the outcome, the culprits would be soon dealt with.

Scott's driver picked up Maxine, and they hurried to the hospital in Long Island. Maxine was worried too. She was there to comfort Scott and be there for Bugsy like he was there for her. She had developed a connection with him.

Scott and Maxine rushed into the hospital lobby with a small army of thugs behind them for support and protection. The dangerous looking men drew attention and intimidation. Scott looked dazed and unraveled. The sharp element of his style had been dulled by one incident after another. He was so tired of seeing the inside of a hospital. If he lost Bugsy, Scott didn't know what he would do. He would be beside himself.

The sliding doors to the lobby opened and in walked Layla and her entourage, including Meyer and Lucky. The tension between the two groups grew thicker than a block of ice. Seeing Maxine in the lobby made Layla furious.

"I don't want that bitch in my son's room," she said.

"That's not your call," Scott said.

Before things escalated, security and police officers got involved. They defused the ticking time bomb, but it was only temporary. Scott and Layla had nothing else to say to each other. They behaved as if they'd never met. It was a baffling situation for the doctors and the nurses. Their child was in the hospital severely beaten, yet the two parents were acting like four-year-olds.

The hallways and the waiting area were crowded with people from both organizations. They congested every area of the lower floor; every seat was taken. Some folks paced back and forth, hoping for the best, but preparing themselves for the worst. If Bugsy were to die, God help everyone.

Soon, the double doors to an adjacent hallway opened up, and a clean shaven white man in blue scrubs and a stethoscope around his neck came walking their way. His look was expressionless. His eyes were fixed on the many groups of people in the lobby and hallway. All eyes were on him.

Once Dr. Charles identified the key people he needed to speak with, he pulled them to the side in private—for the family's ears only. The doctor explained to them that Bugsy was in surgery. He'd sustained serious head trauma. His jaw had been broken, his ribs were fractured in several places, and there was a chance he could lose vision in his right eye. Also, there was swelling in the brain, so he had to be put in a medically induced coma until the swelling went down.

"Will he live?" Scott asked the doctor.

"Absolutely," said the doctor. "But it will be a long road to recovery."

Who was more upset, Layla or Scott? Hearing the news from the physician, it fueled both parents with murderous intentions. Each one wanted to blame the other.

While they were listening to the doctor's prognosis, Meyer and Lucky gave their father the cold shoulder. They stood close to their mother in a protective manner, and the insect caught in their glaring web of anger was Maxine. They both hated her. She ruined everything. Before she came into the picture, though their family wasn't picture perfect, everyone somewhat got along and dealt with each other. Maxine was the catalyst of their civil war in their eyes, and everything was falling apart because of her.

"You do everything you can for my son, doctor," Layla said seriously.

"We are," he responded.

"I mean, I want the best for him. I don't care about the cost. You are responsible for his well-being," Layla continued.

It was an implied threat to him. The doctor looked at Layla; she was a mother in pain, and he understood her. But this was his hospital.

"He's getting the best care from everyone."

Meyer pivoted and left his mother's side. The news about his brother was troubling, but Meyer felt he had other pressing matters to worry about. Meyer knew that if what Luna said was true about Bugsy knowing it was them, then he would tell Scott when he woke up.

Meyer sighed. He felt himself sinking deeper and deeper into the quicksand of conflict and inevitable bloodshed.

The sliding doors to the lobby opened, and Layla walked outside into the cold in her long mink coat and leather knee-high boots. She wiped the tears away from her eyes and lit a cigarette. She needed the nicotine and a break from the dreary hospital. Between seeing Scott and Maxine together and her son in the hospital, if she would have stayed any longer, she felt she would have gone postal on everyone. It took a lot for her not to lash out at Maxine and Scott. In due time, though. She took a few needed drags and walked over to where Meyer was standing alone.

"Luna's got to go, Meyer. I want him dead for this," she said.

He didn't respond to her. He simply stood there, aloof, looking away from her.

"I could have lost another child tonight because of his temper. He dare put hands on our family. He's not family, Meyer. Your brother is," she reminded him.

Layla had no guilt that it was her plan that placed her son in harm's way. To her, it was all Luna's fault. He had no right to attack her son. He needed to go, and she placed Meyer in charge of that task.

"Meyer, do you hear me?"

"I hear you, Ma," he replied quietly.

"You need to show to me that you're fully loyal to me, not him! I love you and I need you to show me that you love me back. You let me down before with Penelope, choosing that bitch over me. This will fully redeem your sins against this family, and I'm not taking no for an answer."

Layla finished smoking her cigarette and walked away from her son. In so many words she told him not to dare choose another person over her. He either did the murder, or he was out of the organization. And Layla would see to it that his father didn't take him back in. Not if she told Scott what Luna had done to Bugsy while Meyer stood by.

Until now, they had the cloak of anonymity because Scott believed it was Deuce attacking his spots. Let them shoot it out and kill each other.

For Layla, it would be killing two birds with one stone.

Meyer felt torn. He had love for Luna. He wanted to give his friend a second chance. He believed Luna when he told him that Bugsy somehow made them. He saw it in Luna's eyes, and he only did what he needed to do to make it look legit. If they'd fucked up everyone but Bugsy, what would that say? It would seem suspicious. However the beating was excessive. Luna had gone a little too far, maybe.

Layla preached about family, but she was willing to throw her son into the fire and watch him burn for this unless he made it right.

Meyer stopped the car in front of the three-story, L-shaped apartment building with the exterior fire escape on the wide boulevard. At two in the morning, the Canarsie area of Brooklyn was peaceful and quiet and thin with activity.

Meyer took a deep breath and checked the clip to the 9mm he carried. It was loaded. He was caught between a rock and a hard place. Tonight, he had to murder his best friend, his partner in crime—the man who'd had his back every single day. There was no way around it. Layla had given him no choice. Either Luna went, or she would try and ruin his life. He didn't want to call her bluff. The bitch never bluffed. She was the real thing—borderline crazy.

He smoked a quick cigarette and lingered inside the car for a moment with the gun on his lap. He became reminiscent of his past with Luna— the good and bad times they shared, the people they murdered, and the bitches they fucked. Meyer felt closer to his friend than his brother. He and Luna could relate on so many things, unlike him and Bugsy.

But this was the game, right? Niggas came and went, lived or died—it was the life they lived.

Meyer stepped out of the car, shoved the gun into his waistband, and walked toward the building. Dressed in a black snorkel with the hood pulled over his head, he trekked toward the front entrance, slid inside from the cold, and took the elevator to the fourth floor. He slowly walked down the hallway and reached apartment 4D and knocked. A short moment later, he could hear someone at the door.

"Nigga, it's Meyer. Open up."

The apartment door swung open, and Luna loomed into view wearing a wifebeater and holding a .380 in his hand. "What's up? Is everything okay?" Luna asked.

"Yeah, I just need to talk to you for a minute—some crazy shit."

"Yo, come in, nigga."

Luna stepped aside and allowed Meyer into the apartment. The door closed. Meyer stood in the spacious living room with the hardwood floors, leather furniture, glass tables, and a huge 70-inch TV. There were posters and framed stills from the infamous *Scarface* film hanging on his walls. Luna was a huge fan of the movie. He lived a full bachelor's life and had the ultimate bachelor's pad, including a king size waterbed in one of his two bedrooms.

Luna stepped into the room and placed his gun on the table. He seemed relaxed around an old friend.

Meyer stood, as did Luna. They looked at each other. Meyer's hard look gave him away.

"So what's this crazy shit you need to talk to me about?" Luna asked. "Everything good?"

Meyer stood silent for a moment. He wasn't himself, and Luna picked up on it.

Luna glanced at the revolver on the glass table, far from his reach. Then he said, "I know what this is about. You came here to kill me, right?"

"You went too far with Bugsy."

Meyer removed the 9mm from his waistband and pointed it at Luna.

Luna didn't flinch. "I tried to protect you. He was figuring it out—his look and demeanor toward you, there was no way he would believe it was Deuce if I didn't attack him the way I did."

Meyer's arm remained outstretched. He looked at Luna and was hesitant in pulling the trigger.

"She wants you dead," said Meyer.

"How many times I been there for you—saved your life? And now you're ready to take mine because your mother is paranoid or angry? She sent us there to rob the place, knowing he would be there. What'd she expect, for it to be easy? Meyer, you need to think about this. It's me, and I'm the only one that always had your back."

It was true—the reason it was making pulling the trigger difficult.

"How many times they made you second to Bugsy? Your mother, she's playing you, Meyer. You think if she had to choose between Bugsy or you that she would choose you? I was more family to you than anyone," Luna proclaimed. "We brothers, nigga!"

So many emotions were welling up inside of Meyer. He locked eyes with his friend and replied, "I know. . ."

He then squeezed the trigger and fired.

38

It was just before dawn when Meyer showed up at his mother's place in the city. He felt like he'd lost a brother. He felt defeated. Luna was gone, and it was painful.

He stood in the center of his mother's place looking withdrawn and sullen. Murder was nothing to him. He'd done it plenty of times, and the blood of his victims was an eternal stain on his soul. But to kill a friend—a man like Luna—it was the only time he would feel any remorse.

Layla walked to her mini bar and fixed herself a quick drink—a tall vodka on ice. Wearing a long, beige robe with fur, she seemed to glide toward Meyer. She wanted to hear it come from his mouth. It looked like Meyer had gone through with it, and now he showed regret. There were no tears—better not be—but sadness was inside of him.

"So, is it done?" she asked.

"Yeah, it's done. He's dead."

"You did a good thing, Meyer. I'm proud of you."

He felt no pride.

"Where's the body?" she asked him.

"Why you ask?"

"I'm going to tell Scott you found out that Luna was behind the ambush at his place and Bugsy's beating. And you killed him for it."

She believed it would take the heat off of Meyer once Bugsy woke up and told his version of the story.

It was suicide, Meyer believed. "You wanna do what?" he said.

There was no way Scott would believe that Luna would go against the grain. He had always been loyal, and he would never attack Scott and Bugsy unless he were ordered to. Besides, he thought she wanted Scott to believe it was Deuce. Why change up the plan?

"It doesn't make sense," he griped.

"Let's get in front of the problem and be proactive, because Bugsy is going to wake up, and when he does, hell is going to break loose."

Meyer shook his head. "We don't know for sure that Bugsy knew it was us! And his brain got fucked up, right? Who knows what he'll remember?"

The gates of hell were already open, he believed. But what was his mother suddenly so concerned about? She hated Scott and she wanted to see the man broken. This was war, right? Not *Let's Make a Deal.*

"My son is strong. He's a West. He'll remember everything."

Meyer thought for a beat. "How much did we score from this lick?"

"Just over seventeen million. Your father won't let this shit go so Luna is the sacrificial lamb, Meyer. Get that shit through your fuckin' head."

Meyer continued, "If you're suddenly so afraid of his wrath, then give him the money back."

Layla slapped her son hard in the face.

"I'm not giving shit back, and I'm not afraid of anyone," she retorted. "And why the fuck you keep telling me to give Scott back *my* fuckin' money? This is the second time you've said that shit. First the fifty million, and now this. Are you fuckin' retarded, Meyer? All I've done to build up this empire and my husband didn't leave me a crumb. Not ten fuckin' dollars to buy a box of tampons."

"What about us? Me and Lucky? We deserve some of that money too! You and Pop ain't build this shit alone."

"Boy, bye with that bullshit." Layla rolled her eyes dismissively and continued with, "I have a plan. And I need Luna's body. Where is it?"

"In the river," he lied.

Her face tightened with distress. "In the river?"

"I had Luna meet me by the docks and dumped his body in the water."

"You fuckin' idiot!" she cursed.

"You wanted him dead, right?"

"I wanted him dead and the body displayed—not made missing. How stupid are you? What's the point of killing Luna if not to show Scott the body?"

Meyer frowned. "You said kill him, and I did! How the fuck I know what your secret plan was? I'm no mind reader."

"You're not a fuckin' child, Meyer. You're a grown man, and you need to think." Layla tapped her forehead repeatedly to make her point. "I can't always hold your hand. I swear, if this were Bugsy, he would understand what I meant without me having to draw him a damn map, like you."

Her sharp comment stung Meyer like a horde of killer bees. Like his father, she was comparing him to Bugsy. She was belittling him. Everyone respected Meyer on the streets, but he couldn't get respect from his own parents.

"Don't go there wit' me!" he shouted.

"Shut up. I need to fix this."

"I do everything for you!" he shouted.

"Clearly not correctly," she rebuked.

"If we tell Pop it was Luna, he won't believe it anyway."

Meyer knew Scott wouldn't fall for any bullshit like that. He would believe they were involved. In his eyes, his mother was playing with fire. She was delusional. One minute she was the big bad wolf, and the next, she was worried about Scott and the consequences. Since when did she care about consequences? Layla did whatever she wanted when she wanted.

Meyer felt like she was ready to wave the white flag. Was it because of Bugsy being hurt? Did the bitch finally have a conscience about something?

When she said to him, "He'll kill us all," Meyer burst open with rage and screamed, "I'm not scared of that muthafucka! He can suck my dick! Fuck him! Fuck everybody!"

Both his parents had pissed him off—and without Luna, he felt alone. He was ready to erupt like a volcano and raise hell.

He had to think, would Scott kill his own flesh and blood? It was on Meyer's mind. He hated to admit it, but he felt a little trepidation. The foundation had been rocked and shaken, and a few pieces crumbled. Bugsy would wake up from his coma, and if he had a hunch Meyer was behind the robbery and attack, it would get ugly. There would be war and bloodshed. Bugsy was always Scott's favorite son, so where did that leave Meyer? Most likely, it would leave him dead.

Meyer had nightmares. He could vividly see his murder happening. Shot in the back of his head multiple times, his body hacked to pieces and tossed into the Hudson River like he was bird food—discarded like yesterday's trash with no remorse from his father and his brother. It would be revenge. They considered Meyer the black sheep of the family anyway.

Meyer felt if Scott had him killed, he would make it look like he was on vacation somewhere chasing pussy. Meanwhile, his body would be rotting in an unmarked grave somewhere. Would his brother be forgiving? Bugsy was unpredictable—or maybe he wouldn't want to see anything bad happen to his twin brother.

Meyer knew that his trifling mother and manipulative sister would somehow be able to weasel their way out of danger, and he would be the one left holding the bag. His family didn't care about each other; they only cared about themselves.

Meyer stood on the terrace of his building shirtless in the cold. His entire body felt numb; he felt nothing. He smoked a cigarette and looked at a wintry and snow covered neighborhood. Six inches of snow had fallen on the city. It was late, and it was a ghost town. The storm made everyone stay inside.

Meyer thought about Zoe, missing her greatly. She was out of town on business, and he couldn't wait until she got back. Until then, he had business of his own.

He turned around to see the curve of her back lying against his bed. Not long ago he had her legs vertically in the air, thrusting his hard dick in and out of her. Everything about Lollipop was delicious—and the hour-long blowjob she gave him was memorable. Zoe was wifey, but Lollipop was his freaky side-piece. He needed to release some stress, and Lollipop didn't hesitate to help him relieve it with her mouth and her pussy.

"You comin' back to bed, baby?" Lollipop asked him.

"Yeah, in a minute. I'm just thinkin' about something."

"Shit, you're not cold out there?"

"I'm good."

"Well, damn, can you close the door a little? I'm starting to feel a draft," she said.

He closed the door and continued to stand outside in the cold. The snow against his bare skin felt exhilarating. He was crazy and he wasn't afraid to show it. Meyer knew that he would never die from pneumonia—nah, that would be the easy way out. He believed that if you lived by the gun, then you would die by the gun. He was ready to die by the gun, but he'd give the triggerman a run for his money. Everywhere he went, he remained armed and dangerous. He moved with caution. Shit, if he couldn't trust his own parents, then who could he trust?

After a minute more in the cold, gazing at the city, he stepped back into the bedroom. Lollipop smiled at him.

"It's about time," she said. "You ready to fuck again?"

"Give me a minute," he said.

He needed to make a phone call. He picked up his cell phone from the dresser and dialed the one person he felt he could still trust. Lucky's phone rang several times before she finally answered.

"Hello?"

"I need to talk to you, sis," Meyer said with urgency in his voice.

"What's going on?"

"You know, not over the phone. We need to meet."

"Okay. Tomorrow's cool with you?"

"Yeah, I'm cool."

"I'll text you." She hung up.

He released a deep sigh. He stood still for a moment, his eyes distant. Meyer had a lot going on, and it was difficult to adjust to living without his friend.

"Come back to bed, baby, and give me round two of that good-ass dick," said Lollipop.

Her sweet voice snapped him out of his trance, and he eyed his little freak spreading her legs and gently playing with her pussy. He loved the way she yearned for him.

✂ ✂ ✂

The following evening, Meyer came to a stop in front of his sister's towering building near Central Park. The snow had ceased falling, but the evidence of yesterday's snowfall covered the city for miles. Almost everything was covered in white—NYC was a winter wonderland. The sanitation department was clearing and cleaning the streets of the snow, and business owners and residents trekked outside to shovel the front of their properties and driveways.

Meyer sat in his idling Beamer, his head swiveling every passing minute, gun on his lap and his eyes watching everything moving. There wasn't much to see besides a few passing cars and pedestrians. It was a day to stay inside, drink hot chocolate, cuddle, have sex, and watch movies. Meyer would be doing none of that. He had to make moves to survive.

A cigarette was lit, and the nicotine became a minor alleviator of paranoia. It felt like everyone was out to get him. He watched cars and people from his rearview and side mirrors. Though the neighborhood was affluent, killers didn't care about zip codes.

Finally, he observed Lucky leaving her building and approaching his ride. She was warm and snug in a white North Face coat, the hood pulled over her head, hands in her pockets. Meyer unlocked the door and she slid into the passenger seat.

"What's going on?" she said.

Where should he start? Meyer took a pull from his cigarette and glanced at his sister, tentative to her question.

"Let me get some of that," she said about his cigarette.

He handed her the Newport. She took a few drags and waited for her brother to say something. She noticed the gun on his lap. He was solemn about something.

"Talk to me, Meyer. What's going on?"

He stared at his sister and released things—speaking to her like he was in some confession room.

"I fucked up, Lucky," he uttered vaguely.

"With who? Scott?"

"We put Bugsy in the hospital," he admitted.

"What?"

Meyer explained everything—the robbery, the beat down by Luna, and the reason. He then explained what had happened with Luna's body and that Layla was flipping the script on him.

Layla was hell to deal with, and she wasn't sharing the wealth. Meyer felt he was doing all the hard work and not being compensated for anything. She was feeding him crumbs, and he wanted more. Everything was becoming complicated. He didn't have Luna's body to offer as a peace treaty—but why would she want a peace treaty with Scott? Meyer felt that his mother had a master plan but she wasn't telling him everything.

Lucky looked bewildered by it all too. Meyer had said a mouthful and it was a lot to process. Layla was fucking toying with her brother and it seemed that killing Luna wasn't only because of Bugsy. Her mother wanted to wave a white flag to Scott. But why? Lucky agreed it made Layla look weak.

Lucky agreeing with him made Meyer amped. Exactly! He knew that he wasn't the dumb muthafucka Layla wanted him to believe he was. She was playing mind games with him, but Meyer wasn't one to play games.

"Maybe I can help you get what you need—money," Lucky mentioned.

"What you mean?"

She stared at her brother. She could see the torture, followed by eagerness in his eyes. He would do anything.

"I know this guy. He got bank and he talks a lot," she said. "The nigga can't stop running his fuckin' mouth."

"Bank—how much we talkin' about?"

"I overheard him talkin' about this exchange happening in Philly. Maybe a few million," she said.

Meyer looked ready to go. At the mention of a few million dollars, he didn't care if it was the cartel he was robbing.

"I'm sayin, maybe we can get this money from this fool, throw some back at Scott, set it up in Luna's apartment like he took it fo' real, and keep plenty for ourselves. Maybe, you and me, we break away from the family—the organization—and start our own shit," Lucky suggested.

Meyer liked how she was thinking. They used to bump heads and argue constantly—but now, they were coming together as brother and sister.

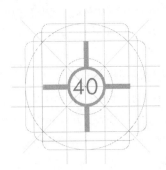

Lucky fed the information she'd received from Carter to Meyer. There was possibly a twenty-million-dollar exchange happening in North Philadelphia. Carter was supposedly a heavyweight distributor for majority of the city. For Meyer, it was a damn good opportunity.

Ogden Street in North Philly was cluttered with a few abandoned row houses, junk-filled lots, and dilapidated homes. Drugs and crime were rampant, and the old, shabby homes were inhabited by poor residents. It was a forgotten neighborhood in Philly. Meyer felt right at home.

It was another snowy night—quiet and cold. The narrow block was mostly empty of vehicles, and the people—shit—it was too cold to look out the window. Meyer sat shotgun in the black Tahoe, watching the entrance to the location Lucky had given him. It was a dilapidated row house in the middle of the block. Meyer and his small crew were laying low. They'd vetted the area—highways, main drags, side blocks, and alleys. It all looked to be in their favor. They figured this Carter character wouldn't even see them coming. They only had to wait for the right moment.

Meyer lit a cigarette and smoked. He was bundled up in a North Face coat and black ski hat. He carried a Desert Eagle and a 9mm. He was prepared for the worst—and the worst always came. He exhaled the nicotine, his eyes fixed on the entrance. Funny thing, though, the place didn't look like it would carry almost twenty million dollars in cash. But Meyer knew that in this line of business, appearances could be deceiving.

"How much did your sister say was inside again?" the driver asked.

"Enough to go around," Meyer said.

The driver's name was Bedrock. It was a name given to him because of his massive frame. He stood 6'3 and weighed close to three hundred pounds. He was a convict fresh home from Clinton after doing eight years for armed robbery and assault. Seated behind them in the truck were Pilo, Kron, and Gallow. Each man was a serious threat to society, and they were eager for a huge payday.

Missing from the crew was Luna. For Meyer, it felt strange not to have him around. In situations like these, he always depended on Luna to have his back. The nigga was a shrewd killer like himself, and he also knew how to watch out for booby traps and setups. Now, Meyer had to depend on these men to execute.

After an hour of laying low and watching, the door to the row house opened and a single figure in a black winter coat exited the premises and walked away from the place. The cold and wind made him walk briskly with his head down.

"Showtime," Meyer uttered as he slyly exited the Tahoe, threw the hood over his head, and approached the man. Nearing his target, he asked, "Yo, you got a cigarette?"

The man looked at Meyer then exclaimed, "Step off, nigga!"

"It's like that?" Meyer returned.

Before the man could answer, Meyer charged at him and thrust the Desert Eagle in his face. The bigger the gun, the greater the fear.

"You know what this is, nigga. We goin' back to where you just came from," Meyer said.

At gunpoint, he had nothing else to say. Quickly, Meyer's crew hopped out of the truck and headed across the street. Meyer shoved the man toward the row house.

"Move, nigga. Let's do this!"

The snow was falling silently, and a thin layer covered the sidewalk. Each man took his position outside the house, their guns drawn and their adrenaline pumping. This was it! If things went as planned, they were looking at a sizeable payday.

"Knock, nigga! Tell 'em you forgot something," Meyer told his hostage.

The man looked reluctant, but he had no choice. Meyer had the huge cannon aimed directly at his face, and if he moved wrong, he wouldn't have a face anymore.

The men hid from the view of the doorway, and they were camouflaged by the falling snow. Visibility outside was bleak. The weather was to their advantage. The cold was bone-chilling, but they were all heated with greed.

Their hostage knocked on the door several times and shouted, "Yo, it's me. Open up. I forgot something."

Everyone waited in anticipation for that steel door to open. A closer look at the place showed how fortified it was. From the high-security steel door, the barred windows, and the security camera pointed directly at the entrance, Meyer knew a goldmine was inside.

They waited and then they heard movement.

"Yo Mick, you always forgetting shit! Fuck is wrong wit' you, nigga?" a voice said as the door was opening up.

The moment the door was opened, Meyer and his goons lunged at the man and rushed inside, and immediately chaos ensued. A gunshot went off—*pop*—someone shot the first hostage in the face. His body crumpled against the snow-covered sidewalk, turning the white snow into crimson. More shots exploded—*Boom! Boom! Boom!*

Another body dropped and intense gunfire ignited inside the rowhouse. There was yelling and shouting and more gunfire. It sounded like war inside the Philly stash house.

There were casualties on both sides. When the gunfire stopped and the smoke finally cleared, Meyer and Bedrock were the only two running away from the place, carrying two duffle bags of cash. They hurried into the Tahoe and sped away—tires slipping on snow and the vehicle fishtailing as Bedrock mashed his foot against the accelerator.

"Go, nigga, go!" Meyer shouted.

Bedrock sped toward Lancaster Ave, and from there, he sped east toward the nearest highway. The snow made the streets empty and slippery, and Bedrock flew through a few red lights and even slid out of control a few times. Being on parole made him edgy, which made him sloppy with his driving. Meyer had to yell at him to slow it down. The last thing they needed was a cop pulling them over.

Immediately, Meyer knew what they took from the place wasn't in the millions. He was pissed. "What the fuck is this!" he shouted.

Each duffle bag had ten-thousand-dollar stacks inside—totaling close to half a million dollars. The robbery didn't even produce even a quarter of what they thought it would. It was a bust!

Meyer right away called Lucky to tell her about the disappointment. She gave him bad information, he assumed. They still had a long road to seventeen million dollars, and it had to be acquired before Bugsy woke up from his coma.

Lucky was pissed off. Carter had more than exaggerated his wealth and his position in the drug game. He was all talk and no show.

41

Alicia sat by Bugsy's bedside with a sad face. Seeing her man in such terrible condition—his face swollen, jaw broken, eyes puffy and bruised—was disheartening. The only thing she could do for him was pray for a full recovery. Then there was the gunshot wound she knew about but he failed to tell her about. It was all becoming too much for her. She was sick and tired, and more than afraid for her thug boyfriend. Yeah, he wore the nice suits and nice shoes and was very polished, but he was still a gangster.

First her home had been shot up and now all this. Her simple life was becoming more complicated and dangerous. She didn't know when a bullet would have her name on it. What if they went after her to get to him? His risky life was eating away at her well-being.

Sure, Bugsy helped her sell the house, allowed her to keep the profit, and bought her a much better place without a mortgage to worry about. It was more than enough to make up for her troubles. Then there were the nice cars, stylish clothing, and expensive jewelry he showered her with. But they were all material things, which wouldn't mean shit to her if she was dead.

Alicia wiped the tears that trickled down her face. Looking at Bugsy with his swollen face like the Elephant Man broke her heart into tiny pieces. She let out a big heavy sigh and closed her eyes, trying to hold back more of her tears, but the floodgates were already open.

"Damn it, Bugsy," she muttered.

It was a hard decision to make, but she had to make it. Her mind was made up. It would take a lot of courage, but she needed to leave him. Her heart could take no more worries and troubles. She loved him deeply—more than she'd ever loved anyone—but she couldn't do this. She would nurse him back to good health, but that was as far as she could go with him. She worked hard and had a good heart. She didn't deserve to be tethered to someone whose clock was counting down. In her profession, Alicia had seen men like Bugsy come into the hospital beat up, shot up, and stabbed, and it was always a tragic sight to see. Whether they lived or died, they would forever be changed, as would the people who loved them.

She strongly felt that Bugsy had an expiration date, and she couldn't sit by and wait for it to approach.

The day Bugsy opened his eyes and woke up from his coma, the first person he expected to see by his side was Alicia. He wasn't disappointed. There his angel was, standing right there by his bedside looking heavenly. He smiled, but it was harder than he thought. His jaw had been wired shut.

He wanted to say something to his queen, but speaking was almost impossible. The only thing he could do was communicate to Alicia through his eyes and hand movements. He hated every bit of his condition, but he thought, *Charge it to the game, right?*

He had been in an induced coma for six days. It took several days for all the medication he was being fed intravenously to leave his system, and then his cloudy head began to clear. Through the slow recovery, Alicia and Maxine hardly left his side. Alicia comforted him the best she could, and Maxine got him whatever he needed. It would be a long road to recovery, but Bugsy figured that if he had Alicia there to support him, he could get through this. He could become whole again, for her.

The moments he was alone, he had time to think. Meyer did this to him. He remembered everything. They tried to hide behind their masks, but their identity was clear to him. The sneakers were the first thing that gave his brother away, then body language and finally the only thing visible—his eyes. It was Luna who had attacked him. And his boy, AJ, was dead.

He had a lot to think about—the audacity of Meyer coming after him and taking from their father.

His body ached, and his face felt like stone. They fucked him up good. It was a miracle he was still alive, but Bugsy remembered Meyer pulling Luna off him. Meyer was trying to save his life, but Bugsy deduced that it was Layla who had masterminded the robbery.

He decided that he wouldn't tell Scott. He would keep things quiet for now. He knew that once Scott found out the truth, then Meyer and Layla would both be dead. No, once he was healed, he would handle the situation himself. He wasn't even going to confront his brother about it— not yet. Revenge was a dish best served cold.

Three weeks went by, and Bugsy was healing well. He felt in good hands with Alicia. Her being a nurse helped him out a lot too. He had been released from the hospital and could finish recuperating in his home. Day after day, Alicia took care of him. Maxine kept him company in the evening while Alicia was at work.

Bugsy's days were spent watching TV, lifting weights, and reading. He had frequent visits to several doctors to check up on his condition. He was receiving the best treatment that money could buy. His speech was still put on hold since his jaw was wired, but he could talk to his girlfriend with a notepad, his touching, and texting. Bugsy wanted to speak so badly, but the condition with his mouth and jaw would last for six weeks.

Ironically, he received a visit from Layla, Lucky, and Meyer. Layla played the role of a worried mother. She hugged her son passionately and shed tears about his condition. Meyer asked the questions.

"Yo, you know who did this to you? Just tell me or write down a name, and I'm on these fools fo' real—gun 'em down, my nigga. I got your back," Meyer said.

He said it in front of Alicia, and she frowned and left the room. Bugsy wanted to curse his brother out. He didn't want that talk around his woman.

He knew Meyer was fishing for information, trying to see if he knew anything. But Bugsy shook his head no. He would play it like that— pretend to be clueless of his brother's involvement for a while until he figured things out.

Meanwhile, he and Meyer played video games to pass the day away, and it was like when they were kids again.

S cott hadn't felt like himself in a long while. It all felt like it was slipping away from him. The thieves that ran rampant in his Long Island location made off with millions of dollars, and it was another small blow to his organization. And with his son beaten, he was looking weak in the streets. He couldn't look weak. The wolves were knocking at his door, and they were eager to take him apart. To take down a large drug kingpin like Scott West would be a glorious victory to whomever achieved it, and the crown would be theirs to wear.

Scott lingered by the window and gazed at his workers and the activity in the scrap yard. The ground was covered with snow, and it was a gloomy day with gray skies and cold wind. He chomped down on the Cuban cigar and took a few puffs. He then brought it back down to hang between his fingers. He looked pensive. If he didn't react now, then everything he'd built would be destroyed. He had to send a vicious message out on the streets and set an example—you don't dare take from him and attack his son. The bang needed to be nuclear. It should be heard and seen for many miles.

He had to stop playing house with Maxine and get his hands dirty again, or else he would suffer additional consequences, and one could be losing another child. Bugsy had done more than hold the organization down against Deuce. He'd proven repeatedly that he was the right fit to lead the empire.

Bugsy had taken out many of Deuce's men, but the head of the snake was still attached. It was time to turn up the heat and burn shit down.

Scott made a few phone calls and contacted some heavy hitters to do the job. They were expensive, but it was necessary. What Scott had forgotten about the game was, it just wasn't about the guns and the soldiers that brought you to the top and gave you power, it was information too. Information was power, and he would pay a lot of money for some information on his rivals. Therefore, he made more phone calls—most were out of town—and he put the word out. Two million dollars was the right bait to lure in any fish.

It took less than a week for Scott to hear something. Mason, one of his trusted henchmen, had been holding down Delaware since Bugsy was attacked and Meyer switched sides. He put pressure on the corner boys, spread out some paper, and came up with some viable information. "You wanna talk to this cop—Sergeant Connelly is his name. He's in Deuce's pocket. He'll lead you right to that muthafucka. I can guarantee it."

"Sergeant Connelly, huh?"

"Yeah."

Immediately, Scott took a trip to Delaware. The three-hour drive had him there by early evening. He rode in an armored Escalade—everything bulletproof, even the tires. It didn't take him long to track down the police sergeant. Scott had his home address, but it wouldn't be polite to show up uninvited, and he didn't want to attract any unwanted attention. He wanted no one, especially his enemies, to know that he was in town.

Once again, he passed some money around, it got into the right hands, and soon word got back to Sergeant Connelly. He was promised fifty thousand dollars for his time, and a note with an address was given to the cop. The sergeant was skeptical at first. He knew the name. Scott

West, a millionaire tycoon out of New York City. What would a man like that want with him?

Connelly couldn't turn down the meeting, but he had a hunch it would have something to do with Deuce.

After midnight the gray Crown Vic arrived at Christina Park. The sergeant brought another corrupt cop with him. They parked in the vacant parking lot, near an idling black Escalade. Connelly eyed the lavish ride with the dark tints. He sat in the passenger seat and took a deep breath.

"You need me to come with you?" the cop asked his boss.

"Stay here. I'll handle this alone."

Connelly climbed out of the car and slowly approached the truck. His gun was holstered to his hip, and his badge was underneath his clothing. He couldn't shake the nervousness he felt. Dealing with these criminals, he didn't know what to expect. They were a different class of offenders, far removed from the local crack dealers, gang members, and fiends he was used to dealing with. Scott West could probably buy and sell his small city.

As he got closer to the Escalade, the driver and back door opened, and two men got out. They were Scott's henchmen, Mason and Avery, and they eyed Connelly carefully.

"Your gun." Mason suggested he remove it from his hip.

Connelly didn't have a choice. He slowly removed his weapon and handed it over to Mason. It was foolish, giving up his police issued Glock to a criminal. But he'd come this far.

Avery then indicated he needed to search him.

Connelly groaned. "Seriously? I'm a fuckin' cop."

"You think we care?"

Connelly lifted his arms and spread them like wings, and Avery patted him down from head to toe. He checked between his legs and squeezed his dick to be extra cautious. It was awkward.

"He good," said Avery.

Mason tapped on the back window and said, "He good to go."

The door opened, and Connelly climbed into the backseat of the truck. The door closed behind him. Scott sat next to him, calmly smoking his cigar. Connelly quickly sized Scott up, and the man was dressed impeccably. His suit and shoes probably cost more than Connelly's house and car put together.

"I'm here," Connelly said

"I appreciate your time, sergeant," Scott said.

"Well, don't waste it."

"I won't. I understand you and I have a common problem."

Connelly chuckled. "You think I have a problem?"

"I know you do, and I want to fix your problem and make you a very rich man at the same time."

Connelly read between the lines. "So you want me to help you kill Deuce?"

"Yes."

"And why should I help you?"

"Two million dollars."

Two million dollars—whoa, that amount of money would be enough for Connelly and his wife to retire. He could buy a house in Florida and fix up his boat.

"I know he has you in his pocket, and whatever dirt he has on you, it's not my interest. My only interest is his demise."

"And when he's gone, then what?"

"For two million dollars, why should you care? I hear you're planning on retiring soon anyway."

Connelly exhaled sharply. Scott's eyes were fixed on him, waiting for his reply. The cigar smoke and the smell of a good Cuban filled the backseat. Connelly wanted to ask for a puff himself.

"No mistakes, you understand me? I can't have this coming back on me. I have a family and kids, and if Deuce figures out I'm setting him up, he'll come for them and then me," said Connelly with uneasiness in his voice.

"We don't make mistakes, sergeant."

The two men looked at each other. They both had authority, and they both were affected by Deuce's ruthlessness and craziness. It had to come to an end. There had to be some balance of respect and control.

"Make the call," Scott said.

"You mean now?"

"Yes."

Scott didn't want to waste any time. While he was in town, he would be hands-on in eliminating Deuce. There was no way he would leave Wilmington without results—without Deuce, Jimmy, and Whistler dead.

Connelly removed his cell phone from his jacket pocket and made the call. Scott listened carefully to every word out of his mouth.

"Yeah, it's me. We have a serious problem, and we need to meet," Connelly said.

It was a quick call, and Deuce agreed to meet with the man. Everything was coming together perfectly.

43

Bugsy stared at himself in the mirror. He'd lost some weight. He didn't look emaciated, just lean. The morning jogs, the weightlifting, and the Creatine shakes were helping him add muscle and weight, but he had a ways to go. The doctor finally removed the wires from his mouth, and he had limited mobility in his jaw. He could finally talk, but he couldn't open his mouth as wide as before. There was a slight change in his tone. His voice sounded lower and raspy and had more of a sinister pitch to it. His voice had always been deep, but when the trauma doctor in the ER had gone to work on him, his vocal cord was slightly pinched.

Day by day, Bugsy was recuperating, and the only thing he could think about was finally proposing to Alicia. He wanted everything to be perfect. He had no more medical restrictions, and he wanted to plan his future with the woman he loved—the love of his life.

Maxine was excited for him. She knew he had a good woman.

That night, he put together her favorite meal—a Philly cheesesteak from her favorite restaurant and French fries with some Häagen-Dazs vanilla bean ice cream and ginger beer. It's one of the things he loved about her; she enjoyed the simple pleasures.

When Alicia arrived home from work, she was surprised by the scented candles burning, flowers in the dining room, and R&B music playing. He had a soothing bubble bath prepared in the bathroom for after dinner.

"Ohmygod," she uttered.

"You like it?" he said quietly.

Everything was beautiful, and it was the reason she was so sad.

"I got your favorite," he said.

He pointed to the table, and she saw the cheesesteak meal. She chuckled as her eyes welled up with tears. It was romantic and well thought out.

Bugsy took her hands in his and pulled her closer to him. The look in his eyes was pure love. He wanted no one else but her. She was his life, and he was prepared to make things official with her. So, before they started their romantic evening together, he dropped down on one knee in front of her. It seemed like the velvet ring box magically appeared in his hand. He smiled up at her and revealed the vintage engagement ring. It was flawless.

Alicia was dumbfounded—this wasn't happening. *Shit!*

"Alicia, I love you so much, and I want you to become my wife. Will you marry me?" he proposed with a broad smile across his face.

She stood there in front of him. Her eyes became more watery. He was waiting for her to happily shout out *"Yes!"* But there was hesitation, and from the look on her face, the tears trickling from her eyes, and the sadness in them, Bugsy knew something was wrong.

"I . . . I can't," she announced sadly.

Bugsy was blown away. Had he heard her right? She couldn't marry him. Why? He remained on one knee in front of her. This was a greater pain than when he was pistol-whipped and beaten.

"I'm afraid for you, Bugsy," she continued. "I don't want to live that type of lifestyle—always afraid of you being murdered or someone coming after me because of you."

"Baby, I promise you, no one will ever harm you. As long as I'm living you're safe with me," he said with conviction in his voice.

He stared at her, pleading with his eyes. By now, he was standing on both legs and trying to take her hands into his and have her reconsider.

"You don't know that. You can't make promises like that."

"I can, and I will. I would protect you with my life," he said.

"That's the problem. I believe one day you will. You have enemies out there, Bugsy. And seeing you in that hospital, beaten like that, my heart was shattered, and I can't go through that time after time . . . and I can't let our kids go through that. I don't want to end up like your mother. I look at her, and I see a miserable woman. She lost three children to that lifestyle, and it made her angry and bitter. I can't—I can't see you in a grave. I would rather walk away than go through that, and that's why I have to leave you now before it gets worse," she proclaimed sadly.

Her words were cutting him deep. By now, Bugsy was teary-eyed. He rarely cried, but it felt like a giant knife had penetrated his heart. He saw the love and the pain in Alicia's eyes too. Where did he go wrong?

"But I told you everything about me and you said you could handle it. I never lied to you, Alicia. Why allow me to fall in love with you if you were going to leave me anyway?"

"I thought I could take it. I fell so much in love, I didn't think it would matter. But it matters because I love you."

"Please, don't do this."

"Baby, just let me go. I will always love you, but I can't be a part of that life," she said.

He looked at her and released a deep breath. It would kill him, but he reluctantly agreed. He loved her so much that if it meant she would be happy elsewhere, then so be it.

He hugged and kissed Alicia one final time, and said, "I love you."

Bugsy collected himself and grabbed a few of his things and left her place. He got into his car and sped off.

Later that evening, he drowned his sorrows with a fifth of Hennessy and playing the blame game. Who did he blame for losing Alicia? Meyer! And that grimy bitch, Layla!

44

Deuce and Jimmy arrived at the isolated location near a set of abandoned train tracks and the Christina River. For a half mile, there was nothing around but the elevated 495 freeway that crossed over the river. It was dark and late, and it was a dark looking area, nothing alive and moving but the animals and insects. Deuce and Jimmy trusted the location. No one could set up on them—no buildings to hide in, no busy roads—nothing. It was a ghostly looking area.

Jimmy had done his surveillance, and he was content with where they were to meet with Sergeant Connelly. They sat inside the Yukon and talked while waiting for Connelly to show.

Connelly had been on point since Deuce had met with him at his home. He fed him information, made arrests that were beneficial to his drug organization, and warned him of snitches. Connelly feared him and had a lot to lose; it's the reason he made the perfect corrupt cop for Deuce.

"Where is this muthafucka?" Jimmy said.

He glanced at the clock. It was 12:45 a.m. There wasn't a soul around—not a sound; it was the cold, the vacant land, and the dark.

"He'll be here. Whatever he needs to talk about, it better be good," Deuce said.

In that moment, the two noticed the headlights approaching their way. Jimmy gripped the Uzi in his hand. Deuce strongly felt it wouldn't be needed. He warned Connelly to come alone and if he tried anything, to think about his wife and kids. It wasn't just his job in jeopardy.

The gray Crown Vic rolled up toward them and came to a stop. Deuce squinted his eyes at the car and saw one silhouette inside. The headlights shut off and the door opened. Connelly stepped out of the car and looked their way. Deuce and Jimmy exited the Yukon and walked toward the cop.

But then, Connelly suddenly stopped in his tracks and appeared to be nervous about something. Deuce read his body language—not good. His eyes shifted toward the 495 freeway. Something was wrong.

As Deuce rotated his head to see what had caught Connelly's attention, Jimmy's face exploded. Blood and brains flew everywhere—looking like a smashing watermelon, and his body violently propelled forward. Before Jimmy could fall, another sniper's shot nearly took off his whole right half. His body crashed to the ground, facedown.

"Muthafuckaaaa!" Deuce shouted.

He attempted to aim his gun at Connelly, knowing he'd been set up, but a deadly sniper's bullet ripped through his chest and pushed him back against the truck. There was a gaping hole in his chest, but somehow, he was still alive. Connelly looked at him wide-eyed, as Deuce struggled to breathe and aim the gun at him once again. He wanted to kill the sergeant before his death. But then another bullet ripped through his face. The splash of blood and bone went all over the place. Deuce fell dead, and between both bodies, there was enough blood to drown a small animal.

Unbeknownst to both men, the van parked on the shoulder of the 495 freeway harbored an astute sniper with a Barrett M82 sniper's rifle. Hired by Scott, Kwame was one of the best killers money could buy. He could shoot the wings off a fly. Through the scope, he observed his handiwork from far away.

Mission accomplished.

He soon aimed the rifle at Connelly, targeting the man in his crosshairs. The sergeant was walking back to his car, but he didn't make it far. Kwame put a bullet through the back of his head and killed him instantly. Direct orders from Scott—no one leaves the area alive—no one. Connelly lay dead, sprawled facedown on the ground near the Crown Vic with a hole the size of a baseball in his head. Connelly had to go too; he wasn't to be trusted. He had sold out Deuce for a promise of a two-million-dollar payout and he was responsible for losing many men and money while collaborating with DMC. A message had to be sent. The era of Deuce and DMC was over.

Ruthless, Scott was. No more Mr. Nice Guy.

Next on Scott's list was Whistler. He didn't know Whistler's fate had already been sealed by Layla and Lucky.

B ugsy continued to drink and grieve over Alicia. He was devastated. He wanted her back, but he knew deep in his heart she wasn't coming back. He felt at fault, but he blamed his family too, especially his brother. The thought of her loving someone else was like a steamroller rolling over him. He couldn't breathe. He couldn't sleep. He couldn't even eat.

He emptied the fifth of Hennessy down his throat and tossed the bottle aside. He sat parked outside an underground gambling spot on Rockaway Avenue in Brownsville. The location was seedy—lots of drugs, fiends, and dealers. Around the corner, prostitutes worked the area flagging down cars and hopping in and out of vehicles. It was where he would find Meyer, inside the unassuming building with gambling, whores, and drinking.

Bugsy shoved the .45 down into his waistband and climbed out of his Benz. Bugsy was in a dangerous place inside his mind. He had murder on the brain and he wanted to find his brother and confront him.

At the door, they recognized him right away—Meyer's twin brother. He was good to enter. Bugsy walked into the dim and seedy place crowded with thuggish locals and loose women and looked around for his brother. Rap music blared. The stench of weed being smoked all over the place lingered in the air. His eyes scanned everywhere, through the thick crowd of debauchery, and he was aloof to it all. He was a man on a mission.

It didn't take long. He spotted Meyer shooting dice with a few men in the next room. Meyer clutched a handful of money and talked shit with his back to the approaching Bugsy.

"You stupid muthafucka!" Bugsy screamed at him before he struck Meyer in the back of the head with the butt of the pistol.

Meyer tumbled forward and stumbled to get his footing, but Bugsy struck him again. He fell over in pain.

"You think I didn't know—about AJ, the robbery? It's because of you that she's gone!" Bugsy shouted.

Meyer was dumbfounded. *Bugsy knew all along?*

Meyer tried to stand up. He felt the warm blood on the back of his head. Others simply stood around the action and observed. They were aware who the twins were. No one wanted any trouble with them.

"Bugsy, let me explain—" Meyer said.

But the moment he tried to open his mouth and talk, Bugsy smashed him in the face with the gun. He wasn't there for an explanation.

Blood gushed from Meyer's nose. He charged at Bugsy and they wrestled aggressively. Meyer smashed his elbow into the side of Bugsy's skull and then tried to grapple him into a headlock, but Bugsy strongly resisted. Their guns went flying and were confiscated by unnamed goons who could get a couple hundred on the streets for them. It was chaos all around, and the twins would not stop until the cops arrived.

Quickly, they were broken up by several uniformed officers, handcuffed, and arrested. Their bruised and bloody faces were evidence of the fight. Bugsy was steaming mad. He could kill his brother.

⚜

In the bullpen, the twins cooled off. They sat on opposite sides of the room and barely looked at each other. They were nursing their wounds. Everything had gotten out of control.

Bugsy looked at his brother and said, "She's gone. It's because of who I am—this life I live—that the best thing that ever happened to me walked out of my life. And you instigated her leaving me by having me beaten within an inch of my life. She couldn't take it."

Meyer looked at his brother and said, "I'm sorry."

"You're sorry?"

"I know she's a good woman and you love her, but this ain't all on me. I wasn't the one calling the shots, Ma was. She put that shit together."

Bugsy continued to frown, but he was listening. He understood where his brother was coming from. Their mother was a brutal and cold woman, and Meyer would do almost anything for her. Still, Meyer was still at fault for agreeing to go through with it.

"You chose to stay with her," Bugsy said.

"I did, because I don't trust Pop. You was always the better son to him, and he always belittled me. How much more was I supposed to take from him? But you gotta admit, both our parents are fucked up."

Bugsy knew Meyer was right. He saw his father's weakness.

"But look, when we robbed that place, you wasn't supposed to be harmed. Ma made that clear to everyone—not to touch you. But Luna, he felt that you made us, so he figured if he came after you, you wouldn't believe we had anything to do with it. We wanted to pin it on Deuce."

"That's idiotic. Deuce is a psychopath. He would have killed everyone in that room, including me."

"Anyway, when she heard the news about you, she went crazy, and she forced me do it—do him anyway," Meyer said quietly, as if others were eavesdropping on their conversation.

This was the first Bugsy heard that Luna was dead. He could see the sadness in his brother's eyes. He knew what Luna meant to Meyer.

The brothers made amends during their time in lockup, reconnecting over losing someone close to them and realizing that friends and lovers may come and go, but they would always have each other. A brother's bond that could never be broken.

I t was sixty-five degrees and sunny with blue skies stretching endlessly. The warm weather meant that spring was approaching. It had been a brutal winter, from the cold and inclement weather to people's evildoing. The springlike day in late winter was needed.

Maxine stepped out of the building lobby in a blue flutter sleeve top, a pair of tight Gucci jeans that accentuated her curves, and a pair of wedge heels. She looked exotic with her dark and glossy stylish hair and pearl necklace. She was the epitome of elegance. The warm air against her skin felt exhilarating. She exhaled. It would be a beautiful day.

She strutted toward the Bentley, where the chauffeur stood near the opened back door and waited for her to enter the vehicle. Maxine had a busy day today—breakfast with Scott, then brunch with a new friend she had met in the building, shopping at a few stores, and just living her life the way she was supposed to—with richness, class, and elegance.

Her stint in prison felt so long ago. She'd come a long way. She was twenty years overdue to live the good life. Scott was in love with her, and he was giving her the world. She didn't want for anything. Their relationship picked up right where it'd left off, and all was forgiven.

As Maxine approached the Bentley, her cell phone rang. She reached into her purse, removed it, and answered the call. The caller was unknown, and she knew her man sometimes would call her from different numbers.

"Hello?"

She expected to hear Scott's voice, but she heard her worst nightmare.

"You fuckin' bitch, you think you and me are over with? Shit just got started," Wacka growled into the phone.

Maxine was shocked and terrified to get a call from Wacka on her cell phone. She stopped walking toward the car. The last thing she needed was the chauffeur eavesdropping.

"How did you get this number?" she asked.

"Bitch, that's the last thing you need to worry about."

It was a valid question. It took connections and sheer luck, but Tarsha had a cousin who worked for a collection agency. Wacka had Maxine's full name, and that was all they needed. Several telephone calls yielded a result. They found her—the woman who had hired Wacka as a hitman.

Maxine looked around. It was a busy area with lots of people and lots of traffic. She feared he might lunge at her from out of nowhere—gun her down where she stood. Wacka was unpredictable and crazy.

"Ms. Maxine, is everything okay?" the driver asked her.

She ignored him. Wacka had her undivided attention. The thought of him coming for her angered her. She stepped farther away from the driver, confusing the man as he waited near the car.

"Listen to me, you stupid muthafucka. I'm not the bitch to fuck with. You understand me? I will hunt you down and have you killed."

She heard an ominous chuckle from him, and then he said, "Not before I tell your boyfriend about our business dealings in the past. I think he would be very interested in knowing that his lady—oops, I meant to say fiancée—had me murder his three young children."

"He'll never believe you," she retorted.

"You think so, huh? Would you want to take that chance?"

Maxine knew she couldn't. If Scott even had a suspicion she was involved with his kids' deaths, it would change everything. It was a secret she wanted to bury deep, but she couldn't while Wacka was still alive.

"He'll kill you too."

He laughed. "But you first, bitch," he mocked.

"Fuck you!" She was losing her cool.

They argued with each other, but Wacka had the advantage.

"Maybe we can work something out, and you pay me for my silence."

Maxine felt it was coming—the blackmail. It was still hard to believe.

"What the fuck you want?"

"I want five hundred thousand dollars."

"Five hundred thousand—are you crazy?" she repeated the price like it was a shocking blow to her. She feigned anger at the amount, but she had to keep from laughing at the price.

"Bitch, did I stutter?"

"No."

She was almost relieved that he'd asked for such a small amount. She could get that with no problem.

Wacka was a dumb fuck, and Maxine was grateful for his stupidity. Did he have a clue how much Scott was worth?

"I need some time to get the money. It's a lot."

"I don't give a fuck how you get it. You have one week, bitch."

"A week?"

"Don't play games wit' me, bitch. You should be dead, but consider this your amnesty fee—five hundred thousand dollars or your life."

He hung up.

Maxine stood there for a moment, taking it all in. She had to be smart on this. She had to get way ahead of him and fix it.

Breakfast with Scott was great. She laughed with him and enjoyed the poached eggs and blueberry pancakes put together by one of the best chefs in the city. Clinton's was a fine place to eat on the lower east side.

Maxine felt it was the perfect time to talk to him about her future.

"I wanna go shopping today, but I need some cash," she said.

Scott reached into his pockets and pulled out a wad of cash—all one hundred-dollar bills. He counted out seven thousand dollars and handed it to her. Maxine took the money, but the look she had wasn't happy.

"You okay?" he asked.

She wanted to tell him how she felt, but she knew that you could catch more bees with honey than shit. So, in a very calm voice, she said, "Thank you, baby. I appreciate everything you give me, but I do want to feel some security. It isn't about the money, but more of me wanting to become my own woman. Why do I continually have to ask you for money like I'm a child? I don't want an allowance from you, but I want an opportunity."

He smiled. "Opportunity, huh?"

Did he understand where she was coming from? Maxine was a smart woman, not some groupie looking for a handout. They had history together and she once had a vibrant future ahead of her.

"Yes, an opportunity. I want to be able to buy my own car."

"I just bought you a car."

"It's not about the car; it's about the financial freedom. Why is it that Layla gets to walk away with fifty million dollars and I get spoon-fed a few thousand dollars here and there?"

Scott's jaw tightened at the mention of Layla and his money. Abruptly, he banged his fist on the table, startling Maxine. "Layla is not going to keep a fuckin' dime of my money! I'll see her dead first. And do I have to remind you that it is because of you that she's still living?"

Maxine still tried to get her point across. "Well, I'm your fiancée, and I should be treated accordingly. I feel that I should have access to certain accounts, and I should have the chance to build something of my own."

"You're starting to sound like her," he said.

Maxine didn't want to be compared to Layla. It infuriated her.

"I'm offended," she said. "After everything I went through to prove how much I love you. I kept my mouth shut and did the time, and you went and started a family with her, and you treat me like I'm her!"

Maxine abruptly pushed her chair away from the table, stood up, and stormed away from him. She couldn't help but to shed a few tears.

Scott took a moment to sit there and cool off. Why was he so resistant in trusting Maxine? She wasn't anything like Layla. She was a good woman. She even spared Layla's life after all she had done to her. And Maxine was never a materialistic woman. She cared about her education and her family. When they were together, he had to force her to take gifts from him. She would hardly wear the expensive jewelry he'd bought for her back in the days. He would always have to ask her to put on the jewelry he bought for her. Scott wanted them to stunt together. She was his woman and she needed nice things.

Scott finally caught up to Maxine outside the restaurant. He grabbed her by the arm and spun her around. She put up little resistance.

"I'm sorry, baby. Forgive me," he said.

She looked at him expressionless.

"I love you," he proclaimed wholeheartedly. "And I'll start making arrangements to have your name added to some of my accounts, properties, and other legal affairs. You do deserve it, after everything you been through."

She still looked at him.

"Look, everything is going to take some time. I want to marry you and spend the rest of my life with you so you'll always be entitled to half of everything I own."

She smiled. But, the kicker was time—Maxine felt that time was what she didn't have. Now she had to go to plan B which made her very unhappy.

The day before the meeting with Wacka, Maxine went to the bank to withdraw five hundred thousand dollars in large bills. The money was from the sale of her parents' home. Years ago, they'd put her name on the deed, so she didn't have to go through probate court to receive her inheritance. Her parents' home was paid in full. Her dad bought the property over forty years ago. She netted the full sale of the home, which was just under six-hundred thousand dollars, after the realtor fee.

Maxine was almost sick sitting with the branch manager for the withdrawal. This was blood money, and she was giving it away to a murderer and blackmailer. She took a deep breath and knew that she had to go through with it.

After over an hour inside the bank, Maxine finally walked out the building with the money in a cheap gift bag. For once, the lady with all the master plans and intricate schemes didn't know what to do to get rid of Wacka for good. She was stumped.

Maxine had to remain patient. She had to think things through, but a lot of issues weren't looking in her favor. Trouble was looming left and right, and it was becoming difficult to handle everything. With Wacka's threats, she realized that she didn't have access to Scott's money—at least not yet. Maxine was agitated by the fact that Layla walked away with fifty million dollars, when Scott didn't give her a bank account or access to any money. Scott was at war, and he was still legally married to Layla. So for her to be his fiancée, it was only for show. If something were to happen to him, then all his legal assets would go to Layla—her archenemy. Maxine would walk away with nothing. She'd come too far, did too many years in prison, along with losing both of her parents behind her decisions, just to walk away broke. And now Wacka had the audacity to blackmail her.

If she pillaged from Scott, would she want to give it to Wacka? And the five hundred thousand—her father worked his ass off to buy that house. Now Wacka wanted to take it from her. She had to think about it. She needed Wacka dead, but how? She couldn't go to Scott and tell him to kill him. Well, she could, but since Wacka kidnapped her Scott would probably torture him first and get him to talk, and Wacka would quickly give her up.

No, she couldn't involve Scott. Scott colliding with Wacka was something she couldn't chance. And she was sure that she couldn't take him out alone. Not like she had with Miguel. There was no way around it. Until she found an appropriate way to get rid of the problem for good, she needed to pay up.

It was Tarsha's plan that Wacka was following. She had become the root, and he was the tree. She made him call Maxine, and the money exchange was set for a public place. It was a very public place—One Police Plaza.

Maxine was taken aback by the location chosen. Why there? What was his motive? What was he trying to pull? Had he become a snitch? She wanted to know. Maxine clarified it to him she didn't like the idea. She was very reluctant to walk anywhere near One Police Plaza with five hundred thousand dollars in cash and simply give it to him.

"I'm not doing that, Wacka. Are you crazy?"

"Look bitch, you either be there wit' the cash or pay the consequences. I ain't fuckin' around. And if you try anything—if I even *feel* I'm walkin' into a trap, you and I are both doing life in prison. I don't give a fuck! I'll be a snitching muthafucka to the cops, the feds, anyone that will listen about the murders you consigned to me. I have all the copies of the letters and photos you and my sister sent me, with names and all that good shit! And if you try to send niggas after me, you'll regret it, cuz I'm letting you know that this shit don't stop wit' my death. I got a crew of muthafuckas who'll make sure Scott will get the info on you. And I promise you, you kill me and you'll follow me to hell. Real talk, bitch!" Wacka said a mouthful. "I hate you, bitch! And the only reason you ain't a dead bitch is because I wanna get paid. Period! So keep talkin' that slick shit, and the money might not mean that much to me."

He was serious. He was angry and he wanted revenge. He blamed his family's death on Maxine, and she could do nothing about it but comply with his every demand.

She was stressed out, not eating, and losing weight. Her mind was spinning out of control. Wacka was taking things too far. He was supposed to be this hardcore thug, not a snitch. But either she paid him or risked life in prison or death by the hands of the man she loved. Both options were bleak.

It felt like Wacka had her in checkmate, but she had to continue playing the game somehow. This couldn't be her end. There was still so much to do. She wanted to crush her enemies, starting with Layla. She still wanted Layla dead, but not before her precious lifestyle was ripped away and Scott married Maxine. She wanted Meyer dead, and she wanted Lucky to see life in prison. Those were her wishes.

It was show time, and Wacka put on his game face. Tarsha bought some black leather gloves, wrapped sticks in duct tape until they were the length of his missing fingers, and secured the gloves to his wrists. With a black hoodie, Timberland boots, and his usual mean grill, he was looking as menacing as ever. Hiding his sudden handicap was important. He had enemies everywhere, and if word got out, the wolves would come charging to tear him and his family apart. And if anyone, especially Tarsha's cousins, knew that the violent and murderous Wacka would most likely never be the same, he was a dead man. They would come for everything, including the cash they expected to receive from Maxine. Tarsha's cousins were ruthless too, and unpredictable, and they wouldn't hesitate to shoot Tarsha and Wacka in the head and leave their bodies in the Buick—money gone.

One Police Plaza was a busy place in lower Manhattan—lots of towering buildings, traffic, and people moving about freely with their busy lives. The place was a stone's throw away from the Brooklyn Bridge, and the block bordered Park Row, Pearl Street, and Police Plaza. Since 9/11, the area had been locked down tightly with police, security, and bomb-sniffing dogs.

Maxine moved around the area nervously in her wool blend coat, clutching a gift bag with the money inside. Also on her person was a .380 for her protection. She didn't know what to expect from Wacka. Would he kill her right there, in front of hundreds of witnesses and police? She didn't doubt him one second. He was crazy enough.

Maxine was never more alert, watching everything within her radius and trying to predict his actions. But he could come from anywhere, and she probably wouldn't see him coming.

A few feet away, watching Maxine wander about with the gift bag, was Tarsha, and sprinkled around the area were both of her dangerous cousins. Wacka sat in the Buick, keeping out of sight. They all had been there for hours staking out the area and looking for a setup. But nothing seemed shady.

Tarsha calmly approached Maxine, watching her every move. The moment she got up close on Maxine, she right away asked, "Is all the money there?"

Maxine pivoted and was taken aback by the woman asking about the money. She looked the ghetto looking bitch wearing the purple bubble coat and bamboo earrings up and down and said, "Where's Wacka?"

"He's around, but you're dealing wit' me."

"I don't think so," Maxine refuted. "I want to see Wacka."

"Look, don't make this difficult. Just give me the money and I'll go."

Maxine hesitated making the matter difficult. The woman caught her by surprise. Who was she?

The two ladies had an exchange of words while trying to look pleasant. No one wanted any attention on themselves.

Maxine feared she was getting played. "I'm only giving the money to Wacka. I don't know you."

"He's around, watching your every move. And if you fuck this up you won't make it back home alive. But let's not continue this dance; I know everything about you putting hits out on children. If that ever got out, you would be so fucked up."

Maxine didn't want to hear any more. It was bad enough she knew. She handed over the gift bag to Tarsha, and while taking the bag, Tarsha eyed everything that she had on. The bitch was classy with it—the clothes and the diamond/platinum engagement ring on her finger, it was a dead giveaway that she was worth more than a simple half million.

Tarsha didn't say another word to her. She walked away briskly and hailed a taxicab. Maxine stood there dumbfounded; praying it was over with, but deep inside, she knew it wasn't. The feeling these people would not go away so easily ate away at her.

In the back seat of the taxicab, Tarsha opened up the bag and smiled. The money was inside, stacks of it; she even leafed through each bill to make sure they were all hundreds instead of singles. Everything was the real deal.

Wacka and her two male cousins followed the taxicab in the Buick. Once they were sure she wasn't being followed, Tarsha had the cab pull over several blocks from One Police Plaza. She paid the driver and hopped out, then slid into the backseat of the Buick with Wacka. The first thing out of her mouth was, "Yo, that bitch is loaded. She's holding out on us. We need to get more money from her."

Maybe had Maxine just handed over the gift bag to a nervous Tarsha, it would have been the end. But Maxine had asked too many questions and delayed the drop. In doing so, Tarsha had time to size her up. She felt that Maxine had played them, and asking for five hundred thousand was stupid—it was punk money. Divided between the four, the cash would be gone within a week or two. They gave her cousins fifty grand apiece and were left with four hundred thousand.

Tarsha had expenses, and Wacka had no fingers or family because of Maxine. She needed to suffer and pay them more money. The ring on her fingers was worth millions. Tarsha had noticed similar rings before from websites, TV shows, and celebrities sporting high-end diamonds and whatnot. The information was golden and Wacka was energized. He wanted to drain Maxine of everything she had and owned. She was living like a celebrity and his entire world had been turned to shit.

No fucking way!

Less than twenty-four hours later, Wacka made another phone call to Maxine and harshly said, "Bitch, you think we stupid? I want five million dollars in a suitcase in the trunk of a Bentley, and you got two weeks to do it. Don't fuck wit' me!"

Maxine was flabbergasted and pissed off.

Wacka had become enemy number-one, and her main goal was to destroy him somehow and someway. She would not be bullied!

EPILOGUE

It was go time for Meyer. He was packed and ready to go—and a few hours from now, he and his lady would be chilling and relaxing in Maui. Passports, plenty of cash, and first-class plane tickets were all in Meyer's possession. He was preparing to exit his home and scoop up Zoe from her place. Downstairs was a limousine waiting to take him and Zoe to JFK Airport for a red-eye flight. He deserved a vacation. This trip to Hawaii would be extravagant—the best money could buy. He had reservations to an elite resort where their cabanas were directly above the beautiful blue sea. The floor was glass, and you saw the sea, sharks, fish, and everything oceanic beneath your feet.

Zoe's ninety-day countdown of no sex was finally coming to an end, and Meyer wanted some pussy. But he wanted to do something special for his beautiful queen—and it couldn't get any more special than taking her on an exotic trip to Hawaii.

As he was moving through his place, checking to see if everything was secured and shut down, he heard nothing, but he felt a sudden presence. It was a feeling he couldn't shake. So he went for his pistol on the night table where he'd left it, only to find it missing. Odd—Meyer never misplaced a gun, unless someone picked it up. He slowly turned around, hoping that it was only an eerie feeling and maybe his nerves were getting the best of him, but no such luck. He stared down the barrel of a .45 snub-nose pistol.

Expressionless, he said, "I let you live."

"Big mistake."

"So you gonna do me like this? I'm ya brother!"

"My brother—we always say that to each other, but then you abandoned me," Luna said.

"What choice did I have? My mother wanted you dead."

"Fuck that bitch, we were all we got. And what life do I have outside of the family—outside of New York? This is all I know, what I live and breathe for—and just like that, I'm supposed to run away and give it up? No crew, no money—nothing! I expected you to go to bat for me, but you didn't."

Meyer frowned. He went to bat for Luna, but his hands were tied.

"So not killing you is not going to bat for you?"

They argued, but there was no getting through to Luna. He raised the pistol toward Meyer. Ironic, now the shoe was on the other foot. Meyer held his ground and glared at his friend, his brother from another mother, and expected the worst to come. And it did. Luna fired—*Bak! Bak! Bak!*

Luna emptied the clip into Meyer, and then he reloaded, placed the barrel of the gun under his chin, and fired.

Bak!

He dropped to the floor near Meyer's body. It appeared to be a murder-suicide, as if it was a love story.

Four Hours Later

Maxine laid nuzzled against Scott on the king size bed, their naked bodies entwined under the sheets with sleep still consuming them both. It had been a passionate night between them—lots of sex and lots of love. Scott came so many times inside of her, she could've sworn she felt herself getting pregnant. It would be a blessing.

The bedroom was dark and still. Things were calm until they weren't.

Bang—the noise immediately lifted Scott from the bed and his woman's sweet grasp. His feet slammed against the floor, and he instantly went for his weapon.

Bang—the noise grew louder, and Scott grabbed his gun believing it was a hit. Maxine startled awake too. Her eyes grew wide with panic. She looked at Scott for answers, but he was clueless too.

"Hide, baby," he said to her.

But she didn't want to hide. He screamed, "Get under the damn bed!"

He then charged into the next room with his gun in hand and aimed at the threat. Maxine heard someone say, "Gun!" and then she heard repeated gunfire—*Boom! Boom! Boom!*

It sounded like a thunderous bomb in the next room. She heard, "FBI, get down! Get the fuck down!"

Unbeknownst to them both, it was the feds kicking down their front door and bursting into the room with arrest warrants, guns, and hordes of agents. There was screaming and confusion. Maxine hurried into the next room to see Scott lying on the floor, bleeding profusely. He had been shot twice; one bullet went into his chest, and the other went into his shoulder.

"Ohmygod!" Maxine screamed.

She attempted to rush to his aid, to grab her man into her arms and comfort him, but the feds prevented her from going anywhere near him. They grabbed her tightly, and she resisted.

"You assholes!" she yelled.

The alphabet boys were rude—and the big bad feds had blown the house down. Things were chaotic inside the large penthouse suite. Maxine was subdued; her arms aggressively were folded behind her, and they threw on the handcuffs. They handcuffed Scott too, even though he was bleeding badly, his blood staining his expensive Berber carpeting.

"Call an ambulance! Please, get him some help," she yelled at them. "He's dying!"

They weren't worried; if he lived or died, they still had their man in custody. Maxine threatened them with legal action, but they felt it was a clean shooting. He'd brandished a gun, and they feared for their safety.

They could've done things the easy way—knocked on his door at a reasonable hour, shown him the arrest and search warrants, and taken him away. But what fun would that be? They came in the wee hours of the morning in full swat gear, disturbing the entire building and capturing their man dead or alive—it's what they lived for.

Not having anything on Maxine yet, they had to let her go. But the damage had already been done. She had to watch EMS carry her man out on a gurney. He was in bad shape, and the paramedics worked on keeping him alive. To make matters worse, the media was outside their building—capturing everything with their cameras. To add fuel to her raging fire, they prevented Maxine from riding in the ambulance with Scott.

She had to hail a cab to the hospital. She hurried toward admitting and explained to them that her fiancé was there for multiple gunshot wounds and demanded to know his status.

"His name?" they asked her.

"It's Scott West."

She had swiped Scott's phone to call Bugsy and his men. But the minute she attempted to make a phone call, it rang. The caller ID showed that it was Layla. Maxine pushed talk and immediately heard chaos on the other end of the phone.

"Scott! Scott, the concierge said the feds are on their way up with a warrant for my arrest! What the fuck did you do? What the fuck is going on? I'm hiding in my panic room! Shit, they're kicking in my door! Noooooo!"

The phone went dead.

All hell was breaking loose, and Maxine found herself in the center of it all.

31901062883493